E.R. PUNSHON
THE DARK GARDEN

ERNEST ROBERTSON PUNSHON was born in London in 1872.

At the age of fourteen he started life in an office. His employers soon informed him that he would never make a really satisfactory clerk, and he, agreeing, spent the next few years wandering about Canada and the United States, endeavouring without great success to earn a living in any occupation that offered. Returning home by way of working a passage on a cattle boat, he began to write. He contributed to many magazines and periodicals, wrote plays, and published nearly fifty novels, among which his detective stories proved the most popular and enduring.

He died in 1956.

The Bobby Owen Mysteries

E.R. PUNSHON

THE DARK GARDEN

With an introduction
by Curtis Evans

DEAN STREET PRESS

Published by Dean Street Press 2016

Published by licence, issued under the
UK Orphan Works Licensing Scheme.

First published in 1941 by Victor Gollancz

Cover by DSP

ISBN 978 1 911413 31 8

www.deanstreetpress.co.uk

To

The members

of that

Battalion of the County of London Home Guard

in

whose guard room

much of this book was conceived and written

INTRODUCTION

THE YEARS OF the Second World War meant not only major changes in E.R. Punshon's personal life but in his Bobby Owen detective fiction as well. After a successful investigation, as part of an unusual personal commission, into the strange slaying of a British citizen in a French village in *Murder Abroad* (1939), Detective Sergeant Bobby Owen left Scotland Yard and joined the county police force of Wychshire, where he doubles the parts of, as Punshon explains, "head of the not very extensive Wychshire C.I.D. with that of private secretary to the chief constable," Colonel Glynne. Along with *Four Strange Women* (1940) and *Ten Star Clues* (1941), previously reprinted by Dean Street Press, seven additional Bobby Owen detective novels are set within the mysterious confines of Wychshire: *The Dark Garden* (1941), *Diabolic Candelabra* (1942), *The Conqueror Inn* (1943), *Night's Cloak* (1944), *Secrets Can't Be Kept* (1944), *There's a Reason for Everything* (1945) and *It Might Lead Anywhere* (1947). In addition to being set in Wychshire, these seven novels constitute, along with *Ten Star Clues*, Punshon's body of wartime crime fiction, though the war only starts to intrude significantly into Wychshire everyday life with *The Conqueror Inn*. Bobby takes the lead in all of Punshon's fictive Wychshire murder investigations from *The Dark Garden* onward, Colonel Glynne being conveniently sidelined for various reasons. (In *The Dark Garden* he is suffering from a "bad attack of pleurisy," while in later novels he often is in London, trying to obtain, despite being overage, some sort of overseas post in the armed services.)

In contrast with Bobby Owen and his newlywed wife Olive Farrar, E.R. Punshon and Sarah Houghton, Punshon's spouse of nearly four decades standing, never left London during the war, steadfastly remaining in the city even as German bombs rained down around their house on Nimrod Road, putting them in peril of their lives. In correspondence from October 1940, Dorothy L. Sayers and Anthony Gilbert (Lucy Beatrice Malleson), two of Punshon's colleagues from the Detection Club, a social organization of many of Great Britain's finest detective novelists, worriedly discussed the fortunes of the couple, both of whom were now nearly in their seventies. For her part Gilbert professed belief to Sayers that any bomb surely would deliberately go in another direction rather than fall anywhere in the vicinity of kindly Mr. Punshon. (See my 2011 CADS Supplement *Was Corinne's Murder Clued? The Detection Club and Fair Play, 1930-1953*, p. 21.) Indeed, far from being put out by a bomb, Punshon during these months managed to complete *Ten Star Clues*, despite having to spend a great amount of time on duty with the Battalion of the County of London Home Guard. The sixteenth Bobby Owen detective novel, *The Dark Garden*, which followed *Ten Star Clues* into print later in 1941, fittingly carries a dedication from the author to his fellow members of the Battalion, "in whose guard room much of the book was conceived and written."

Set in June 1940 ("that dreadful month when all the world held its breath to watch the British Empire fall, when a Marshal of France was earning himself that title—"enfant chéri de la défaite" [darling of the defeat]--by which history will know him, when German officers were jovially inviting each other to dinner in London, when Britain, all unaware of the doom so unanimously pronounced, was making her public preparations and going about her private affairs in her usual and accustomed manner"), *The Dark Garden* presents Inspector Bobby Owen with a thorny problem involving Messrs Castles, a well-known firm of lawyers in Midwych, the county town of Wychshire. It all begins when Osman Ford, a farmer of most forbidding aspect, makes his way into Bobby's--or rather Colonel Glynne's--office, complaining that Nathaniel Anderson, the senior partner in Castles, is refusing to turn over to him funds the firm is holding in trust on behalf of Ford's wife, funds which the proud and ambitious farmer needs to finance the expansion of Roman Ends, his 750-acre landholding located "on rising ground on the outskirts of the great Wychwood forest." With some difficulty Bobby manages to send Ford packing, telling the outraged petitioner that his dispute with Castles simply is not a police matter. Soon Anderson goes missing, however, and Bobby finds that there are additional people besides Osman Ford who might have had some desire to do away with the lawyer, including the passionate Ann Earle, a secretary at Castles and Anderson's reputed mistress, about whom there is "something oddly impressive ... belonging much more to some heroine of old tragedy than to a twentieth-century office worker." With *The Dark Garden* E.R. Punshon once again crafts a complex and compelling drama about the lethal interplay of powerful human emotions.

Punshon himself would learn firsthand the challenges confronting those entrusted with funds when in 1946 he accepted, after much importuning from Dorothy L. Sayers, the office of Treasurer of the Detection Club. On account of the war the Club had essentially gone defunct for six years, and, at the time Punshon became Treasurer, no one was quite sure where what remained of the Detection Club's prewar treasure actually was located. Commencing a lengthy search for the lost funds, Punshon eventually discovered a cache of Detection Club savings certificates, then worth about £185, which had been deposited to the Westminster Bank a few days before the London Blitz began on 7 September 1940. After an audit held with Richard Hull, an accountant and fellow Detection Club member best known today for his droll inverted mystery *The Murder of My Aunt* (1934), Punshon was pleased to report to Sayers that the Club had a bank balance of just over £300, close to £10,000 today in real price (see *Corinne*, p. 23). As far as we know, no one was murdered in the process.

Curtis Evans

CHAPTER I
OSMAN FORD'S WRATH

IN THE SEAT of the mighty, that is to say in the office chair of Colonel Glynne, chief constable of the Wychshire County Police, sat Inspector Bobby Owen, who doubled the parts of head of the not very extensive Wychshire C.I.D., with that of private secretary to the chief constable, just now absent from duty with a bad attack of pleurisy.

On the table before Bobby was piled a formidable heap of the war-time instructions, counter instructions, circulars, regulations, with which he was dealing. Some he was reserving for future consideration, some required immediate attention, others he was putting aside for action by the deputy chief constable, Superintendent Allenson, an old time officer on the point of retirement and only too glad to leave to Bobby everything with which Bobby was willing to deal.

At the moment he was wrinkling his forehead and rubbing perplexedly the tip of his nose over an elaborate scheme for a network of police blocks and controls whereby, necessity arising, parachutists, either as hordes of invaders or merely as solitary spies, could be swiftly dealt with. The scheme seemed to him clever enough but extremely complicated, so much so as to be very likely to break down in execution. It had been drawn up by one of the younger officers, and Bobby knew its author was very proud of it, so that any modification would have to be suggested with great tact, unless mortal offence were to be given. Bobby's introduction into the force from London had roused a certain amount of jealousy and suspicion, since there were several of the senior officers who still held him for an intruder and thought his probable succession to the office of chief constable on the retirement of its present holder, in the nature of a slight to themselves. The measure of success he had achieved during his service with the Metropolitan police had earned him his present position, but that had not prevented murmurs about 'favouritism' and 'influence', and these prejudices he was still trying his best to overcome by showing himself as friendly as possible and very willing to accept help and advice.

But it was going to be a difficult task to suggest the simplification he felt necessary without causing a good deal of that heart burning which makes difficult the smooth and efficient running of any organization, and so it was with a touch of relief that he relegated its solution to the future as he looked up to greet the visitor who had just been introduced. This was a tall burly man of middle age, with the weatherbeaten complexion of the outdoor worker, heavily built, with heavy, strongly marked features and small, close-set, suspicious eyes. He sat down with a kind of ponderous deliberation in the chair Bobby indicated, but did not speak, and Bobby, looking at the card brought to him, said:

"Mr Osman Ford, isn't it? What can we do for you?"

Mr Osman Ford made no answer for a time. He continued to stare darkly and angrily at Bobby, his large hands planted on his knees, his square, powerful-looking body leaning stiffly forward. The impression he gave was of a forceful, somewhat arrogant personality, one intent on pursuing its own aims and possibly not too scrupulous about the means employed to attain those ends. There was even something a little disconcerting about the way in which he sat there, silent, still, and watchful, and it was with a touch of being, as it were, on guard in his voice that Bobby repeated:

"Well, sir, what can we do for you?"

"You're the detective chap they fetched up along from London, for by way of being smarter than the chaps here?" Mr Ford asked, or, rather, asserted, in a voice like himself, deep, compelling, in it a curious undertone of suspicion and hostility.

"I served in London before being transferred to Midwych," Bobby agreed, not best pleased by the other's remark. No business of his, Bobby thought. But a non-Midwych man had to be careful about treading on Midwych toes, and there was often a directness of speech about these people that was apt to sound challenging and even offensive to a Londoner, though not meant to be either. Bobby said: "I understood you wished to see us on a matter of some importance."

"That's right," Mr Ford answered. His small eyes grew angrier, his expression darkened, but still he did not explain. It was as if he were brooding over a secret grievance he was unwilling to bring into the light lest thereby he should lose some part of it. "That's right," he repeated. "Important."

"Well, sir, what is it?" Bobby asked, making now no attempt to conceal the impatience in his voice. "We are exceedingly busy. As you may see for yourself," he added with a comprehensive wave of his hand towards the various small piles of papers covering his desk. "So I should be very glad if you could be as brief as possible."

But all the same he was well aware that nothing would persuade to haste the slow, angry obstinacy of the man before him.

"Aye, I'm busy, too," Mr Ford answered. "Maybe you'll know the name—Osman Ford." He paused, evidently expecting assent and Bobby was almost childishly pleased to shake his head even more emphatically than was necessary. "Of Roman Ends," he said, and again paused as if for the sign of recognition that Bobby was still pleased not to be able to give since in fact he had never heard either of Osman Ford or of Roman Ends. "Seven hundred and fifty acres of the best and all in good heart," Mr Ford continued, "and now seemingly I'm to break up old pasture that's fed cattle since most like the Romans themselves were here tens of thousands of years ago."

Bobby thought this estimate of time a trifle exaggerated but made no comment. He waited, convinced now that the quickest way of getting rid of his visitor was to let him tell his story at his own pace, but sighing at the thought that every minute expended now would have to be made up later on. Mr Ford continued in his slow, forceful way:

"That means capital. Capital. Up there in London they seem to think all land is just land, and as easy to switch from grain to pasture and back to roots as for a London politician to change his coat. Well, it ain't. You've got to have your plans laid all ahead. So many head of cattle requiring so much pasture, so much home grown feed, so much to be bought, so much in roots, so much in grain, all settled and not so easy to unsettle again as them thinks that does it all on paper. There's machinery to think of and labour that's scarce even when it's worse than bad, but at the end of it, it all comes back to capital. You've to feed the land if you want a return, just as you have to feed calves if you want fat steers."

"I'm afraid we can't help you there," Bobby said. "This is a police office."

Mr Osman Ford took no notice.

"Capital I want and it's my right to have," he went on, "and I won't say I haven't it in my mind to take over the Roman Middles, two hundred acres, that is, and only needs handling to be better than good, even if the Middles will never be same as the Ends." The anger left his small, dark eyes. A sort of heavy enthusiasm took its place, yet an enthusiasm still charged with defiance and mistrust, as if he foresaw an enmity it would be necessary to overcome. "The money's there," he said, "and Castles' have it. But they won't part. And for why? Not along of what they say but along of it's not being there."

To Bobby, this last reason seemed adequate, even though in conflict with the remark made just previously. He said:

"I'm sorry, Mr Ford, but all this does not seem to be in any way a police matter. I'm afraid we can't help you."

He said this with great decision and as he spoke rose from his chair, hoping that Mr Ford would follow his example. He was disappointed. Mr Ford remained more solidly, more securely seated than ever. It looked as if nothing but physical force—and considerable physical force at that—would ever get him out of it. He said:

"Aye, it's a police matter all right. You'll see. Or I wouldn't be here."

Impressed in spite of himself by the heavy, slow power of the man, Bobby sat down again. It was almost as if he were in contact with some elemental force of nature it was useless to attempt either to deflect or to resist.

"Castles'," Mr Ford said suddenly. "You'll know them." Without giving Bobby the time to signify the assent he could not on this occasion deny, Mr Ford continued: "Five thousand pounds it is, them sitting on it tight as a broody hen on her nest and not with one penny will they part. For why? Where is it? That's a police matter all right, isn't it?" he asked triumphantly. "That's your job, Mr Detective that's for you to find out—where the money's gone. That's what I want done."

He relaxed, letting his square, stiff body sink back into his chair as at a task accomplished. He said again while Bobby watched him in puzzled silence:

"That's a police matter all right. Five thousand pounds. That's a job for a Grade One detective. I've heard of you. Stick to a job like a pup to a root, they say, till you have it all worked out. Well, work that out. That's what I want. My wife's money. Five thousand pounds. Detect it."

"Mr Ford," said Bobby, amused, annoyed and a little puzzled too, "do you mean that you are accusing Messrs Castles, the lawyers, of being in possession of money that is yours?"

"Aye. That's right. My money. Belongs to my wife. I want it. For the farm. I don't say that I mightn't take over the Dry Fields, as well as Roman Ends and the Middles. That'd make all of twelve hundred acres." He spoke those last words, longingly, almost lovingly, behind them still the slow force that seemed characteristic of the man. "Castles'," he repeated. "The lawyer's. Not Georgie Blythe. It was him humming and hawing and being uneasy like that put me on it. Old Nat Anderson it is, him as did down young Castles, and got the firm into his own hands same as he got my money and means to stick to it if he can."

"Mr Anderson is connected with Castles', and you are accusing them of having embezzled your wife's money?" Bobby asked.

"That's right. That's what I want you to detect. See? Embezzled. That's the word I wanted only I couldn't rightly lay my tongue to it. Get on with the job, eh? Police matter all right, eh?"

"What proof have you," Bobby asked, "that this money has been in fact improperly dealt with?"

"Proof?" Mr Ford repeated with great scorn. "If a field's bare, do I want proof it's never been seeded? If the money's not there, do I want proof it's gone?"

"You have seen Mr Anderson? What does he say?" Bobby asked.

Seldom had Bobby seen a man look more darkly angry than did Osman Ford then. It seemed almost as if he glowed with an inner flame of rage. He spoke slowly, each word heavy with his wrath. He said:

"He had the impudence to up and say it wasn't my money but my wife's, and he wouldn't discuss it with me, or with her, neither, if I was there, but only if she was all alone, no matter what writing of hers I had, though I showed it him all writ down clear. And he told me to get out. So then I came straight here."

"I see," said Bobby, beginning rather to approve of Mr Anderson, though with an approval slightly checked when Ford added:

"The old rip. There's things I know and maybe I'll tell some day. Him and his lady clerks."

He would have gone on perhaps to say more had not Bobby stopped him.

"That'll do, Mr Ford, please," Bobby interrupted in his most official tone. "I don't want to hear anything like that. Apparently you believe your wife's money has been embezzled. What is said here is confidential and won't be repeated, but I should advise you to be careful what you say anywhere else. There are such things as actions for slander and sometimes the results are serious. The only advice I can give you is to consult another firm of lawyers. It is not a police matter."

Mr Ford stared at him—glared would be a better word.

"Meaning," he said with the slow, hidden anger that seemed as it were to be the core of his character, "meaning to say, you won't do anything?"

"Nothing," Bobby answered firmly, "beyond repeating that if you aren't satisfied, you must consult a lawyer. Not a police matter at all. Good morning."

He picked up his pen again as he spoke and drew some papers towards him, but even that broad hint was not enough to dislodge his visitor.

"You been hearing tales about Youngman?" he asked, more heavily, more darkly even than before.

"I don't know anything about any young man," retorted Bobby, impatiently, and this time pressed the bell on the table.

Promptly there appeared Sergeant Wright, a brisk young man whose recent promotion was partly due to a favourable report made by Bobby.

"Oh, sergeant," Bobby said as he entered, "you might show this gentleman the way out, will you? I'm afraid I'm too busy to go to the door with him myself. Good morning, Mr Ford. Sorry not to have been more helpful."

Sergeant Wright was quite sufficiently alert to guess what all that meant. It was not the first time that importunate and troublesome visitors had had to be got rid of.

"This way, sir, if you please," he said, with considerable emphasis on the 'if'.

Osman Ford sat on, taking no notice of Wright, bending on Bobby a glance of fury and of menace, so fierce a glance indeed that Wright, a little startled, took a hasty step towards him. There was a moment of tension. Then Ford apparently realized that he had either to go voluntarily or offer a physical resistance that would be as foolish as useless. For Bobby, too, was on his feet now, and powerfully built as was Osman Ford, he was certainly no match for the two of them. Neither Bobby nor Sergeant Wright had much the air of men to be trifled with.

"Aye, I'll go," Ford said and rose heavily from his chair.

In his slow, ponderous way he moved towards the door Wright was now holding invitingly open. In the doorway Ford paused and turned and said with immense scorn:

"Call yourself a detective and won't even try."

He moved a step onwards and paused once more. Over his shoulder he said with scorn greater even than before:

"Detect—you couldn't detect a cow in a turnip field. Take legal advice, that's what you would say."

"That's enough of that," Wright said sharply and laid a hand on his arm.

"Keep your hands to yourself," Ford snarled at him with such sudden cold ferocity that Wright was startled again.

He did not loosen his clasp for that, and for a moment there was again tension in the air as once again Bobby was on his feet prepared for any eventuality. But now Ford moved away, down the passage towards the street, and yet as he went managed to preserve still that same air of anger and of threat, so that his slow retreat had about it something strangely ominous. Wright followed him, wishing silently and intently for an overt act on the other's part that would justify him in action. Bobby called after them:

"Sergeant, I want to see you for a moment, please, after you've seen Mr Ford out."

"Very good, sir," Wright answered and was soon back. "Went off quiet enough, sir," he said, "though looking fit to murder every one near. I did think we were in for a bit of a rough house," he added regretfully, for the other's manner had annoyed him so much he was very disappointed at not having been given an opportunity to show his disapproval by appropriate action.

"A nasty customer," Bobby said. "Do you know him?"

"Oh, yes, sir," Wright answered. "He's well known. He farms in a big way. Got on wonderful, his old dad was cowman on the same place where he's master to-day."

"Well, that's to his credit, I suppose," Bobby said, and Wright looked as if he did not think anything could possibly be to Osman Ford's credit. Bobby went on: "He seemed worried about some money belonging to his wife. I told him it wasn't a police matter, he must take legal advice if he wasn't satisfied. He said something about a young man he seemed to think I had heard about. Have you any idea what he meant?"

"I expect he meant the Youngman affair," Wright answered, "not a young man, it's a name, Youngman. He used to come courting Miss Vigors that's Mrs Osman Ford now. Old Mr Vigors farmed Roman Ends and Osman Ford worked up to be his bailiff. He did good work by all accounts, pulling the farm together. He's a born farmer, as tender to the land as he's hard to all else. Old Mr Vigors had been letting it go downhill, losing his grip he was, with illness and age. In the end Osman Ford had it all in his own hands so he got to look on himself as master. Mr Vigors had only the one child, a pretty lass they say in those days, and there was this young fellow—Youngman by name—a Midwych chap, something in the cotton trade—used to visit there so often every one thought it would be a match between him and the girl, most like with Osman Ford staying on as bailiff, as every one thought would be good enough for him with his old dad having been a cowman on the place. But then Mr Youngman was found dead in the canal near Ends Bridge and how he got there there's no saying, but plenty of gossip all the same. Mr Vigors died soon after and Miss Vigors married Osman Ford, so he is boss now, not bailiff."

Bobby had listened thoughtfully and now he rubbed the end of his nose still more thoughtfully.

"Quite a story," he commented. "Was there any real ground for suspicion against Ford?"

"Well, sir, it was before my time, I couldn't hardly say," Wright answered. "Anyway, there was lots of talk and gossip but not an atom of proof that ever I heard of. It was a week or so before Youngman's body was found. It was winter and a cold night with thick mist.

There's been more than one walked into the canal thereabouts. The verdict was found drowned and as far as I ever heard Ford was never even questioned. But the gossip still goes on, and there's a way he has, as you saw yourself, sir, just now, of looking as though he would as soon murder you as not, if you crossed him."

"He certainly looked murderous enough," Bobby agreed. "Was this money he talks about left by old Mr Vigors too? "

"No, that came from the mother's side—an uncle who had done well in Australia. Maybe he had heard stories about Osman Ford. He left it tied up with Castles', the lawyers, as trustees, and she can't touch a penny without their consent."

"Have they a good reputation?" Bobby asked.

"Oh, yes. There was a time, in old Mr Castles's day, when they were counted the leading firm in Midwych. There was Black-lock's, of course, but their dealings were chiefly with the county folk. Agents for Earl Wych and such like, they are, and most of the Midwych people went to Castles'. It's not like that now, but they are still very well thought of."

There was a touch of hesitation in the sergeant's voice as he said this and Bobby remembered one remark Osman Ford had made.

"Ford was trying to hint at some sort of scandal connected with a Mr Anderson," he remarked. "I shut him up. Mr Anderson seemed to be the partner Ford had been dealing with. He is a partner, I suppose?"

"Yes, sir, the senior partner. He took it on when old Mr Castles died. I have heard he is a little inclined to choose his lady clerks for their looks as much as for their typing, and I do happen to know one girl left because she thought Mr Anderson was a bit too friendly. But then some said she left because he wasn't friendly enough."

"Are there other partners?" Bobby asked.

"Mr Blythe is the junior partner. Very well thought of gentleman, and gives up a lot of time to Hopewell House."

"Hopewell House?" Bobby repeated. "Isn't that a hostel for boys?"

"Yes," agreed Wright with a touch of enthusiasm. "Fine place. Some of our own lads have been through it. It's for boys with no home of their own; boys who would otherwise be at a bit of a loose end and likely to drift into mischief if not looked after. Hopewell

House gives them a real home they pretty well run themselves. Mr Blythe sort of supervises, gives a lot of time and money, too. He's there every night. The boys pay as much as they can, and there are subscribers, but they do say Mr Blythe finds half the expenses out of his own pocket."

"Sounds jolly good idea," said Bobby approvingly. "I think I've heard about the place. Must come pretty heavy on Mr Blythe, though, if he stands much of the cost himself."

"Oh, he has a good subscription list, too," Wright answered. "He got £5,000 from an anonymous giver not so long ago for a new swimming bath and engineering shop. Mr Blythe's handy with tools himself and keen on all the lads knowing how to use them."

"Very sensible, too," Bobby approved once more. "Any Castles in the firm now?"

"Well, yes, in a manner of speaking," Wright answered, again with a certain hesitation. "Only not a partner. Managing clerk. I don't know the rights and wrongs of it, but some say Mr Anderson that's boss now did him out of his rights and that he ought to be boss himself and head partner instead of only managing clerk. Others say Mr Anderson did everything for him when he was left an orphan, gave him his articles free, provided his education, everything, and that he has to thank Mr Anderson for being what he is with a good screw instead of a two pound a week clerk. I daresay it's worth a bit to the firm to have a Castles in it, even if only as managing clerk. The name's remembered still in Midwych."

"I expect," Bobby said thoughtfully, "Ford will make trouble if he can. He's that sort. Most likely Castles are acting within their rights and duties as trustees, though," and with that he dismissed the matter from his mind till a few days later there came to see him Miss Anne Earle, describing herself as from Messrs Castles, the lawyers.

CHAPTER II
THE FARM

IT WAS ON some quite unimportant detail of a fund in aid of the Red Cross for which Colonel Glynne, still absent on sick leave, had undertaken to act as treasurer, that Miss Earle had come to ask Bobby's advice. Bobby indeed, overwhelmed as he still was with the task of carrying out the instructions that since the outbreak of war had descended upon the police authorities in a daily avalanche, would have felt considerably annoyed at being bothered with such small details, had he not somehow guessed immediately that some other purpose lay behind this visit.

Remembering Sergeant Wright's tale of gossip to the effect that the feminine members of the staff of Messrs Castles were occasionally chosen more for looks than for efficiency, he soon found himself reflecting that Miss Earle seemed to qualify on both grounds. In the execution of her errand she showed herself brisk, business-like and well informed, and there was no denying the strange beauty that was hers, though its dark and sombre appeal would not have been thought attractive by all. There was indeed more than a hint of a latent and hidden power about the girl; and her voice was one to be remembered, deep, soft and low, and yet with a ringing note in it that seemed to lend a weight of meaning to every syllable she uttered. He noticed, too, how, beneath brows so heavy and so strongly marked as to be something of a blemish, her eyes could change from a dull, indeterminate hue to an intense violet. Eyes that could, Bobby felt, blaze with depths of passion and emotion. The odd idea came to him that she was one who moved in an almost perpetual disguise, a disguise only rarely laid aside, so that only in rare moments did her real self appear. A little frightening, Bobby thought, this manner of concealment that hinted at such unknown depths beneath, that suggested that in some queer way she stood upon one side of a gulf and all the rest of the world upon the other. An aloof and solitary spirit, he told himself, and then he reflected that very likely he was merely being fanciful, that behind the veil she seemed to wear there was probably very little, nothing perhaps. All the same he was conscious of a certain relief when she rose to go, of relief as from an overpowering and unknown presence. Then at the door she turned and paused, and in that deep, soft voice of hers, that seemed so curiously to combine in itself the purr of the contented cat with the back tones of the crouching tigress, she said:

"I know I oughtn't to have bothered you with all that. It wasn't so very important. Only, you see, I am afraid."

Bobby looked hard at her. She returned his glance as steadily, as searchingly. He saw, as it were, a small and distant fire begin to glow in the depths of those strange eyes of hers, whereof the hue changed, as he watched, to deep violet. Instinctively he felt that if this woman were afraid, it was not without good reason. He said:

"Why are you afraid?"

"Not for myself," she answered with a slight, backward movement of her small head, as if to say that for herself she would not soon or easily be frightened.

Something oddly impressive about her. Something, he thought, belonging much more to some heroine of old tragedy than to a twentieth-century office worker.

He felt he could well imagine her as one of the Valkyria, riding the storm above the battle to choose those about to die. She for her part was still looking at him steadily, but also a little doubtfully, as if not sure of the wisdom of her appeal, as indeed she might always be doubtful of the wisdom of making any appeal to anyone instead of trusting only to herself.

"You had better tell me about it," Bobby said and went back to his chair.

She remained standing in an attitude that gave an odd illusion of height greater than that she actually possessed, as though an inner force of the spirit had made her taller for the time. Lifting one hand, she said:

"There is a man named Osman Ford and he has been making threats against Mr Anderson."

"Mr Anderson is the head of the firm you work for, isn't he?"

"Yes," she answered, and now her face was like a mask and she withdrew the fire in her eyes, sinking back, so to say, into her normal, everyday self, and all that so plainly that Bobby said to himself:

"Why, she's in love with him."

That, he supposed, explained the gossip of which he had heard recently. Still, it was not his affair. He said aloud:

"What sort of threats and why?"

"Mr Anderson won't let him have his wife's money. He wants it to spend on his farm. Mr Anderson thinks that under the terms of the trust deed, the money ought to remain invested in trustee or similar securities. Mr Anderson doesn't think a farm gives that sort of security. He has complete discretion."

"I see," Bobby said, remembering that Osman Ford had made a direct accusation of fraud. "Obviously, if Mr Ford is not satisfied with Mr Anderson's handling of the trust money, he should consult another solicitor. Has he done that, do you know?"

"No, of course not, what would be the good?" Miss Earle answered contemptuously. "Mr Anderson is acting in the interests of his client, following his instructions. Osman Ford knows that. So he has been making threats. I heard him. At the office. He said he would wring Mr Anderson's neck and Mr Anderson told me to be ready to ring for the police. Once before, a long time ago, Osman Ford got rid of a man who was in his way. Pushed him in the canal. It could never be proved. Now he's been saying in a public house that there's always room in a canal for more. It's not only that. I saw the way he looked when he was with Mr Anderson. He looked like murder. I told Mr Anderson. He only laughed. He won't take care of himself. I made up my mind to tell you. You must see he's safe."

A note of anxiety had come into her voice, a note Bobby felt no peril for herself would ever have put there. Not now was she a Valkyr, chooser of the slain, but simply a woman afraid for her lover.

Bobby said:

"I want to remind you of one thing first. What is said to us here is confidential and will not be repeated. But please be very careful what you say anywhere else. It might lead to very serious trouble, very serious trouble indeed."

"There's that now," she answered moodily. "Serious trouble, I mean. At least I think it's not far off."

"You take these threats seriously?"

"I saw the way he looked."

"Can you produce any evidence that threats have been made in public?"

"Oh, yes," she answered. "It was at the 'Rose and Dragon' one night." Then she paused and seemed to consider. "I see what you mean," she said. "It's possible the men who heard him wouldn't want to come forward. They are all afraid of Osman Ford."

"Would you have thought what he said important if you hadn't known of his quarrel with Mr Anderson?"

"It was the way he looked," she repeated.

"I am afraid it is impossible to take police action on a look," Bobby said; and probably he would have let the matter rest there had he not himself seen Osman Ford and been struck by the dark, glowing anger of the man.

"You mean you won't do anything?" Miss Earle's voice broke on his thoughts, and there was a hard tone in her voice that reminded him oddly of how Osman Ford, too, had said almost the same thing in almost the same manner. Curious, he thought, how much these two, the young girl and the middle-aged man, seemed to resemble each other, not only in physical bearing, but also in the impression they gave of passions and emotions stronger than the ordinary.

"I think all I can do," Bobby said presently, "is to have a talk with Mr Ford and try to give him some sort of discreet warning. But it will have to be very discreet," he added with a faint smile, for he felt that unless he was very tactful indeed he might easily get Mr Ford sending in complaints of officiousness and meddling.

"Thank you," she said.

She stood still for a brief moment, proud, impassive, vaguely challenging. Then in a second she was gone, leaving him wondering a little at the impression she had made on him.

"A dangerous, vivid, vital sort of girl," he reflected, and he wondered much how one who seemed so violent, so primitive even, in her emotions, fitted in the dull ordinary routine of a lawyer's office.

She ought to have lived, he thought, in a more highly coloured, more picturesque age, not one in which even war has become a factory product, and death is dealt out by machinery.

He crossed the room to the window. In the street below, her tall, thin form and long, swinging stride made it easy to pick her out amidst the hurrying crowd on the pavement. Again he was struck by something aloof, almost elemental about her—primitive was the word that had occurred to him before. The thought came to him that it matched curiously with something equally primitive, or elemental perhaps, in the Osman Ford of whom she seemed so much afraid, though less for herself than for her employer. Was that, he wondered, because instinctively she recognized in him a spirit akin to her own, and therefore knew, by instinct also, what headstrong strength of passion it concealed?

That night at dinner, chatting with Olive, his wife, he described the impression made on him by these two visitors and remarked that he thought they would have been well suited to each other had they chanced to meet in favourable circumstances and had they been more of an age. But Olive shook her head.

"It's not always like that suits like best," she said. "Like and unlike often get on better."

Bobby rubbed the end of his nose and thought this over. Possibly this remark of Olive's explained the attraction Anne Earle apparently found in Mr Anderson. Bobby had never seen him, but the picture in his mind was of a staid, elderly, shrewd, calculating lawyer, as different as possible from the enigmatic young woman who had come to see him. He said presently:

"Well, of course, he is old enough to be her father. I think I'll try and see Osman Ford. We don't want any trouble if we can help it. I could drop him a hint."

"It will have to be a very tactful hint," Olive warned him. "He sounds the sort of man likely to turn nasty."

Bobby agreed that that was possible, but knew also that if it did chance that serious trouble developed, and it transpired that he had taken no action on warning received, then he would probably be blamed. Another of those continual dilemmas of which a policeman's life is almost wholly composed, he told himself sadly, but decided that on the whole the best horn of the dilemma to choose for impalement was that of dropping a discreet, even a very discreet, hint to Mr Ford.

On the afternoon of the following Monday an opportunity presented itself. He had occasion to visit one of the county police stations, one situated so close to Roman Ends farm that to call there would hardly take him out of his way.

The farm lay, he found, on rising ground on the outskirts of the great Wychwood forest, and had the air, as even Bobby with his small knowledge of farming could tell, of a prosperous, carefully looked after, well managed place. Hedges, ditches, fences were all trim and in good repair and condition. The live stock evidently received the most careful attention. The out-buildings seemed equally well cared for, not a nail or a tile out of place, no lack of paint or whitewash. Even the farm implements, wagons, and so on, were all carefully ranged under cover, which is not always the case on even well managed places. Through the fields of the farm ran a small stream that had its origin somewhere in the forest. In two or three spots, it had been dammed up to make convenient watering places for the live stock and to form in front of the house a small, well sited ornamental pond.

The house itself was a low, weather beaten building, unpretentious but comfortable, mellowed by age to a beauty of its own. The farm buildings lay to one side and a little in the rear, and Bobby noticed, running from the house and between the buildings, wires that suggested Mr Ford made good use of electric power. Apparently an up-to-date as well as a prosperous establishment. Money had evidently been spent freely, and Bobby wondered whether it had all come from profits or whether there had been perhaps an overspending of capital. If so, that might account for Osman Ford's need to make use of his wife's five thousand pounds. If he had really been overspending on the place, then that money of hers might be very badly needed indeed, possibly even needed to avoid bankruptcy.

If a man were threatened with the loss of all this for the lack of a little more cash, and if he were refused, by a narrow-minded lawyer, the use of money he might think himself entitled to, he would be quite likely to feel very deep resentment indeed. Little wonder perhaps that Osman Ford's anger had seemed to glow within him like a living fire.

Bobby noticed, too, that in front of the house was a very well arranged garden, at the moment gay with flower beds. It was a really fine display, and Bobby looked at it with admiring envy. Since his marriage and his removal from London to Wychshire he, too, had been endeavouring to cultivate a garden but with a success so far strictly limited. This garden was not much larger than his own, but it had been laid out with unusual skill and taste and tended evidently with equally unusual care and knowledge. Bobby had been told more than once that farmers as a rule despised gardening, considering it a waste of time and energy and grudging fiercely every hour that garden took from farm. Surprising, Bobby thought, to find grim and dour Osman Ford an exception to that common rule, for gardens such as this are not made by sitting in the shade, and evidently much care and labour had gone to its cultivation.

He pushed open the gate and entered, and all at once there stood up and faced him a small, pale, scared-looking little woman, who seemingly only controlled with difficulty her first impulse to take to instant flight. She had been bending so low over a flower bed with which she was occupied that he had entirely overlooked her proximity, and indeed her whole appearance gave an odd impression that she was always likely to be overlooked. She had on an enormous gardening hat, and a huge gardener's apron provided with innumerable pockets for all the appliances of the craft. The gauntlets she wore to protect her hands looked almost as big as herself. In fact, a fanciful person might have been excused for supposing that she was not actually there, but only existed as a kind of impalpable background for apron, hat, gauntlets, and the other gardening paraphernalia that alone possessed substantial reality.

Trying to make his voice as reassuring as if he were speaking to a small, frightened child, Bobby explained that he had called to see Mr Osman Ford on a matter of business.

"Oh, yes, yes," she answered, edging away a step or two as she spoke, as if she felt safer at a distance. "I expect they will tell you at the office where he is, the small building on the left."

Bobby turned to look and when he looked back she had vanished, merged apparently in the garden, for just at first he could see no sign of her till he discovered her behind some tall-growing hollyhocks.

With an amused shrug of his shoulders Bobby walked on along a path that took him in the direction of the indicated building, a small one-story affair and apparently a recent addition. He noticed it had been planned with some skill to harmonize with its surroundings and to leave unobstructed a fine vista across fields and stream towards the great mass of the distant forest.

"Certainly a good deal more in Mr Osman Ford than you would think at first," Bobby decided.

He thought, too, how curious are the contrasts between human beings, between the vivid, vital, passionate Anne Earle for instance, formed to attract attention in any surroundings, and the small, timid, frightened little mouse of a woman he had just been talking to. If, as he supposed, she were Mrs Osman Ford, the former Miss Vigors, Bobby told himself it was no wonder she had been unable to offer much resistance to the wooing of so dominating, tempestuous a personality as her present husband and former bailiff. "As much chance as a lamb against a wolf, a dove against an eagle," Bobby told himself, and felt very sorry for the poor little woman, who would hardly dare nowadays, he supposed, call her soul her own.

"I don't expect he actually ill-treats her," he decided, "but she'll have to toe the line and quick about it. Most likely after her father's death she was all alone without any male relation to help her."

He was still feeling very sympathetic when he reached the office building. Telephone wires ran between it and the house and buildings. A complete system apparently. The door was half open and through it came the busy rattle of a typewriter. Before the typewriter was seated a brisk, efficient-looking young woman who glanced up, saw him, and said:

"Please come in. Mr Ford is out on the farm. Kindly take a seat. If you will state your business I will try to call him."

Bobby accepted the invitation and found himself in a very modern, well fitted office. There were two filing cabinets, a card index cabinet, a small safe, a house telephone exchange, everything in fact that up-to-date business requires. A farm to-day, especially in war time, demands so much clerical work, so much filling up of official forms, keeping records, giving, receiving and delivering orders, that the farmer needs to be not only a farmer but also accountant, correspondence clerk, filing clerk, cashier, in fact a whole office staff in one. Osman Ford, who grudged every moment taken from the land, had, like some other farmers on a large scale, thought it worth while to employ skilled clerical labour in the person of the young woman now busy with her typewriter, sharing her services with another farmer to whom half her time was allotted.

Bobby said as he seated himself:—

"You might tell Mr Ford Inspector Owen of the county police would like to see him for a moment or two, if convenient."

The young woman looked at him with indignation. In these days of multitudinous orders and regulations police are visitors to farms both frequent and unwelcome. She said sternly:

"There's no foot and mouth disease on this farm or in this district either. Or any swine fever," she added still more sternly.

"I'm sure there isn't," said Bobby amiably, though he knew very well that there had been disturbing even if unconfirmed rumours of the dreaded foot and mouth disease having appeared in the district, and though he knew, too, that sometimes farmers were apt to ignore the trouble on its first appearance in the hope that it would disappear of itself and so they would be saved the loss and inconvenience of the stand still order. "It's nothing of that sort I've come about," he added.

The young woman gave him a frowning and suspicious look as if she did not much believe him and then turned to her small private exchange. She plugged in to 'Pigsties' first, got no response, tried 'Silos' and 'Stables' with equal lack of success, said 'Tcha' impatiently, and remarked that she didn't know where every one could be, and then got a return call from 'Pigsties'. She listened and said to Bobby:

"Mr Ford is on his way here. He won't be long."

It was in fact only a moment or two before he appeared. He was dressed now in his working clothes, heavy boots and gaiters, a loose Norfolk jacket with large bulging pockets, filled no doubt with samples of grain and oilcake, packets of seed and so on, and he was carrying a pitchfork sloped over one shoulder. When he saw Bobby he halted in the office doorway and favoured him with a stare of slow hostility. Bobby said:

"Oh, good day, Mr Ford. I was driving by here on some business, and I wondered if I could have a word or two with you in private."

"No," said Osman Ford.

Bobby raised his eyebrows.

"Well, really, Mr Ford, that's a little abrupt and decided, isn't it?"

Osman said nothing. He had a way of saying nothing that was very expressive. Bobby made a little bow and moved towards the door. Osman drew back to let him pass. Bobby closed the door behind him as he went out. Now they were alone on the threshold of the office, the closed door behind them, through it coming the renewed rattle of the typewriter to show the efficient young woman was briskly at work again. Bobby said:

"I merely wanted to inform you, Mr Ford, that we have received complaints that you have uttered certain threats. I don't know if the complaint is justified. I hope not. I have not thought it necessary to inquire. But I may remark that uttering threats is very clearly a police matter. If the complaints are repeated, inquiries will have to be made. You understand that at present I am merely mentioning it privately and unofficially, simply so that you may know what is being said."

"You are on my land," said Osman. "Get off it."

"Well, I've certainly no desire to stay on it any longer than is necessary," Bobby answered, "but don't you think you are being rather needlessly offensive?"

"No."

"And just a little foolish as well?"

"I've told you," Osman said, still more threateningly. "Get out or I'll throw you out."

"Good day, then," Bobby said and walked away, trying to look as dignified as it is possible to look when retiring under threat of personal violence.

He knew well it would never do for the secretary to the chief constable and the head of the Wychshire C.I.D. to get involved in a scuffle with a bad-tempered, bad-mannered farmer.

"Hi," shouted Osman after him.

Bobby, still dignified, took no notice, though he did walk just a trifle more slowly. Osman shouted again, bellowed rather:

"Hi! You!" And, when Bobby, continuing to be dignified, still took no notice: "If you are so keen on detecting, why don't you try Rose Briar Cottage? Plenty to detect there."

Bobby still took no notice. If the man had anything to say, he could say it properly and decently, not bawl like that, breaking the peace and quiet of this lovely garden with his raucous shouts. Bobby's indifference evidently exasperated Osman as much as, perhaps, it was meant to, and he let out another bellow that ended abruptly in full volume. Bobby, his curiosity this time really aroused, looked back. Osman, staring hard at the sky, as though all at once it had begun to interest him enormously, was shuffling nervously with the toe of his heavy farming boot in the gravel of the well-kept path. He had exactly the air of a clumsy, coltish school boy, aware of the eye of authority and more than half expecting stern rebuke. At the door of the house little Mrs Ford was visible, just visible, that is, her small faded self hardly noticeable against a background of wall and Virginia creeper. Had it not been such an absurd idea, one might almost have supposed that here were cause and effect—Mrs Ford's appearance, Osman's silence and embarrassment—and that Mrs Ford did not approve of noisy shouting in her quiet garden.

She disappeared back into the house or somewhere. Difficult in fact to notice where or when so insignificant a presence did disappear. Osman turned and went back—it wouldn't be fair to say, crept back—to the office. Bobby, faintly puzzled, walked on towards his waiting car and then forgot all about the incident as he wondered what Osman had meant by saying there was much 'to detect' at Rose Briar Cottage.

CHAPTER III
ROSE BRIAR COTTAGE

IT WAS NOT difficult for Bobby to invent some excuse for calling again at the small police station he had previously visited, and as he was leaving he remarked to the sergeant to whom he had been talking:

"By the way, is there a Rose Briar Cottage near here?"

The sergeant gave him a quick look, wondering evidently what had produced this inquiry that sounded so casual but that he guessed had a purpose behind it.

"Yes, sir," he said. "It lies on the Chester road a little past the London fork. Occupied by Mrs Augusta Jordan and a niece of hers, Miss Anne Earle. Miss Earle works in a Midwych office."

Bobby had more than half expected it might be Anne Earle's name he would hear and there seemed to rise before him a memory of her dark and passionate face, her eyes in which deep fires could glow so clearly and so easily. The sergeant had paused but his manner made it plain there was more to come if Bobby wished to hear it. Bobby said:

"Know anything about them?"

"One or two reports. Gossip mostly, nothing to take action on," the sergeant answered. "You know what villages are for gossip, all of 'em knowing all about their neighbours and inventing a lot more."

"What sort of gossip?"

"Oh, they say a man has been seen leaving the cottage early in the morning. No reason why an elderly lady and her niece shouldn't have a man friend visiting them, but he slips away as if he didn't want to be seen and that's set tongues going. Then there's a story that at week-ends Miss Earle goes for a walk and she meets a car and she hops in and doesn't turn up again till she gets back from town on Monday evening. Visiting friends perhaps. Why not?"

"Anyhow, no business of ours," Bobby agreed. "We aren't guardians of people's morals, thank goodness. Your men haven't made a report of that, surely?"

"Oh, no, sir, that's just the talk that's going about and leaving out the nods and winks that go with it. It was Smith made a report. He saw a young man climbing out of an upstairs window and sliding down the drain-pipe. Looked like breaking and entering and there had been a complaint already so Smith started to challenge him and then someone—Smith couldn't see who—fired a couple of shots out of the window, either at the young chap or just to give him a scare. Smith yelled up to the window to stop that and pounded off after the young chap. Well, sir, you know yourself, you don't get quicker on your legs as you get nearer pension age and so that was no good. Smith says that anyhow what with the shooting and one thing and another the chap had so good a start no one could have caught him before he got to the forest. That's as may be, but anyway he got there all right and of course once in the forest he was safe enough. We never traced him. Fair haired, long legged young chap was all the description Smith could give and not much to go on."

"Hardly enough," agreed Bobby, who remembered Smith as a sound and comfortable presence with a good many years of service to his credit, but not likely to be at his best across country.

"The funny thing," the sergeant went on, "is that when Smith got back the window was shut and when he knocked he couldn't get an answer at first. When Mrs Jordan did come to the door, she as good as accused Smith of being drunk or lying. Said she had been indoors all the time, and nothing had happened and no one had fired any shots. Smith sticks to his story and he says, too, that Mrs Jordan was all hotted up and had a bruise under her eye that showed plain, though she had been plastering powder and stuff on it. Smith says when he asked her about it she just used some more language and banged the door in his face."

"Probably she had her reasons for keeping the young man's name quiet," Bobby remarked. "Not to mention the shooting, didn't care to have police know she took pot shots out of bedroom windows."

"Yes, sir, only what was that young man sliding down drain-pipes for? Miss Anne Earle wasn't there, she's in town during the day." He permitted himself a faint smile. "If you had ever seen Mrs Jordan, Mr Owen, sir, you wouldn't think any young man would want to go sliding down drain-pipes on her account."

"You said something about a previous complaint?" Bobby remarked.

"Attempt at breaking and entering. Two or three weeks earlier. One morning when there was no one at home, Miss Earle at her office and Mrs Jordan in town—she takes the bus in for shopping or a show once or twice every week. She rang up and I went round myself. There had certainly been attempts to force both the doors, both at the front and the back, and one of the ground floor windows as well. It hadn't been managed, though. Interrupted perhaps or got the wind up, if it was an amateur. But why did Mrs Jordan complain then and next time swear black and blue nothing had happened? Besides as good as telling Smith he was drunk. Hurt Smith cruel that did, him being strict chapel and T.T. since birth. Why, they say he wouldn't take his mother's milk till he was sure she hadn't had any drink to keep her strength up."

"Nothing we can do about it, anyhow," Bobby remarked. "Probably she knew she hadn't a firearms licence and was afraid of being fined and having the pistol confiscated."

"It might be that," agreed the sergeant, but doubtfully. "After that, Smith kept an extra special sharp look-out there whenever he was on that beat, on account of Mrs Jordan's telling him he had been drinking, making him a bit resentful like, not to say spiteful, which seemingly you are apt to catch from being extra strict chapel and T.T. I reckon human nature being what it is it's got to find a way out somehow."

"That, Sergeant," said Bobby, much impressed, "is a remark of profound psychological significance."

"Yes, sir," said the sergeant suspiciously, thinking that if any one but an inspector had said that, he would have given him his choice of taking it back or having it pushed down his throat.

Would Smith know the drain-pipe-sliding young gentleman again?" Bobby asked.

'He said not, he only saw his back and his long legs going as he made off. City clothes, bare headed, light-coloured hair and that's about all."

"Smith's extra special watch produce anything else?" Bobby asked next.

"It was what he heard—threatening language like," the sergeant answered, and Bobby looked a little startled, for here it seemed was talk of threats again.

"What threats? Who?" he asked sharply.

"Last week it was, Wednesday. Smith was on day duty and seemingly he hung about Rose Briar Cottage a bit, feeling sort of sore and brooding like over being called drunk, and he heard quarrelling going on. A woman and a man, he said."

"Did he see who they were?"

"No. He hung about so long I ticked him off for keeping me waiting or I don't suppose he would have said anything. He must have been in the garden close up, to hear all he said he did, and he might have got ticked off again for entering private property without reasonable cause, it not being part of police duty to listen at windows. He said they were fair shouting at each other. The woman was yelling she wouldn't put up with it and he had better mind what he was doing, and the man telling her to mind herself, because if it was blackmail she meant he knew how to deal with that all right. And she said something about him trying to push her in the canal and he back answered he was sorry he hadn't, because then she wouldn't have bothered any one any more. But Smith didn't seem too clear about which of them said what, what with their both shouting at each other at once and him uneasy about listening at all."

Bobby liked this talk of the canal and people pushed therein even less than he had liked the mention of threats. Confused and doubtful as it all appeared, like passing glimpses of sketches for a picture not yet completed, there seemed to him to be ugly, underlying implications. He was aware of a feeling that the picture when completed would be no pleasant one. But these scant scraps of knowledge, these vague and doubtful hints gave no ground for action. Nothing to be done. Bobby asked a few more questions but learnt no more. Constable Smith stuck to his story, had plainly the very worst opinion of Rose Briar Cottage and everything connected with it, admitted he had possibly exceeded the strict limits of his duty by entering the Rose Briar garden to overhear a private conversation, stuck to it that threats had been exchanged and that they sounded as though they had been meant, regretted that he was not sure of being able to recognize the voices, though certain that one was that of a man, one that of a woman, and, finally, hinted a determination to keep a sharper eye than ever on the cottage, its inmates and visitors.

"Me drunk?" he complained through a heavy walrus moustache, "folks who say things like that about other folks did ought to be respectable folks themselves."

Bobby did not much think that 'respectability' would in any case justify unfounded accusations, but agreed it might be as well to keep a careful but discreet—he laid an emphasis on the last word—watch on the cottage. It also came out as a result of this talk that the unfavourable opinion held in the village of Rose Briar Cottage and its inmates was at least in part due to the fact that Mrs Jordan made all her purchases in Midwych, buying nothing in the neighbourhood unless it was some trifle she had forgotten to get in town. It was also matter for comment that all that came from Midwych came from the best and most expensive shops there. There had even been deliveries of cases of champagne, a fact that had stirred the village to its depths, for while the production of champagne at any special festivity, a wedding or other unusual celebration, met with approval, even with awed approval, its use as an everyday beverage suggested somehow extreme depravity. The complaint was general that the only money of Mrs Jordan's the village ever saw was that paid to the woman who went to the cottage three mornings a week to help in the housework and brought back tales of the lavish, careless, and untidy style of living prevalent there.

"Everything of the very best, money no object, fair chuck it about so they do," she would say.

Bobby went away in a puzzled and uneasy mood. There was nothing in all this on which police action could be taken, and yet it seemed to him a situation unstable and full of menace with so many vague ominous hints coming from so many different quarters. Nor did he like this tale of a pistol fired from the cottage window at an unidentified fugitive or the recurrent mention of the canal that had already been the scene of one sudden and mysterious death linked in some way with those people of whom he was already beginning to think as centring upon Rose Briar Cottage.

Nothing to be done. Any inquiry about the firing of the pistol would only be met with renewed denial. Nothing to be done but await the event that it was to be hoped would never occur. But mingled curiosity and unease combined to make Bobby think he would like to have a look himself at this cottage around which there seemed to revolve so much that was ominous, mysterious, and disturbing.

The way took him over the canal of which so often mention had been made. He crossed it by a high, steeply arched bridge known as Ends Bridge. On the further bank he stopped, got out of his car, and went back, descending from the roadway to the canal bank by steps running down from the side of the bridge. The water ran dark and sluggish, stirred at the moment to faint oily ripples by a chill, damp breeze that blew beneath the bridge. The towing path in spite of recent dry weather, was wet and muddy. Probably the water seeped up through the foundations of the bridge. One had the impression that here the sunshine never came, that always it lay under the brooding shadows cast by the bridge overhead and the steep embankment of the road. Just about here, Bobby knew, young Mr Youngman, once Miss Vigors's suitor, had walked into the canal one dark night and been no more known in the world of living men. The water lapped lazily, softly, evilly, on the bank of the towing path. Bobby, his hands in his pockets, stood staring at it thoughtfully. A man bemused with drink might drown easily enough on a dark night. Or, in panic, he might splash away from safety and the bank into the middle of the water and so drown there. Or, on a cold night, an old man or a man with a weak heart, might lose consciousness as a result of the sudden shock of immersion. But, normally, there seemed little reason why any one who had slipped accidentally into the water, should not rescue himself easily enough by catching hold of the brick-lined edge of the path and hauling himself on to the land again.

Bobby found his mind oddly obsessed by thoughts of that past tragedy. A young, strong man should not have died so easily, he thought. But all that had happened long ago. Useless now to wonder or ask questions.

The dead, swollen body of a drowned cat came floating down the canal's slow, greasy current. With a shudder of repugnance Bobby turned away. A lonely spot, for the road by which he had come was not much used, and the canal carried little traffic, since the railway company to which it belonged preferred that goods should be carried on the more expensive and more profitable railway line and took steps to see that that happened. A hidden, solitary spot, fit indeed for stratagems and treasons—or for worse. Bobby did not like to think of any fellow creature choking out his life in the darkness in that yellow, sullen flood.

Quite a relief to come presently to a cheerful-looking village where the gentle, accustomed life of the everyday world was pursuing its ordinary course. There were even no signs here as yet of the war strain that was fast approaching. Young men were still going about their work, and friendly signs on cottage windows still offered teas with severe rationing as yet only a distant speculation. Beyond the village, following the directions given him, Bobby found the fork in the road he had been told of. Taking the westerly branch he came soon to Rose Briar Cottage.

A pretty, almost theatrically pretty place, it seemed, with its steep thatched roof—though this was a district in which thatching was not practised—its dormer windows above and bow windows below, all with diamond panes twinkling in the sun, its creeper-clad walls, its ostentatiously rustic porch. A lovely little garden, too, bright with flowers all neatly bedded out, and a lawn on which not a blade of grass was out of place. Charming, Bobby thought it at first, and then the longer he looked at it, the less he felt it so. Something was wrong. Too artificial, he decided presently, out of touch with its surroundings, a business man's idea of what a country cottage ought to be, founded probably on unconscious memories of musical comedies. Bobby would hardly have been surprised to see the heroine come round the corner and begin singing some popular air.

He had stopped the car to get a good look at the place. A window opened and a woman thrust out her head and stared at him suspiciously across the flowering hedge. A woman not young, now, with hair of so intense a raven hue as instantly to suggest dye, with red inflamed eyes that had rolls of swollen flesh beneath, a great hooked nose, a thin rat trap of a mouth. A plentiful application of powder, an equally lavish use of rouge and lipstick, had removed all human expression from the face, except that implicit in the small, uneasy eyes and in the hungry, thin-lipped mouth. An unpleasant face, Bobby thought, but he thought also the opportunity was not one to be lost. He got down from the car and opened the garden gate. He noticed that it was a lich gate and he wondered, as he had done before, if people knew the meaning of the word 'lich', or what was the original use and purpose of the lich gate. He went on up the flagged path, under a kind of pergola of climbing roses, and at the cottage door found waiting him, hostility and suspicion expressed in her every attitude and movement, the woman whose face he had seen at the window. A big woman, he saw now, fat and unhealthy looking, with a suggestion about her that she both ate and drank too much, sloppy and untidy in appearance as well, with her hair ill arranged, her dress unfastened at the throat, one stocking holding itself up in uneasy wrinkles, her feet in loose slippers. Nor were her hands too clean, and from her there exuded a strong odour of some cheap scent.

"She is expecting something, she is afraid of something," Bobby thought, and he wondered if between this woman and Anne Earle there could be either kinship or friendship or any kind of mutual sympathy and understanding, such different types they seemed. This woman would never know a scruple or a hesitation save those dictated by fear or self interest. The girl would probably know many, both scruples and hesitations, though her inner demon might drive her on to override them all.

Lifting his hat, adopting his most conciliatory manner, Bobby said:

"Excuse me, madam, I'm so sorry to trouble you but could you put me on the right road to Midwych?"

"Turn back the way you've come," she answered, her voice harsh and grating. "There's a sign post there. You must have passed it. I suppose you can't read?"

"Oh, I can read," Bobby assured her. "I must have over-looked it somehow."

"Pity you haven't better eyes," she retorted, and added viciously: "Mr Policeman."

If there was one thing that annoyed Bobby more than anything else, it was being recognized and greeted as a policeman when he was in plain clothes. He was quite sure he did not look like a policeman, and he thought it strange and unfair that so many people should make what were, he was convinced, merely lucky guesses thrown out at random. He felt he disliked and mistrusted the woman—Mrs Jordan, he supposed—more than ever, and he asked crossly:

"Why should you think I am a policeman?"

"Snooping around," she retorted.

"Is that what you call asking the way?"

"Asking my hat. You aren't in uniform so you aren't a soldier, though you're young enough to be called up. But you've a straight back, a well drilled back, a policeman's back if it isn't a soldier's."

With that she banged the door in his face and he went back to his car, convinced now that not only did he dislike Mrs Jordan but that she was a formidable as well as an objectionable person.

CHAPTER IV

MESSRS CASTLES

It was only the next morning that Bobby, returning from one of the numerous conferences on A.R.P. at which he had for the time to represent the absent Colonel Glynne, found on his desk the card of Mr Nathaniel Anderson, the senior partner in Castles.

Bobby looked at it thoughtfully. Something else about Rose Briar Cottage or about Osman Ford, perhaps. Was it possible that these reported threats Osman was supposed to have uttered Mr Anderson took so seriously that he was going to apply for police protection? The address, that of the firm, was Chief Building; a large, new and imposing block of offices in the centre of the town, just off Market Street, where, from time immemorial, until comparatively recent years, a market had been held twice a week. But the market had waned as the town had waxed, and now was little more than a collection of cheap stalls banished to that Bye Street which now crept humbly along at the back of magnificent Chief Building.

Mr Anderson had left no message or hint of the nature of his business, and Bobby found himself wondering what this man could be like, this sober business man, head of a responsible firm of solicitors, who apparently kept a country cottage for the benefit of one of his staff; who seemed to have aroused in her who was no common type such strong emotions; who equally had aroused in Osman Ford such strong emotions of quite another kind; who again, according to what current gossip you chose to listen to and believe, had swindled the son of his former chief out of his rights and installed himself in the place rightfully belonging to the boy, or alternatively had treated the young man with extreme generosity, providing him with his education and his opportunity in life.

It was near lunch time and Bobby decided suddenly that even if it meant cutting down the time he allowed himself for his midday meal—the war had long since ended that comfortable arrangement of the leisurely days of peace by which he had been able to motor home each day at noon—he would spare a few minutes to call at Messrs Castles's office. One could always judge a man better if one saw him in his accustomed surroundings. Osman Ford's smouldering anger; Anne Earle's brooding passion; unpleasant Mrs Jordan; Rose Briar Cottage with its artificial appearance, its mysterious visitors climbing out of first-floor windows and its pistol shots subsequently denied; in the background, the tale of the man who years before had died in the muddy canal to clear the path for a rival; all that had combined to awake in Bobby's mind a foreboding of ill things to come. Yet he hoped they might still be avoided by a more complete knowledge and a wider acquaintance with the characters of those concerned.

He arrived at Chief Building. Messrs Castles's offices were on the first floor, to which there was access, not only by the lifts, but by a fine spreading stair, whereof the dignified upward sweep added much to the imposing character of the entrance. True, it ended on the first floor, thence succeeded by a narrow winding stair no one even thought of using. But that great sweep of stairway facing the entrance almost compelled use, and Bobby, ascending it, found himself facing a large double doorway on which was painted the name of the firm, and, in smaller letters, an injunction to 'enter without knocking'.

Obeying the invitation Bobby pushed open the door. Within was an enormous room, well lighted, extremely well fitted up. Desks for the staff were arranged round the walls, and in the centre stood a large shining mahogany table, on which lay most of the morning and financial papers. Mr Anderson, the senior partner, during a visit to America, had there seen and approved the new fashion of accommodating all the staff, senior and junior together, in one big room. It was a fine idea, democratic, friendly, intimate, making for goodwill and understanding all round, Mr Anderson had declared. When the firm moved from the dingy old offices previously occupied into this modern building, he had made it a condition of his tenancy that this enormous room should be provided for the staff. It had the further advantage, Bobby reflected, of keeping the whole staff continually collectively, and comfortably under the eyes of their employers, so that opportunities for gossip and general slacking were limited. But that no doubt was merely, so to say, a by-product.

Near the door, on the right as one entered, was a large writing table, marked 'Enquiries', spelt with an 'E'. At the moment, there was no one there. Bobby, glancing quickly round with eyes trained instantly to take in details, saw that all the members of the staff, even a small office boy, were furnished with big, brightly polished mahogany writing tables, all, even the office boy's, covered with masses of papers calculated to impress the casual visitor and possible client with the great amount of business being done. At one end of the room were three doors, marked respectively, Mr Anderson, Mr Blythe, Mr Castles. Another door was marked 'Registry'. Two other doors were marked, the one, Reception Room; the other, Waiting Room. Later, Bobby found out that the Reception Room was for ladies, and for clerical and country clients or others presumed to be of the most unsophisticated type. It was furnished in a comfortable, homely, friendly style likely to induce a pleasant confidence in the possibly nervous client little used to visiting solicitors. The Waiting Room was for business men, and was furnished in an efficient, plain, no-nonsense-about-it style, equally calculated to inspire confidence in the man of affairs.

So again in the great outer room the writing tables, where the lady members of the staff sat, were graced with flowers, while the men had to be content with desk 'phones, though as they could all communicate with each other by getting up and walking across the floor these were but little used. The whole place indeed gave an air of careful arrangement, of a belief in the value of appearances very natural in an age that judges chiefly by appearances. It breathed friendliness (flowers) and efficiency (desk 'phones) against a background of knowledge and experience suggested by shelves lined with works of reference and bound volumes of legal periodicals.

It was all quite impressive at first sight; and only later did Bobby come to recognize here the same thing he had noticed at Rose Briar Cottage, where the first impression of rural charm and innocence had come so soon to wear an arranged and artificial air, just as here also there was too much carefully arranged show. Something 'phoney' both about the cottage and the office, Bobby came presently to tell himself. At the cottage, innocence; here, confidence and trust, were so loudly suggested as almost to suggest the opposite, that neither innocence nor trust-worthiness existed where both had to be so violently suggested; 'forced', so to say, on the visitor as a conjuror forces on his unsuspecting victim the one special card he intends to be chosen.

No one for the moment took any notice of Bobby. The staff had been allowed to understand that notice should not be taken too quickly of the entrance of visitors. So constant was the flow of clients, it was to be subtly indicated, that the appearance of one more was altogether likely to escape notice.

Coming towards Bobby as he stood by the door was a plump, fair, blue-eyed girl, with fair, curly hair that seemed exceptionally to owe its curls to nature rather than to the genius of Monsieur Marcel, with a complexion of cream and roses surprisingly unspoilt by that craze for cosmetics by means of which so many women seem to think they can enhance their charms in presenting to the world a countenance strongly resembling an egg. And though eggs have many and striking, occasionally very striking, merits, charm is not among them. It was this newcomer who presided apparently at the 'enquiries' table. And Bobby noticed, too, that at a table near sat Anne Earle, busy at her typewriter with that same air of doom she had shown before, as though indeed these were death warrants that she typed.

To the fair-haired girl as she came up to him, Bobby said:

"Is Mr Anderson in?"

"I'm so sorry," she answered. "He had to go out to an important conference and I hardly think he will be able to get back just yet. Our Mr Castles would be at liberty in a few minutes, I think. I could inquire, if you would like him to see you."

"Oh, I won't trouble Mr Castles, thank you," Bobby told her. "I daresay I can see Mr Anderson some other time. It's nothing very pressing."

He was turning away when Anne, who had not seemed to be taking much notice, got to her feet. She had a swiftly sudden, somewhat disconcerting speed of movement. She had left her seat and was standing between Bobby and the fair girl before Bobby realized she had stirred. In that deep, harsh voice of hers with the ringing undertone, she said:

"Ursula, one moment." Then more directly to Bobby: "Miss Harris didn't mean Mr Anderson would be so very long. I am sure he would like to see you." To the fair girl she had called Ursula, she added: "It's Inspector Owen."

Her full deep voice had great carrying power, and large as was the room, and busy as was, or appeared to be, every one in it, they all turned and stared, for Bobby's name and status were by this time well known in Midwych. The sudden interest thus shown Bobby understood, for he was a policeman, and the visits of the police on duty bring often their own excitement with them, but it was plain that there was also unease, almost apprehension, as though beneath the smooth surface of this ordinary, busy solicitor's office ran under-currents of doubt, of suspicion, and of fear.

One young man, for instance, when he heard the words 'Inspector Owen', turned round so quickly that he knocked a book from his table to the floor. It was a heavy book, it fell heavily with a resounding bang, the noise of its fall made everyone start afresh and turn and look, but of all that he himself took no notice, so entirely did his interest seem absorbed by Bobby's appearance. He was a tall, fair-haired youth, long limbed, a little thin as yet but likely to fill out in a year or two; his face pale, thin, and long like himself, with a smudge of a moustache beneath a big aquiline nose and above a small mouth with red, curved lips, a mouth indeed that in a girl would have been called a rosebud of a mouth. Not that there was anything effeminate about the thin, eager face, a face indeed that narrow and pointed as it was gave him almost a predatory look. His eyes were concealed behind thick, round glasses in heavy horn frames, and above these were thick and heavy, overhanging brows. Those heavy brows, the thick glasses, gave an odd impression of ambush, as though they hid a searching and intent gaze that little escaped but which itself often went unsuspected.

"That chap's more upset than the others, what's he so nervous about?" Bobby found himself thinking, and, remembering Constable Smith's account of how easily he had been outrun, reflected that this young man's long legs would soon take him out of the reach of most people, especially out of that of a stout middle-aged country policeman. Smith's description, too, had mentioned 'fair hair', and this youth's hair was of a noticeably pale tint.

This was neither the time nor the place to stress such suspicions though, and then he became aware that the attention of the office was concentrated not only on himself but on someone who had just entered, but so quietly that Bobby had not heard him come in and with his back towards him had not known that he was there. Turning now he saw a man of middle height, made less by an habitual stoop. He wore, against the present fashion, a small beard and moustache, and his large head was crowned by a mass of snow-white, still curly hair that he wore a little long, and that served to give him a dignified and even impressive appearance. Those snow-white locks were belied, however, by the brisk youthfulness of his manner and his movements, and indeed his actual age was well under sixty, which is young enough in these days. Not now is a man of those years addressed as 'venerable' as was the philosopher Hobbes when he could count as many. His eyes, for instance, were as bright and keen as those of any youngster, though deeply sunk in a thin, ascetic face, of which the fine bones showed clearly beneath the pale, almost transparent skin. An unusual face, Bobby thought, the face of a keen, determined man, but one whose interests and ideas would never be bounded by the conventional or the commonplace. He said with a very friendly and pleasant smile:

"Inspector Owen? Oh, I've heard of you. I'm not often in court. Mr Castles looks after that side generally, but I think I remember you there once. Come along into my room. I've been wanting to see you. Colonel Glynne is laid up, isn't he? It's about the county police band. I've been wondering if I could get hold of it for a fête I'm getting up. Hopewell House, you know. Perhaps you could see the colonel for me and let me know what he thinks."

He went on chatting amiably as he swept Bobby, who knew that the police band was one of the chief constable's chief interests, through the door marked 'Mr Blythe'. "I'm Mr Blythe, George Blythe, you know," he explained in parenthesis as he hustled Bobby along in a way that suggested he never recognized an obstacle to his wishes or was much used to consult the will of others, and so into a comfortable, light, plainly furnished room, that would have resembled that of any other solicitor in good practice had not the walls been covered by rows of photographs—Hopewell House, itself, its workshops, its gardens, its swimming bath, Hopewell House cricket, football, swimming teams, the Hopewell House dramatic society presenting various plays, Hope-well House old boys who had done well in life, a whole series, in fact, representing the life of Hopewell House in every aspect. He motioned Bobby to a chair, took another himself, offered cigarettes and a drink, and nodded approval when Bobby declined both on the plea that he was bound to set an example to the rank and file who were strictly forbidden to smoke or drink on duty.

"I'm a teetotaller and non-smoker myself," Mr Blythe explained. "I don't mean I have any strict views about it. I certainly can't imagine there's any more harm in a cigarette or a glass of beer than there is in a lollipop or a cup of tea that's been brewing in the kitchen all day long." He laughed pleasantly. "Example, in my case, too. I want my boys—Hopewell House, you know—to realize a man can be a teetotaller and non-smoker and quite a normal person all the same, not the least a Stiggins. The man who doesn't know when to stop and the sour-eyed fanatic, are equally a nuisance, I think."

Bobby agreed politely and Mr Blythe, rising from his chair, began to talk about the photographs on the walls. For several minutes he talked about them with a pride and an affection that showed how thoroughly he entered into the Hopewell House life, and that Bobby found a little touching. Then he checked himself and turned away apologetically, murmuring that he was always boring people to death with Hopewell House.

"You must forgive me," he said.

In his eyes, though, there still shone a gleam of something like fanaticism that seemed to find expression, too, in his thin, finely-drawn features and general air of the ascetic who cared nothing for the ordinary pleasures and aims of life, who indeed lived as it were outside the common orbit of humanity. Bobby was oddly reminded of a picture, 'The Inquisitor', he had once seen in some picture gallery. It represented a white-haired ecclesiastic, the crucifix in one hand, the other pointing to a rack. But for the difference in costume, it might have been the same man, so strongly resemblant were attitude and expression, and even the thin, fine features. Not much, Bobby felt, that this, by definition, hard-headed, dry-as-dust solicitor would not sacrifice to further the interests of his beloved Hopewell House. Then once more Mr Blythe's expression changed and again appeared that pleasant smile, which so entirely altered his expression till he seemed neither the fanatic nor the lawyer, but just the pleasant, easy-going, friendly man of the world.

"I know I've been boring you," he apologised once more, and waited for the denial that Bobby gave with much sincerity, for he felt that Hopewell House was in fact doing exceedingly good work for boys at the dangerous age of adolescence when it is so easy for lads to go wrong. Not only girls, by any means, can take heedlessly that 'wrong turning' which leads to ruin and a wrecked life, to a fate truly 'worse than death', instead of to what might so easily have been a useful and honourable career.

"I got the notion from a place in London that I heard about," Mr Blythe went on. "I developed Hopewell House on the same lines, though according to my own ideas. Before I took over, it was being run like a reformatory—regulations, restrictions all the time, the lads treated as a bad lot, collectively and individually. Of course, the consequence was, they became so. I've changed all that. And I think the lads appreciate it. Look what they gave me last Christmas." He showed Bobby a fine pair of motoring gauntlets, lined with an expensive fur. "They put their pennies together," he said. "Two or three guineas, or more, those gloves must have cost. Far too smart and expensive for me, of course, but I have to use them in spite of the risk of making our clients think hard about our fees. Of course, I gave the money back in a subscription from my very useful friend, Mr Anon." He paused and smiled to himself with a kind of odd, almost secret satisfaction, so that Bobby wondered if 'Mr Anon' had not proved even more useful on some other occasion. He put down the gauntlets. "Well, I mustn't lose them," he said. "I'm a little apt not so much to pick up unconsidered trifles as to strew them all around where I've been. Well, Mr Owen, I didn't lure you in here to chat about Hopewell House. Or even to sting you for a subscription, and doing that has cost me a client or two, I believe. The fact is, I'm seriously uneasy."

CHAPTER V
MR BLYTHE'S PROBLEM

ONCE AGAIN THE same note of fear, of warning. It seemed to Bobby that in connection with this office, he was hearing it a little too often. He glanced up sharply. Mr Blythe was not looking at him. The lawyer's gaze was fixed on one of the Hopewell House photographs, one showing a group of the senior boys and members of the staff seated on the lawn before the building. He said:

"All those boys in that photo have had a good start in life and they are all doing well, one or two very well indeed. One of them is training for his wings in the R.A.F. That counts," he added with almost fierce emphasis.

Bobby nodded gravely. He did indeed believe that no better work could be done than to rescue a boy from the handicaps of neglect and ignorance and to give him a reasonable equipment for the battle of life where equipment counts for as much as it does in modern war. But he was faintly puzzled by a remark which seemed to have so little connection with what had been said before. No threat or menace could possibly come from that group of boys all fully launched on their careers. Mr Blythe spoke again. He said, as if referring to what he had said before:

"Everything told the police is strictly confidential, isn't it?"

He said this more as if making a statement rather than asking a question that required an answer, but Bobby replied quickly:

"Nothing told the police is confidential if it in any way affects the course of justice."

"Of course, of course, that's understood," Mr Blythe agreed at once. "But everything else." Without waiting for Bobby's confirmation, he apparently took for granted, he went on: "We always try—it's a tradition with Castles, we've tried to carry it on—to take a real interest in our staff. We try not to interfere but we do want them to feel we are all friends together. Well, one result is that we do know a good deal about them, and one thing I happen to know is that one of our staff paid you a visit the other day. Miss Earle. We have to employ women nowadays, everyone does, but I often wish it wasn't necessary. Complications. I must say I like the purely masculine atmosphere at Hopewell House." He paused for a moment as though he liked to linger on the name of the place that meant so much to him. "Not a woman in the place. Cooks. Sickbay attendant. All men. The lads do their own chores. Fatigue party for this, that, and the other in regular rotation—even one for mending socks. I like it. I think they do. I agree I'm a crabbed old bachelor. I get told so sometimes by some of my friends' wives. They hate it because they can't marry me off." He paused and laughed pleasantly. "I tell them Hopewell House is my wife, my child, my family, and they look indignant and say I could have a wife as well. So I tell them I don't believe in bigamy and that makes them still more cross. All the same, if you get men and women working in the same place, things are bound to happen. Complications. Nature, I suppose. Mind, I don't want you to think I take it too seriously, but it seems Miss Earle does, and when I heard she had been to see you I thought I had better mention it, too." "I don't suppose," Bobby said, "I should have paid Miss Earle much attention, only that the man himself had been in a day or two before. He did rather give me the idea that he had to be taken seriously."

Mr Blythe looked very surprised, even uneasy.

"I had no idea of that," he said. "That's curious. Disturbing, too. What did he come to you for?"

"He wanted advice. I had to tell him that for that he must consult another solicitor."

Mr Blythe was looking more and more surprised.

"Can't understand it," he said. "What advice? Why go to you? It's not a police matter, not from his point of view. It may be from ours. I can't imagine what Dwight was after."

It was Bobby's turn to look surprised.

"Dwight?" he repeated in a puzzled tone.

"Weren't you speaking of him?" Mr Blythe asked. "Dwight is the young man I wanted to talk to you about. An articled pupil here. Did you mean someone else? Not Dwight?"

"No," said Bobby. "I've never heard of him. My caller wasn't Mr Dwight."

"I suppose I mustn't ask who it was?"

"I had rather you didn't."

"But I can guess, can't I? Osman Ford, I expect." He gave his light, pleasant laugh. "You've got what they call a 'poker face'. Not an eyelid quivered. But I think I'm right."

Bobby did not answer and Mr Blythe rose from his chair and began to walk up and down the room. Now and again he paused to look at one or other of the Hopewell House photographs, almost as though he derived strength, encouragement, inspiration, from them. He began to talk slowly as he paced up and down and again it was almost as though he spoke as much to the photographs as to Bobby. He said:

"Osman Ford. Another complication. I didn't take Osman Ford seriously. He and his suspicions. It all seemed so silly. That's what he'll be told if he does try to consult another firm. Anderson may have taken a strict view. I don't say he didn't. I don't say I should have looked at it in quite the same light. But he is fully justified under the terms of the deed, and lawyers have to go by the letter. There would be all sorts of complications if we tried to put our own gloss on the wording of deeds. But Osman Ford was furious. A stubborn, stupid, formidable man."

"I got the impression that he was stubborn and formidable," Bobby agreed, leaving out the middle adjective however.

"Complications," Mr Blythe repeated, throwing the word over his shoulder as though he were discharging a shot. He was still standing facing the Hopewell House photographs, almost like a devotee before some shrine wherefrom he drew courage and inspiration. "Cross currents. I hadn't any idea of this Osman Ford business; I mean, not that he was taking it like that. I suppose it's the war. Everything's the war to-day." He was looking in succession at his beloved photographs, apparently finding in them an exception to the universal war that was absorbing all human activity. He went on: "It's the war that makes Osman Ford want to get hold of his wife's money. He wanted it before but the war gives him a good excuse—national need to develop the land to the utmost and capital needed to do it with. Ourselves, too. The firm. Our practice knocked flat. You can't wonder. People have something else to do today than think of litigation. Ordinary business at a standstill. People evacuating. Or serving with the forces. No time to think of anything but the war. And if there's a scandal on top of it all, the firm will be pretty well finished as a firm."

Bobby made no comment. For some time he had been wondering where all this was leading. But for the feeling he had that the Rose Briar Cottage pistol shots, the dark anger of Osman Ford, conveyed a threat for which it would be well to be prepared, he would have tried to cut the interview short and get that lunch wherefor the time was now growing woefully short.

"I don't want you to think," Mr Blythe continued, "that I haven't every sympathy for Anderson. A man can be tried too highly. His wife ran off with a younger man five or six years ago. He was hard hit. He hasn't made any attempt to divorce her. I think for a time he hoped she might return. Then when he gave that up, he thought he had finished with women. Besides, divorce scandals don't help solicitors. She would have thrown all the mud she could. He thought it better not to give her the chance. So did I. I daresay I took too selfish a line. Thinking of the firm. I admit I was very relieved when he decided to let her go her own way. Gave her a generous allowance, too. Generous even then. Far too much for his resources now and now Rose Briar Cottage as well."

"Rose Briar Cottage?" Bobby repeated.

"Oh, I know you've been there," Mr Blythe told him smilingly. "That's why I made up my mind to have a talk with you. I didn't want you to get wrong ideas. And I did want your advice."

"How did you know I had been there?" Bobby asked.

"Oh, you're too well known for people not to notice it when you make calls. It was all over the village at once. I gather they were disappointed you didn't march off the Jordan woman in handcuffs. One of our staff heard about your visit, and what one hears they all hear, and what they all hear—well, I hear it, too, before long. I suppose it was about young Dwight and his pistol practice that you went there?"

"Is he here today?" Bobby asked, evading this question by asking another, though remembering, too, both Constable Smith's tale of a fair-haired, long-legged young man and his own glimpse of the nervous and again fair-haired, long-legged young man in the outer office.

"Articled pupil," Mr Blythe repeated. "You must have seen him when you came in. Sits at the third table on your left as you enter. Tall boy. Very bad sight, eye trouble of some sort, so the army won't have him, though he swears he'll wriggle in somewhere, some time. I didn't worry much, till I heard about this pistol business. Apparently he was trying to bluff Mrs Jordan into telling names. Perhaps he knew already. Anyhow, the pistol business upset me considerably. I didn't know what to do and then I thought I would see what you thought about it. Sometimes that sort of thing is only working off steam, but sometimes it's serious."

Bobby nodded agreement. That was one of the ever recurring difficulties of police work. People were always talking, and nine times out of ten—nine hundred and ninety-nine times out of a thousand—it all ended in talk. Only sometimes it didn't, and if the police had been informed of that talk and had failed to take action, then all the blame was theirs. A little odd, though, that while Constable Smith's report stated clearly that the shots were fired at, or at any rate, after, the departing Dwight, Mr Blythe seemed to think they had been fired by him. But perhaps that had been Mrs Jordan's story and Mrs Jordan had not struck Bobby as a person likely to be very careful about strict accuracy. She might easily have felt nervous about admitting the firing and have decided to shift the responsibility elsewhere. Or again, it might have been some other person who had fired, whose name she wished to conceal. He said presently:

"Do you mean that Miss Anne Earle is Mr Anderson's mistress and that he provides Rose Briar Cottage for her, with Mrs Jordan to keep up an air of respectability?"

Mr Blythe looked a little taken aback. He made a deprecating gesture with his hand, uttering at the same time a kind of expostulating murmur.

"Of course, if you like to put it like that," he admitted. "The police way. The statement for the prosecution. Sometimes I think the greater the truth, the greater the lie. If I were defending, I should say that when a man's wife deliberately deserts him and refuses to return, then it's a divorce morally if not legally. To him, she is dead, and you can't blame him if he marries again—because in Anderson's case it is marriage even if marriage outside law and church. Law and church allow marriage if your wife's dead, and deliberate desertion is a kind of moral death. I do want you to understand, Inspector, Anderson is not in any way a loose liver. This has nothing to do with the ordinary case of the wealthy employer—not that Anderson is wealthy—seducing a young innocent trusting employee. That's how young Dwight sees it. All wrong. In Anderson's view—and in mine—he and Miss Earle are as much man and wife as if they had been properly married."

He paused and looked at Bobby, evidently expecting a reply, evidently hoping for acquiescence. Bobby said:

"These are very difficult questions. I'm glad I haven't to decide them."

"Ah, you are cautious," smiled Mr Blythe. "Learn that in the police, I suppose. I wish more people were like that. Most of them are only too anxious to decide—condemn rather. If it comes out— well, it won't do the firm any good. It might come to dissolving partnership. Oh, I'm not Don Quixote," he added with another smile as Bobby gave him a quick look. "I want to swim with Anderson if I can, not to sink with him. I've got to think of Hopewell House as well." As always when he spoke of Hopewell House, his expression softened and changed wonderfully, he looked as a lover looks when he speaks of his adored. "You see, that's really why I wanted to talk to you. If young Dwight does anything silly, the whole business is bound to come out in the most unfavourable conditions."

"Why should he?" Bobby asked, though indeed he guessed. "What is his interest in it?"

"Complications," sighed Mr Blythe. "I believe he fell in love with her as they say, at first sight. I saw him when she first came to the office, the first day." He indulged in a short, deprecating laugh. "Do you know, I actually thought the lad was unwell? He went pale, he gasped. Actually gasped. I heard him. It made me look round. You would have thought someone had hit him. I suppose it was like that. As for his work since then—well, hopeless. She seems to have a sort of—fascination, that's the only word I can think of. She came to us with first-class testimonials. Nothing to complain of in her work. I don't know how to express it. She seems to walk apart, but not in light and beauty. Like a tragedy queen rather, a tragedy queen going about her work in a solicitor's office. Sounds silly, doesn't it? But there it is and sometimes I feel that if I believed in the evil eye—well, I should think she had it. Nonsense, of course. All the same, I heartily wish she had never come to us. Young Dwight and Anderson as well, and I don't know which is the worst. Mind, I've nothing against the girl. She's perfectly well behaved. I quite believe she hasn't an idea of the effect she produces. I tried to talk to Anderson once. I don't pretend to be at all broadminded or modern or have any sympathy with some of these new ideas, but Anderson was so plainly, so utterly sincere, in such deadly earnest, that I had to let it go. He said he had never known what love was till he met Miss Earle and now he had met her and now he understood, nothing else mattered. I don't pretend to understand his state of mind, but there is it. He offered to dissolve partnership then and there but that's the last thing I want if it can be avoided. Of course, if the scandal does break, you know what everyone will say. Elderly solicitor seduces girl typist. That'll be the story everywhere, though really it's not a bit like that. More like Romeo and Juliet, or like Antony and Cleopatra rather, and the world well lost. It wouldn't be so worrying if it wasn't for young Dwight having been hit the same way. There's the money side of it, too. It's all costing Anderson a pretty penny, and then there's the allowance to his wife as well, on top of an income knocked all endways by the war."

"Do the staff know about this affair with Miss Earle?"

"I don't think so. I don't think they have any idea. Except young Dwight, of course. And I'm not sure how much he really knows and how much he only suspects."

"You are sure Dwight isn't merely trying to pry, but is genuinely in love with Miss Earle?"

"I think that's quite certain. A grand passion as they call it." A faint note of contempt, of dislike indeed was now in Mr Blythe's voice as he used this last expression. "Neither grand nor a passion if you ask me, just an obsession, but then I don't pretend to understand that sort of thing."

He paused and Bobby found himself thinking that this elderly solicitor, like his senior partner, was also the victim of a grand passion, though for no woman, for his beloved Hopewell House that Bobby felt meant as much to him as Anne Earle could mean to Mr Anderson.

"Quite changed," Mr. Blythe said suddenly. "Young Dwight I mean. I don't believe he ever thinks of his examinations now. But I didn't think it was serious till I heard about this pistol business. It will be bad enough if anything gets out about Anderson's affair, but if it's to be complicated with shootings as well—"

He shrugged his shoulders with a look of something like despair on his thin, ascetic features. Bobby said:

"How many people do you think know about Miss Earle and Mr Anderson?"

"Heaven knows. I don't. Anderson assures me he takes every precaution not to be seen when he visits the cottage, and at week-ends he apparently picks her up on the road and they go where they aren't likely to meet anyone they know—little, out-of-the-way places. But it isn't easy to keep that sort of thing quiet for long."

"What was it you heard exactly about the shooting?"

"That pistol shots had been heard at Rose Briar Cottage and young Dwight seen running away."

"Whom did you hear that from?"

"My gardener in the first place. It was all over the village. Shooting at Long Barsley and three people killed. That was the first story. I shan't forget what I felt when I heard that. I seemed to see Dwight, Miss Earle, Anderson, all dead in a heap together. The worst half-hour I have ever known till I got to Long Barsley myself and found there had been shooting all right, but no one knew what it was about and no one was hurt. Burglary seemed the general idea. I recognized young Dwight from the description. Well, what's to be done? After all, there's been shooting."

"Suppose Dwight simply denies knowing anything about it? There's no proof."

"I know. It was Dwight. There's no doubt of that. It's worrying. Am I making a mountain out of a molehill? It's the intensity of their feelings, all three of them, that frightens me."

"Does Mr Anderson know about this shooting business?"

"He won't take it seriously. I do. I believe the boy is half crazy with jealousy. Doesn't call it jealousy, I expect. Calls it avenging a young girl's honour. Or punishing elderly betrayer. Sees himself as a hero putting wrongs right. You can understand his point of view. He might give way to a youngster like himself, but not to a rich old man, which I expect is what he calls Anderson, though Anderson isn't so very old and is very far from rich. I see his point of view quite well. I've tried to show you Anderson's. Miss Earle's, I suppose, is that her life is her own and she can do what she likes with it. My point of view is frankly that I'm scared—scared of what Dwight may do, scared of the scandal breaking, scared all round. Well, there's the problem. What do you think ought to be done?"

CHAPTER VI
MISSING

A DIFFICULT QUESTION, BOBBY thought. Reflectively he rubbed the tip of his nose. On the whole he did not see that there was anything to be done, either by himself or by anyone else. A boy up an apple tree can be dealt with, even though he has touched no apple. But not a boy who from the road outside is merely casting speculative eyes on the fruit. Certainly police duty is as much the prevention as the detection and punishment of crime. But the first duty is the more difficult. No doubt a man could be detailed to keep watch on Rose Briar Cottage, but—a very big but—with all the multifarious duties developing on the police in war time, where was that spare man to be found? A warning could be administered to young Dwight, but that, too, was of doubtful wisdom and more doubtful utility. The previous attempt to warn Osman Ford had not been a great success.

Very much did Bobby wish he knew why Mr Anderson had called on him that morning. He found himself wondering a good deal what sort of man this Mr Anderson was, who seemed the storm centre round which so much revolved. A talk with him might help a decision. Bobby said as much to Mr Blythe, who nodded in agreement. But again he urged the advisability of Bobby's having a word with Dwight.

"What I do feel so strongly," he said, "is that it might help the boy to realize the position better, make him think a bit."

Bobby felt that most likely he would simply be told to mind his own business. But it might be useful. Once again, if there really were serious developments, he would certainly be asked what action he had taken in view of the various warnings received, and it was always so much better if some sort of reply was ready. Besides, a talk with Dwight would help in forming an estimate of the young man's character. He hesitated, and Mr Blythe saw that he was hesitating, and appeared to assume that according to the old saying, hesitation gave consent.

"Anderson won't be back just yet," he said. "You could use his room. I'll send Dwight to you there. You had better see him alone."

Leading the way out of his own room in which they had been talking he opened the door of the room adjacent, that marked, 'Mr Anderson'. He began to say to Bobby:

"Sit down a minute and—"

Then he stopped and stared, startled apparently and even alarmed. Bobby looked, too, wondering what had given Blythe that intent and startled air. Opposite to them as they entered, at a table occupying the centre of the room, stood a short, stocky, youngish man, whose flat nose, narrow eyes, sallow complexion, gave him a curiously Mongolian look. On the table before him was a small, open ledger, over which he was poring with an absorbed attention. He looked up as the door opened. His expression did not change. Bobby had the idea that his expression very seldom did change. But physically he seemed to draw himself together, though whether for attack or for defence Bobby could not be sure. His hand dropped on the ledger before him and grasped it firmly, almost like a weapon, Bobby thought, and that slow gesture of his did in some subtle way convey a curious suggestion of coming threat. Threat. Menace. Warning. That was always the prevailing note; a murky and a doubtful menace that seemed to start up on every side, though against whom there was as yet no clear indication.

Abruptly he closed the ledger. His narrow eyes half shut but watching the newcomers closely, he said:

"Yes. I'm here. Anderson's out. I didn't expect you back so soon, Blythe. I thought the Arlham conference would keep you longer."

"It had to be put off," Mr Blythe said. "Rogers rang through to say his car had broken down and he couldn't arrive in time."

"Bad luck," the other said, and whether he referred to the breakdown or to Blythe's return, Bobby thought doubtful.

Mr Blythe said to Bobby:

"This is Mr Castles, our managing clerk. Castles, you know Mr Owen. The county police, you know."

"I know, I've seen him in court," Castles said, but without looking at Bobby, for it was on his employer his attention seemed concentrated and it was to him he spoke now as he said:

"I wanted to look up an account."

"The Osman Ford account," Mr Blythe said, apparently having recognized the page of the ledger being consulted. "The Osman Ford account," he repeated. Then he said:

"Why?"

Castles made no reply, and in his silence Bobby felt he recognized once more that obscure note of menace, of warning, he seemed so continually to be aware of. Later on in the war, he would have been reminded of the atmosphere perceptible in city streets when the raid warning had sounded and all still went about their everyday affairs, but with an expectant and a listening air. Waiting for the explosion. So here and now in this affair, all gave him the impression of waiting for an explosion. Mr Blythe said again:

"Why the Osman Ford account?"

"Oh, there are others as well," Castles answered. "Or are there?" and across his impassive features flitted the semblance of a smile, but not a smile that had in it much of goodwill or amusement.

Deliberately he took up the ledger, opened it again, turned its leaves lightly and carelessly, and then replaced it in a safe, of which the door was open. Mr Blythe said:

"Did Anderson leave it open? I've never known him do that before."

"It is unusual, isn't it?" Castles agreed with again that almost imperceptible, quite unamused smile of his. He moved towards the door of the room. Over his shoulder he said: "Good day, Inspector. I expect we shall meet again."

He went out, shutting the door carefully behind him. Mr Blythe who was looking seriously disturbed, said with a laugh that again seemed anything but amused:

"Sounded as if he wanted to say 'At Phillipi'. Oh, well, I suppose Anderson knows, but that's his own very private ledger. I've never even seen it before, except its back, I mean not open. I suppose it's all right. Castles is a very able man, very able indeed. We shall be taking him into partnership some day."

"I suppose he's an admitted solicitor?" Bobby asked.

"Oh, yes. Yes. Thanks to Anderson. Anderson has done everything for him. Provided for his education. Gave him his articles. Everything. Promised him a partnership. That's understood. He'll strengthen the firm. I don't know why it hasn't been done long ago. It keeps getting put off." He went up to the safe and pulled at the door, but Castles had banged it to, and the lock had caught. "Oh, well," he said. "No doubt Anderson knows all about it."

"Mr Castles is a son of a former partner, isn't he?" Bobby asked.

"His grandfather founded the firm," Anderson explained. "Made it the leading firm in Midwych. Everyone always came to Castles' first. His son—our Mr Castles's father—kept the firm in the same leading position till—well, till he started trying to get rich quick on the London Stock Exchange. Gold mines. Clients don't like that. It might be their money. It wasn't, of course. No suggestion of such a thing. All the same there was gossip that did the firm a lot of harm. Clients got nervous and the firm lost a lot of business. Castles—the father, I mean—didn't worry much at first. His speculations were turning out well. He was actually getting rich quick. But the old story. He went on too long. They always do. The luck turned. There had to be a reconstruction. Every debt was paid to the last farthing but there was nothing left. He didn't live long. Left his boy without a penny. Literally. Only enough to clear up liabilities, not a penny more. Anderson stepped in. Anderson had been his managing clerk. Anderson took over. I came in. Anderson found the money for the boy's education, did everything for him, gave him his articles, made him managing clerk, promised him his partnership. I must say I think Castles has earned it. Very able man and his name counts.

Midwych people still remember it. At the reconstruction the reputation of the firm had almost gone—goodwill worth nothing. But that's altered now. After all, no one lost a penny except old Mr Castles himself and to-day the name has its value. Castles would be worth his partnership for that alone. Well, I'll tell Dwight."

He went out, leaving the door open. Through it Bobby could see into the outer office. He watched Mr Blythe walk down it, past the double row of desks, a busy worker at each one. Bobby wondered if they were always so busy, or if their industry only increased to such a pitch when a partner opened his door. The rattle of typewriters, the scratching of pens, the rustling of papers or of leaves as ledgers or reference books were consulted, now and again a sharp, brief question, an equally brief reply, all gave an impression of the usual activity of a busy solicitor's office. Yet well Bobby knew that behind that every day façade, human passions of love and hate, of greed and of ambition, were working themselves out dangerously to their appointed end. He found himself wondering how many more such offices, legal, commercial, dull to all appearance with the utter dullness of everyday routine, hid beneath their drab, commonplace exteriors such human dramas of terror and of passion.

Mr Blythe was talking to the tall, pale young man Bobby had already noticed. He noticed, too, how Anne Earle, pausing in her work with her hands lifted above her typewriter, was watching them from under her heavy brows, as if she both guessed the purport of their talk and resented it with all the formidable intensity of emotion that somehow her slightest gesture seemed able to convey. When her hands came down upon her machine as Dwight rose to walk towards where Bobby was waiting, it was as if she struck downward blows at a defeated enemy.

"I don't understand that girl," Bobby thought. "I don't know whether it would scare me more to be her lover or her enemy."

He moved back into the room as Dwight came up. Dwight stared at him from behind his thick, heavily-rimmed glasses that seemed as much a concealment and a disguise as a protection or an aid. Bobby closed the door of the room, so that they were alone together, and went and sat down on one of the chairs. Dwight remained standing. His attitude was watchful and hostile. In a pleasant tenor voice and speaking slowly, he said:

"You're a cop, aren't you? Well, what's it all about? Think you've got something on me?"

"Oh, no, not at all," Bobby answered. "At least, oh, yes, to what you said first. I'm a cop all right. But why should you think I have anything on you? Not a bad conscience, I hope?"

Dwight made no answer. He moved across the floor and leaned against the mantelpiece. He did not wish to sit and yet he had felt at a disadvantage standing while Bobby remained seated. Now, leaning against the mantelpiece and looking down on the seated Bobby, he felt on more than equal terms.

"Well, what's it all about?" he asked again.

"About an incident that has been reported. I wondered if you could give us any help or any information?"

"Why should I?" Dwight retorted. "Some of us don't see why we should have anything to do with police snooping and spying."

"If you had your pocket picked or a burglar broke into your house," Bobby countered, "would you call it snooping and spying if the police tried to find out who it was and to recover your property?"

"That's different," Dwight snapped.

"You mean it's different when you want us and our help from when you want nothing less," Bobby suggested. "I know. It's often like that. Well, never mind. A complaint has been received that pistol shots were fired at or from or near Rose Briar Cottage, in Long Barsley. Discharging firearms to the common danger is an offence, even if not a very serious one. Can you tell us anything?"

"Why ask me?"

"Because we have been informed that the shots were fired at you. Is that true?"

"First I've heard of it."

"If you don't mind, I should like a direct answer."

"Well, no one was firing at me, if that's what you mean."

"Is there any foundation at all for the story?"

This time there was a perceptible pause, but the steady fixed stare remained unchanged and the answer came:

"None that I know of. I know nothing about it."

"Are you sure?" Bobby asked. "Our information is definite. You don't wish to make any complaint?"

"Nothing to do with me," Dwight repeated.

His attitude was unchanged, impassive. His fixed stare from behind the heavy glasses he wore, never wavered. Yet Bobby could see plainly that beneath that impassive exterior was an extreme nervousness. Small signs, a deliberation of breathing, a rigidity of attitude, an obvious and careful control of every nerve and muscle told their tale plainly. Only one very much on guard would think it necessary to keep so close a watch upon himself, a watch of which the very intensity defeated its own purpose of achieving a semblance of ease.

"For you to say, of course," Bobby continued. "Then I am to understand that you know nothing of the incident reported to us, that you make no complaint even though, if we can believe what we are told, your life was in danger."

"I can look after my own life."

Bobby looked up sharply. He did not know why, but somehow the words seemed to him a challenge to fate, that fate might well take up.

"It's not always easy to do that," he said, half to himself.

"It's nothing to do with me," Dwight said again. "I'm not responsible for what your village cops choose to tell you."

"What makes you think it was a village cop?" Bobby asked smoothly. When he got no reply, only another fixed, expressionless stare, he said:

"Is it because you know a village cop was there to see?"

"Clever, aren't you?" snarled Dwight.

"Oh, no," Bobby protested. "That's almost libellous. Call a man clever in England and everyone mistrusts him at once. Instinctively they add 'By half'. No, not clever. Efficient. That's the word in this country for real heartfelt praise. Say 'Efficient' won't you?" he pleaded.

Dwight did not respond. That fixed heavy stare of his was beginning in Bobby's thoughts to take on a fresh aspect of menace and of threat. That clear, pleasant tenor voice of his grew harsh and muttering as he said now:

"If you've got a report about something you say happen- ed somewhere, it's only natural to suppose it comes from one of your snoopers. You can't make anything of my thinking that, try as you like."

"It doesn't take a snooper to notice pistol shots fired in broad daylight from a country cottage," Bobby pointed out. "Mr Dwight, I wish you would believe me when I say that all I am trying to do is to prevent trouble developing. Quite frankly, I don't like this story of pistols. I don't know what it means but I don't like it. Bullets ask no questions where they hit, they can't be controlled once they've been fired, and sometimes a man, especially a young man, loses his head and does something in a minute that may ruin his whole life."

Dwight yawned.

"If you've nothing more interesting to say," he remarked, "I'll go and get on with my work. I've got some to do, if you haven't."

He yawned again, straightened himself from the lounging position he had preserved while they talked, and went back to his desk. Bobby followed him, feeling that again his intervention had been a complete failure. More than words, more than a warning, he felt, would be needed to influence Dwight. Possibly what had been said might in the long run have its effect, but of that Bobby did not feel too sure. He remained aware of an uncomfortable sensation that beneath the smooth surface of everyday life events were hurrying to a climax he had no power to stay or alter. There had seemed to him a quality in young Dwight's sustained effort at concealed control as ominous as had seemed Osman Ford's glowing anger he had cared so little to hide. He noticed as he walked slowly through the big outer office that all the staff were watching him, watching with a cautious expectation.

"They all feel something's wrong, something's going to break," he thought.

As he let himself out he glanced back and the last glimpse he had of Dwight showed him the lad's features no longer set in a firmly held control, but contorted with some deeply felt emotion that he was doing his best to conceal behind some papers he was examining.

"Fear? Hate? Love? Which? Or all three together?" Bobby asked himself, and, descending slowly the great stairway that led to the building's entrance hall, he saw Castles standing there, waiting for him apparently. Coming forward, Castles said:

"I'm just going out to lunch, I'll walk along with you if I may."

As he spoke, he fell into step by Bobby's side. In the street, Castles said:

"I expect you are wondering what I was doing in Anderson's room."

"Not at all," Bobby answered. "Why should I? Nothing to do with me."

"Sure?" asked Castles, looking up. He seemed to have a trick of keeping his eyes on the ground and also he was a head and shoulders shorter than Bobby, but now the keenness and suddenness of his upward glance was a trifle disconcerting. He added: "You see, I've a pretty good idea why Blythe brought you in."

"Have you?" asked Bobby cautiously.

"Oh, you needn't be so careful," Castles told him. "The Osman Ford account. You heard Blythe say that was what I was looking at."

"Well?"

"I am wondering what to do."

"Are you?" Bobby asked. "Well, what are you driving at?"

"What am I driving at?" Castles repeated in a voice suddenly shaken as it seemed by an abrupt fury. He flung out one hand. He gripped Bobby by the arm with such force that that evening Bobby found faint bruises where his arm had been held. "Listen," he said. "Perhaps Anderson ruined my father. I don't know. I do know Anderson sits where my father used to sit and I'm a hired servant where my father was boss. There's another thing I know. It was Anderson saved me from the workhouse. If it hadn't been for Anderson, I should have been a pauper, with a pauper's upbringing. He's treated me like a son, but did he ruin my father and was it that killed my mother? That's the problem."

The man spoke with an intensity of emotion that shook him from head to foot. Bobby stood still and looked at him with bewilderment. One or two passers-by gave them curious, interested glances. Bobby did not speak. He did not know what to say. Castles took out a cigarette case and held it in his hand. He muttered:

"Yes, that's just the point."

"What is?" Bobby asked.

Castles began to walk away. Some instinct of doubt or of mistrust born of the excitement Castles was showing, made Bobby call after him:

"Where are you going?"

"I don't know," Castles answered over his shoulder, "That's the question," he said and walked on.

Bobby stood still for a moment or two looking after him as he hurried away, lost to sight soon in the busy traffic of the street. A good deal in all this, Bobby told himself, that he did not understand, and that he could only hope it would never be his business to understand. From the door of Chief Building he saw emerge the girl Anne Earle had called Ursula. By her side was another young man Bobby had noticed in the office of Messrs Castles. His name Bobby now knew was Roy Green. They were walking side by side. They passed close by Bobby without noticing him, without noticing anything for that matter, for they were conscious only of themselves. They did not seem to be talking but somehow they managed to give the impression that for them talk was unnecessary. In the busy traffic of the street they, too, disappeared; and Bobby found himself thinking that something sweet and wholesome and altogether natural had passed, far removed indeed from those rumblings of underground, hidden fires of passion and of doubt of which before he had felt so strongly aware. When they had vanished from sight he glanced again at Chief Building and this time he saw standing plainly visible at one of the windows on the first floor the tall, brooding, distinctive figure of Anne Earle. She was bending forward, looking down on the crowded pavement beneath, and once more he was reminded of one of the Valkyria of old, stooping over the battle, the chooser of the slain.

As he walked away Bobby told himself that he wished he had seen Mr Anderson. Everything seemed to revolve round him and yet of him, of his personality, of his character, Bobby had no knowledge whatever. It would, he felt, be much easier to decide whether all these hints and warnings and those pistol shots denied by all concerned, had any mischievous intent. He wondered, too, very much, why Mr Anderson had called to see him.

But in these strenuous days of war, there were many other things to attend to and to think of and provide for. Bobby thought little more of Mr Anderson, of Castles, of Rose Briar Cottage, till thirty-six hours later, on the morning of the following Thursday, when there came before him officially the information that Mr Anderson was missing.

He had not been seen since Tuesday night—it was on a Tuesday that Bobby paid his visit to Messrs Castles' office—and no one knew what had become of him.

CHAPTER VII
FACTS AND SURMISE

THE POLICE ARE well accustomed to reports of mysterious disappearances. Usually they mean little—a domestic upheaval, for example, or a sudden desire for a change of scene. Sometimes there is a more serious origin in the nature of trouble in cash accounts. Now and again, the reason is tragedy.

Bobby, indeed, would not have worried too much even over the disappearance of a well-known solicitor had it not followed so closely upon so much that had seemed ominous and menacing. Even as it was he hesitated to take more than routine action, since it was still possible that Mr Anderson had simply been called away on urgent business and had had reasons of his own for keeping his business secret. The inspector who brought in the report to Bobby was, too, very strongly of opinion that it would be better to wait for further developments before becoming too active.

"You go chasing round after these disappearing blokes," he said, "and ten to one in the end you find 'em back home with their wives— or else away from home with someone else's wife. Then all you get for your trouble is an all round cursing. Let 'em alone and they'll come home," he quoted, "bringing their tales with them all right."

Bobby was inclined to agree with this somewhat cynical view, but all the same he sent for Sergeant Wright, whom he had noted as not only intelligent but careful and painstaking, which is even rarer, and told him to make a few discreet inquiries.

Then he dismissed the matter from his mind till the next morning, when on his arrival at his office he found Anne Earle waiting to see him. More than ever like a tragedy queen she looked as she came into his room—Colonel Glynne's room, really—and stood gazing at him steadily from under her dark, straight brows. He offered her a chair but silently she waved it aside. Tall and still and silent she stood, waiting, apparently deep in thought, till a little puzzled, he said:

"You wished to see me? You have something to say?"

"Yes," she answered, and was silent again.

They remained looking at each other and there began again to glow in the depths of her eyes that appearance of a small and distant fire Bobby had observed before. He said:

"There is something special you wish to tell me?"

"You know Mr Anderson has disappeared?" she asked.

"We have a report," Bobby answered, "that he has not been seen at his home or his office since Tuesday. Mr Castles, your managing clerk, says they are very uneasy."

"He is dead," Anne said. "I think he has been murdered."

"Why do you say that?" Bobby asked, though he had felt from the moment of her entrance that that was what she had come to say.

"Last night I dreamed that he was drowning."

"Dreams have causes," Bobby said. "Or, if not, they are only dreams and don't matter. What caused that dream?"

"How else could he tell me except in a dream?"

"I am afraid police cannot act simply upon dreams."

"If he were alive he would let me know," she told him, and then abruptly: "You know about us? You know we lived together, that I am what they call his mistress?"

She flung the word out with passion proudly, like a challenge, like a flag that she was proud to fly. Bobby said:

"In itself, that is a private matter with which police have no concern."

"We loved each other," she told him. "We were more truly married than most of those who go to church. It wasn't our fault if we couldn't. I didn't care. It made no difference to me. What mattered was what we felt for each other. It bothered him sometimes. Never me."

"I haven't to discuss that with you," Bobby said. "People who live in society and yet break society's rules bear their own responsibility. If you have any solid grounds for believing that Mr Anderson has been murdered, please tell me. You understand you have made a very serious statement."

Her gesture then was full of a supreme contempt.

"Does a fact only become serious when it is spoken?" she asked. "I want you to understand. I've come because he has no relations likely to bother much. I shall bother a good deal." She paused and put her hands together, holding them strongly in position. "I shall not rest," she said, "till I know. Then I shall not rest either till his murderer has been punished. You see, we loved each other. I don't suppose you understand that. Why should you? I don't suppose you believe it. Why should you? People generally don't. Understand I mean. Or believe. Because they don't love either. Women want a man to look after them and give them a home and children. Women call that love. It isn't. It's a need. Love is different. It's to give and to receive, both at once, both utterly. Men want a woman as they want their dinner. One woman or one dinner is as good as another. It's an appetite. That's not love either. But we—he and I—we were different. We loved each other. Now he has gone. But he would not if he were alive. So he is dead. But he did not wish to die. Why should he while I am alive? If it was an accident, there would be some trace of it. What else is left but murder?"

"It may be so," Bobby said. "I don't know. But police need facts to act on. Have you any facts to give me?"

"The fact that no one knows what has happened to him," she answered. "Isn't that fact enough? Why do you want more? Isn't it a fact he would never have left me like this without a word?"

"I don't know," Bobby answered. "You have told me your own feelings. I believe you. But I have only your own statement of how Mr Anderson felt. Police soon learn never to accept any other than first-hand statements."

She regarded him steadily and with a faintly surprised air, as though that point of view had never even occurred to her. So certain was she of their mutual affection, she had not thought till now that anyone could doubt it. Indeed that such a doubt could exist appeared to her a little absurd, even wilful, as though one should pretend to doubt the existence of the sun at noon.

"Would I feel what I do for him," she asked presently, "if I did not know that he felt the same for me?"

Bobby did not attempt to answer. He realized that her conviction was absolute. For him that conviction was necessarily open to doubt. True, it was confirmed to some extent by the story Mr Blythe had told. She remained standing, motionless, upright and silent, for she still refused to seat herself; alight, as it were, with a kind of inner passion, a passion that Bobby felt to be akin to hysteria but that yet he felt also was held so firmly in control there was no danger of its breaking loose. Watching her in a silence not unlike her own, he was oddly reminded of Osman Ford, who had been not long before in this same room; who, too, had in something of the same way, glowed with an inner passion that in the same paradoxical manner seemed at once uncontrolled and yet held tightly reined.

"Won't you sit down?" he asked again.

She did not seem even to hear him, her sombre and heavy gaze never wavered, he had the idea that she saw quite other things than those her eyes rested on. There crept into his mind the ugly thought that women such as her, in the grip of an emotion and a passion so intense, had been known themselves to kill. He thought, too, that it would be wise to encourage her to talk as freely as possible. The more she talked, the better he would be able to judge her character. Not that that, he supposed, would be easy. There still persisted in his mind that first impression he had had of her—that she was one who hid herself, who walked indeed in a perpetual disguise, a disguise that even she herself had perhaps never penetrated. He said:

"I wish you would tell me everything you can think of. You see, we really can't do much until we have more facts."

"Oh, facts," she exclaimed with an energy of repudiation that made him smile faintly.

"They have their importance, you know," he said. "Merely symptoms of thought perhaps, but it's always symptoms both doctors and police have to deal with. To be frank with you, I don't see at present, from the strictly police point of view, what standing you have in the matter, or that you have told me anything on which I can act."

"You mean you don't believe me?" she asked scornfully. "You don't believe me when I say we were everything to each other and that I shall never rest till I know what has happened and why, and till whoever has done it has been punished. I suppose you want to see a properly executed deed, duly stamped and witnessed, explaining it all? Well, I can tell you one thing. He gave me five thousand pounds."

"Oh, yes?" Bobby said, a little startled, and he wondered why the sum had a familiar sound to him till he remembered that it was the amount of the Ford trust fund that Osman Ford had accused Mr Anderson of misappropriating.

A coincidence, probably, and one without significance, but all the same Bobby tucked the fact away in his memory as one not to be forgotten.

"You don't believe me?" she asked again, noticing, but misinterpreting, his quick upward look at her. "Do you think me such a fool as to tell you lies about something you can easily check? Or else you think it only means an old man paid for his pleasures? I suppose you would think that." There was deep scorn in her voice. "Is it so utterly impossible that two people should really care for each other?"

"When they do," Bobby observed, "they are generally more of the same age."

"I was the older," she told him. "He had stayed young. Young in body, young in spirit. I have never been young, never. Do you know anything about me?"

"Only what you have told me yourself."

"I thought you might have heard things. Perhaps you have, only you don't want to say. Everyone is generally quite keen to tell everyone else. They all do, in the office, everywhere. If you really don't know, I'll tell you. You would hear soon enough. I am a workhouse brat. Nobody's child. A foundling. On a doorstep."

She paused abruptly, and it was easy to see how much that had meant to her, how deeply her proud and aloof spirit had suffered from, and been influenced by, the circumstances of her birth.

"Well, that wasn't your fault, was it?" Bobby asked. "You couldn't help it. I thought Mrs Jordan was your aunt."

"That is how I know my name is Earle," she said. "I was called Durban before, because, when I was picked up on my doorstep it was in Durban Street. When Aunt Jordan found me she told me my mother's name was Earle and so it was mine."

"I see," Bobby said, though hesitatingly, for in fact he did not quite 'see'. "When was this?"

"Three years ago, when I was eighteen. Aunt Jordan had been living in Australia and then she came back and she made inquiries and she found me. It meant a good deal to me, to know I had a name of my own and someone belonging to me. It meant more—" She paused and repeated the word 'more' with the deep, almost solemn emotion her strong, soft, passionate voice with the ringing undertone seemed so well fitted to convey. "It meant much more when we met—Mr Anderson and me." Again she paused for a brief moment and then continued: "We both knew at once what it meant. Our meeting." After another short pause, she added: "Now he has been murdered."

"There is no need yet to feel so sure of that," Bobby said. "When did you see him last?"

"Tuesday evening. He came to the cottage."

"How long did he stay?"

"Until after supper. Aunt cooked it. Aunt is a very good cook. It is the thing she likes doing best of all. He left about half-past nine."

"By car or on foot?"

"He had left his car a short distance away. He generally did. I walked with him that far. He got in and drove away. It was about ten minutes altogether. He would be on his way home by a quarter to ten or thereabouts. He had to be in the hotel by half-past because he was expecting a long distance 'phone call."

"Was it made?"

"Yes. He was not there to answer it. It was that made us really uneasy at the office. We were surprised he hadn't come at the usual time. We thought something might have delayed him. Then we heard the long distance 'phone call had been made and he hadn't been there to answer it."

"Apparently, then, if anything did happen to him, it happened between a quarter to ten, when you saw him leave in his car, and half-past ten, when he failed to answer a 'phone call."

"Yes."

"Did you see him every evening?"

"No. But I always knew."

"Did he say anything about his next visit?"

"He told me to expect him the next evening—Wednesday. But only for a few minutes. He was busy. He was going to London this week-end and I was to meet him there. It was my Saturday off. We have one Saturday off in three at the office. We were both looking forward to it. If there had been any change in the arrangements he would have let me know. He hasn't. He is dead. Not accident. Not illness. Not suicide."

"You came here once before and complained that Mr Osman Ford had used threats against Mr Anderson? Do you want me to understand that you suspect him?"

For the first time she seemed to show some hesitation. Then she said:

"I don't know. It wasn't murder I was afraid of that other time. Somehow one doesn't think of murder—not till it happens. It seems so—so remote. What I was afraid of was that he might try to knock him about. Osman Ford is a big, strong brute, like one of his own farm animals, a great cart-horse or something. Mr Anderson was gentle and delicate. He wouldn't have had a chance to defend himself. I wanted to make sure he wouldn't be attacked. I knew he was half expecting it. It would have made a scandal, too. He was worried about business. Business has been very bad since the war began and a scandal might have been fatal. That's why, too, he was so careful about us. Of course, that doesn't matter now."

"He was hard pressed for money and yet he found five thousand pounds for you?"

"Yes. That was why. To make me secure, he said. Because sometimes he said he thought he was going to lose all his money. So while he still had some he wanted to give it to me so as to make me what he called safe. Of course, money doesn't, money can't, but it's how he felt."

For the first time she smiled faintly, as if at the memory of a lovable and touching but also futile and even childish precaution. To Bobby it seemed she was genuinely unconscious of the other and graver implications that this transaction so clearly carried with it. Yet of that he could not be sure. There was nothing about Anne Earle, he told himself with exasperation, of which he could be sure. She might, and quite possibly did, understand very clearly indeed, and yet for obvious purposes wish to give him an impression of complete indifference and ignorance.

He wondered whether to ask her any more questions and then made up his mind not to do so for the present. If the affair were to take the serious turn suggested, there would be plenty of time and many occasions for further questioning. He thanked her formally for what she had told him, promised to take such steps as were possible, and as would indeed become necessary if Mr Anderson's absence remained much longer unexplained. But with that she did not seem content.

"What you mean," she interrupted abruptly, "is that you will do in your official way what you are officially obliged to do. That's not enough. It only means wasting time till it's too late. I don't mean to let it be like that."

Therewith she turned and went swiftly away in her quick, unexpected manner; and Bobby, too late to get to the door to open it for her, saw her pass through and along the corridor beyond, as one intent upon her own purposes. A little uneasily he went back to his desk to get on with the more pressing of the war-time work by which he was being daily overwhelmed.

CHAPTER VIII
THE GLOVE

LATE IN THE afternoon of the following day there reached Bobby a report to the effect that a young man, unidentified, had been seen to throw a glove into the Midwych, Wychshire and Southern Canal, near Ends Bridge. The young man had immediately hurried away, but a small boy chanced to be in the vicinity, observed the incident, and, being as curious as small boys are and should be in so strange a world, promptly retrieved the glove. He took his booty home, but there his mother, seeing that the glove was fur-lined and of an expensive make, sent him off with it to the police. Now, awaiting a claimant, it reposed in the charge of the Long Barsley sergeant.

The incident was curious, Bobby thought, for why should any young man, or any one else for that matter, throw an expensive glove into a canal where probably it would have sunk and been lost for ever but for the curiosity of a small boy? Curious, too, that it had happened near Ends Bridge, since Ends Bridge lay on the road between Rose Briar Cottage and the small, private, and somewhat expensive Upper Forest Hotel where the lost Mr Anderson had made his home after his wife left him. Curious incidents needed explanation, Bobby told himself, and he picked up his 'phone and asked for the number of the hotel. In reply to Bobby's inquiry, a slightly surprised manager declared that he had never noticed that Mr Anderson possessed motoring gauntlets of the kind described. Mr Anderson, he said, always dressed very quietly, and had he owned such gloves, the manager thought that either he or one or other of the staff would have noticed them.

Bobby thanked him and put down the 'phone. He was hardly disappointed. No real reason to suppose the glove had belonged to Mr Anderson; or that there was any connection between it, the odd manner of its disposal, and whatever had or had not happened to the missing man. All the same Bobby was remembering very clearly that a motoring gauntlet resembling that of which he had just been reading the description, had been shown him, a trifle proudly, by Mr Blythe. But then it was Anderson, not Blythe, who was missing, and no doubt there were other people who owned expensive fur-lined motoring gauntlets. All the same Bobby wished so worrying an incident had not been reported from the vicinity of Ends Bridge, a locality that was beginning to take on in his mind an ominous and threatening significance.

From a drawer in his desk Bobby took the report of the routine inquiries carried out by Sergeant Wright. It stated that Mr Anderson had left his office half an hour or so earlier than usual. He had seemed in his usual health and spirits. He had evidently driven straight to his hotel since he had been seen there and had spoken to one or two of the staff and fellow guests about half an hour later. He had not dined at the hotel, but that was not unusual. Breakfast was the only meal covered by the weekly payment he made, extra meals were charged separately and were only taken very irregularly. Not until the Wednesday morning, when the maid, taking him his usual early tea, had found the room unoccupied and his bed unslept in, had his absence been noticed. Even then no alarm had been felt. The maid had assumed that, as sometimes happened, he had gone away for a day or two on business or for other reasons, and that the management had omitted to warn her. No one had given the empty room, the unslept-in bed, the uneaten breakfast, a second thought till his office—Mr Blythe in actual fact—rang up to inquire. Then it was found that Mr Anderson's car was in the hotel garage as usual and that his bag and small personal possessions—shaving tackle and so on he would naturally take with him when he was going away—were still in his room. The car had been found by the garage attendant standing in the yard about midnight, just before he went off duty. He supposed it had been left there for him to put away, and that he had accordingly done. In the morning he had given it its usual routine cleaning.

Possible, Bobby supposed, that Anderson might himself have brought the car back, left it there, and either on foot or securing a lift from a friend, have gone on to Midwych to catch the midnight train for London, or a later one that left in the small hours for the north. But it hardly seemed likely; and if that was really what had happened, curious that no one at the hotel, staff or guest, had seen him. On the whole it seemed to Bobby that probably some other person had driven back the car and left it where the garage attendant had found it.

A disturbing thought and one with ugly implications, Bobby felt.

He sent for Sergeant Wright again and instructed him to try to ascertain if any one answering Mr Anderson's description had travelled from one of the three main Midwych stations by the trains leaving at or after midnight. There would be a good chance that any passenger at so late an hour might have been noticed—in Mr Anderson's case even recognized, since he was fairly well known in the city. Afterwards Wright was to make inquiries all along the route from Rose Briar Cottage to the Upper Forest Hotel on the chance of something having been seen, either of Anderson or of his car. Later, an appeal might be made to motorists who had passed along that road about the relevant time in the hope of thereby securing some scrap or other of useful information. Necessary, too, to try to get in touch with the young man who had so summarily disposed of the gauntlet, but that would be difficult, perhaps impossible, unless he were prepared to come forward of his own accord in answer to the public appeal Bobby decided would have to be made. But as that action of throwing the glove into the canal suggested strongly a desire for secrecy, Bobby did not feel that any such appeal was very likely to be answered. And if not, how was a young man to be traced when of him nothing else was known but that he was young?

All this, of course, was the ordinary spade work of detection, in which so much more depends on team work than on individual brilliance. Sergeant Wright had already left on his errand, and, for his part, Bobby decided that he would like to have a closer look at the retrieved gauntlet, even though it was entirely probable that the thing possessed neither importance nor significance. An odd glove is of small value, and quite possibly the finder had merely decided that he didn't want to be bothered with the thing and so had adopted the quickest way of getting rid of it. But somehow this suggestion did not much appeal to Bobby. No doubt he would have been more willing to adopt it had the locality been other than Ends Bridge.

He had a long evening before him, for this was June, that dreadful month when all the world held its breath to watch the British Empire fall, when a Marshal of France was earning for himself that title—'enfant chéri de la défaite'—by which history will know him, when German officers were jovially inviting each other to dinner in London, when Britain, all unaware of the doom so unanimously pronounced, was making her public preparations and going about her private affairs in her usual and accustomed manner. His office work finished therefore, Bobby rang up his wife to tell her he would probably be busy all evening, received a tart reply that he was never anything else, made the trite and unacceptable excuse that there was a war on, and then got out the small car he had been supplied with for use on official errands, and drove over to Long Barsley.

There the Long Barsley sergeant, though a trifle surprised by the interest Inspector Owen was taking in the thing, produced the gauntlet, now carefully cleaned and dried and showing little trace of its immersion in the muddy waters of the canal.

"Given it a thorough good cleaning, haven't you?" Bobby remarked gloomily.

"I have so, sir," agreed the sergeant, not without some pride. "All mucky it was. Cost real money that did, and now as good as new."

Bobby agreed. No use blaming the man. Quite right and natural he should give it a cleaning, just as it had been quite right and natural for the hotel attendant to give Anderson's car its accustomed rub over. For that matter, very likely there had been no clue of any importance to destroy. But Bobby could not help thinking that there might have been. Might have beens are little use, however, and anyhow neither car nor glove would now show anything to help. All the same Bobby examined the glove very carefully and the longer and the more closely he looked at it, the firmer grew his conviction that it exactly resembled one of the pair Mr Blythe had shown him.

Impossible to be quite sure though, and in any case, how did its appearance in the canal fit in with the disappearance of Mr Anderson? Or was there nothing here but a meaningless coincidence? But Bobby did not much think so, for his dislike of coincidence was always strong.

"Do you think we can take it that the lad who brought the thing in was telling the truth about its having been thrown into the canal?" Bobby asked.

"All boys are liars," said the sergeant, speaking not in haste but with calm thoughtfulness, "but he stuck to his story and you don't see why he should invent such a queer like tale. Dead cert. it had been in the canal some way, that was plain all right."

"He gave no description of the young man he said he saw, did he? Was he quite clear about the chap being young?"

"It's what he said. Maybe he just meant it wasn't any one very old. I tried to get a description but it was no good. He didn't wear a hat and that was all. The boy said he didn't notice much, being busy watching the glove and the splash it made and making up his mind to get it out again."

"I wonder if he would know him again?" Bobby said, and on that point the sergeant had no opinion to offer.

He suggested questioning the boy again but Bobby told him not to bother doing that but to keep the lad's interest up by promising him a reward of a shilling or two.

"He shall have something if I have to produce it out of my own pocket," Bobby said. "It may turn out important. One never knows."

The sergeant looked politely incredulous and Bobby made a note of the youngster's name and address, deciding privately that if any questions were to be asked, he would put them himself. Questioning, especially the questioning of children, has to be done with care and skill, if it is not to produce the wished for rather than the accurate reply. Bobby decided, too, to take charge of the gauntlet himself. It might be as well to have the thing where it would be in safer custody and where it could be more conveniently referred to, if necessary. He told the sergeant that any claimant for it was to be sent to headquarters and then he drove on to Rose Briar Cottage.

When he knocked, Mrs Jordan came to the door and stood looking at him doubtfully.

"Heard anything?" she asked, and when he shook his head she said gloomily: "I don't suppose you will."

"Why not?" he asked.

"People don't vanish for nothing," she answered. "Better come in," she added.

She led the way into a large sitting-room, furnished with a taste Bobby credited to Anne, with a touch of luxury he put down to the lost Mr Anderson's money, and a display of a general untidiness he attributed to Mrs Jordan. An alcove at one end, before a window facing east, was evidently where meals were taken, for on a table there stood some uncleared tea things, a lump of rich sugary cake, and an open and partly empty box of chocolates. The rest of the room was fitted up as what is now called a lounge, since that term seems to suit better our less conventional days than the old word 'drawing-room'. Mrs Jordan cleared a chair—every chair had something on it, even if only an ash-tray—motioned to Bobby to seat himself, swept to the floor two current film periodicals from another chair, seated herself, and then said abruptly:

"Anne says she's sure something has happened. She has had dreams at night. I can hear her. Perhaps he's done a bunk. Men do. A dirty lot," she pronounced.

"Have you any reason to think that's what's happened?"

"No," she answered. Then she said: "I shouldn't wonder." After a pause, she added: "A regular man's trick. Don't I know?"

"Miss Earle seemed convinced Mr Anderson was far too fond of her to leave her without a word," Bobby observed.

"Hard to tell what a man really feels for you," Mrs Jordan pronounced. "You can't ever be sure of 'em. Anne thinks she knows. So you do till you find out different. Feel like that all right, men do, when there's kisses to be got, but once their backs are turned—well, you're only a fool to trust 'em." Once more she paused and added heavily: "I know. Anne's young. She don't."

"Then you think that possibly he has left her?"

"Anything possible with a man," she declared. "You're never sure. Trust a man, trust thin ice when there's a thaw."

"What about women?" Bobby could not help asking.

"Women cling," she told him. "They're like that."

"If it's what you think," Bobby said, "Anderson has apparently left his business, too."

"Perhaps it's his business left him," Mrs Jordan suggested. "He's been worrying about money. I know that. The war and all."

"Did you know he had given a large sum of money to your niece?"

"Anne told me. I haven't seen the money. If he's done a bunk, can she keep it?"

"I suppose that depends," Bobby answered cautiously. "Miss Earle was quite open about the connection between them. I suppose you knew?"

"Think I ought to have stood up on my hind legs and been shocked, I suppose?" she retorted. "If his wife gave him the go by, hadn't he as good a right to get another woman if he could, same as if she had died on him?"

"There is a good deal of difference in their ages," Bobby remarked.

"He wasn't as old as all that," she answered, "and Anne was born middle aged, I think. Never young like other girls. You can't blame her. Dumped on a doorstep, she was. You knew that? I don't suppose her mother wanted to, but what's a girl to do?" She stared at Bobby silently, challengingly, as if daring him to reply. When he made no comment, she went on: "My sister, it was. Well, now then, you can take it from me, him and her—Anderson and Anne—they took to each other all right. Deep it went with her, deep. I don't know about him. I mean to say, it went deep all right while he was with her, but a man forgets so soon. A man forgets so soon," she repeated half to herself, and Bobby thought it was her own past she was remembering. With a sudden change, a sudden darkening of her expression, a sudden malice as it were abruptly gripping her, she muttered: "Only sometimes they aren't let."

"Yes?" Bobby said, hoping she would go on talking, but she gave him a quick and cunning look.

"No business of yours, young man," she said. "You don't go pumping me."

"But that's exactly what I'm here for," Bobby explained amiably. "I want to pump you of anything that can help me to get a line on what has happened. You want to help, don't you? If only for

Miss Earle's sake, you want to know what's become of Anderson. I wonder if you would like to say anything more about that affair we had a report of—when a young man was seen climbing out of a window here and pistol shots were fired after him? I should very much like to know who that young man was. It might help if you could tell me that."

Mrs Jordan appeared to consider. Evidently she was not troubled overmuch by any memory of her previous denials.

"Young fellow at Anne's office," she said. "Articled pupil, they call him. Means he's going to be a lawyer himself. Name of Green, Roy Green."

"Oh, yes," Bobby said, wondering if she had given the wrong name on purpose, since the description supplied by Constable Smith plainly indicated young Dwight. More probably, since any such attempted deception seemed aimless, she had got hold of the wrong name in some way. "What did he want?" Bobby asked abruptly.

"Mad jealous he was, if you ask me," she answered. "Came along thinking he was going to catch 'em together, but not too sure about it, or who it was, but wanting very desperate to know. Just as well there was no one here. Anderson, he was always mighty careful. Came late. Left early. Always left his car well hidden and made sure there was no one looking and kept his hat down and his coat collar turned up. I said: 'Better have a false beard and moustache while you're about it, or a mask.' He didn't like that, not half he didn't. That young man was keen on making sure. Just as well there was no one here, him and his pistol."

"He brought a pistol with him? Bobby asked.

"More than a bit frightened of it, too, if you ask me," Mrs Jordan answered. "But a frightened boy with a pistol can easily mean a bit of trouble. He was still here when I came in from the village That scared him all right. I was scared, too. Took him for a burglar. There was his gun lying on the table where he had put it down when he found there was no one in. I grabbed it and he was scared and so was I and I don't know which was scared the most. He did a bunk out of the window and I let the gun off after him, not meaning to hit, just in the air like. Don't you go for to bring that up against me, young man. If you do, I'll swear you invented it all to back up your blinking copper, all out of esprit de corps."

"Have you the pistol still?" Bobby asked.

She looked at him sideways and cunningly and then said:

"No. I took it down to the canal and chucked it in."

"Oh, yes," said Bobby, not believing this for a moment. "If you come across it any time and let me have it, it might be useful. Just think it over, will you?"

"You don't suspicion that young man, do you?" she asked.

"You say he was mad jealous. He had a pistol with him that day. Miss Earle talks of murder."

"I wish she wouldn't," Mrs Jordan muttered. "Murder. I don't like it. Once is enough. My God, once is enough."

"Was there a once before?" Bobby asked softly, but he had the impression that she had not heard him, that her thoughts were far away, and it was very strange as he sat and watched her to see how slowly her whole gross, overfed body began to quiver, with slow, long shudders as though an uncontrollable memory had risen from the depths, held her in a grip she was powerless to shake off. Over-powdered, over-rouged as she was, too crimson as was her mouth from too free a use of lipstick, yet all that could not entirely conceal how deeply moved she was by thoughts that word of murder called up in her. Recovering herself a little she said hoarsely:

"Don't look at me like that. I haven't murdered anyone."

Bobby did not answer. Very puzzled he sat still, waiting. The suggestion of 'murder' had deeply shaken her. That much was evident. But why? Could she know that in fact murder had been committed? Not probable, he thought, and yet a possibility to keep in mind. He reflected that by her own story she had at least known how to use a pistol and possibly she had been less complacent to the liaison between her niece and her niece's employer than she professed. Or was there something in that story of the gift of money to the niece to account for a quarrel? If it is true that when poverty comes in at the door, loves flies out of the window, it is equally true that when money comes in by door or by window, hate and conflict often enter, too. She said again:

"What are you sitting there for like a great dummy? You get out. I've had enough. I don't know what's happened. Anne doesn't know either. She went with him to where he left his car. He always left it a little way away. He never brought it here. She went with him and he drove off and she came back. She sat a bit. I had gone up to bed. She'll tell you the same. I suppose you think it's us. I suppose you want to dig the garden up and see if he's buried here."

Her voice had risen to a shriek, then died away. Bobby sat silent and waiting, for when self control goes, truth may come out. They heard the front door open and Anne came in.

"Oh, it's you," she said to Bobby. To her aunt she said: "What are you shouting like that for?"

Mrs Jordan pointed a shaking finger at Bobby.

"He thinks we've murdered your Nat. He thinks we've got him buried under the floor or somewhere. He wants to dig up the garden and see."

"Do you?" Anne asked.

Bobby shook his head.

"No suggestion of murder has yet been made," he said, "except by you and your aunt. At present I have no evidence to support the idea."

Anne made no attempt to seat herself. Bobby wondered if she ever did sit down. Upright and brooding she stood, bending slightly forward, her heavy gaze upon the ground.

"I don't know anything about evidence," she said, "but I know that he has gone," and in the last word was the desolation of those who have lost and know not why. "That's evidence," she said, and went heavily and slowly from the room.

"You clear out, too," Mrs Jordan said angrily to Bobby. "There's nothing we can tell you."

"I wish I were quite sure of that," Bobby answered, and she gave him another angry scowl as he got to his feet. "Oh, by the way," he added: "There is one thing more I meant to ask you only I nearly forgot. I understand there was nothing found on Miss Earle to identify her and yet you were able to tell she was your niece. I was wondering how."

"You want to know a lot, don't you?" she muttered. "It's quite simple. My sister's last letter hinted she was going to have a baby, and when I got back from Australia I tried to find her but I couldn't. No one knew what had become of her. So then I wondered about her baby, and I found out there had been a baby picked up in Durban Street and it was Durban Street she wrote from last, my sister, I mean, so I went to ask and they showed me the woollie the baby had been wrapped up in. It was one I had knitted myself. I knew it at once and that was good enough for me. Then when I saw Anne I knew her, she's got the family look about her. Haven't you noticed it?"

There was an almost wistful note in her voice as she said this and Bobby agreed that there certainly was a family resemblance, though not a very strong one, and so took his leave.

"A pretty thin tale," he said to himself as he drove away. "I suppose it may be true. I wonder what's behind it. I don't see there can be any connection with Anderson's disappearance. I suppose perhaps her story may be true. You never know. Or near true, anyhow."

<h3 style="text-align:center">CHAPTER IX</h3>

<h2 style="text-align:center">INQUIRY AND DISCOVERY</h2>

THE NEXT MORNING Bobby made an early opportunity for a word with Sergeant Wright, whose inquiries were proving none the less useful for being so far entirely negative.

"Do you know Durban Street?" Bobby asked.

Sergeant Wright rubbed the tip of his nose, a gesture which, ever since Bobby had been observed indulging in it, had become popular in the Midwych county police force.

"Well, sir," he said finally, "I'm Midwych born and bred and I thought I knew every stone in the place, but I can't call to mind any Durban Street. Perhaps," he added hopefully, "it's one of these new corporation housing estates."

"I looked in the directory," Bobby said. "It seems to run out of St. Peter's Square."

The sergeant clicked his tongue and made other sounds expressive of annoyance and apology.

"Why, of course," he said. "I know it quite well only I didn't just think. Runs behind the Art Gallery and the new library building, and there's a small alley outlet leading into Lord Street. It's not a thoroughfare, only for foot passengers, so it's not much used except for delivery to the Art Gallery or the library or the warehouses across the way."

"Any dwelling houses?" Bobby asked, and when the sergeant said "No", added: "Caretakers, I suppose?"

The sergeant didn't think so. Certainly the Art Gallery and the library had resident caretakers, but they did not consider themselves residents of Durban Street and he did not think their apartments even had back doors in it. The warehouses had no caretakers as far as he knew. Warehouses seldom had.

"I want," Bobby explained, "to trace a Miss Earle who is said to have lived in Durban Street twenty-five years ago and to have abandoned a baby on a doorstep there."

"Near where she lived?" asked the sergeant doubtfully. "They don't often do that."

"It does seem a bit unusual," Bobby agreed, "but that's the story. Anyhow, I want you to try to check up on it as far as possible. Find out if there's ever been a caretaker named Earle and so on. There may be some connection with the Anderson case but keep that to yourself."

Wright accordingly departed on his errand, and Bobby, having made sure that none of the work waiting for him was of immediate importance, went on to Chief Building, where the porter told him, as he had hoped might be the case, that Mr Blythe had not yet arrived.

"He'll be here almost any minute now," said the porter. "Very regular gentleman. On the dot as you might say."

"Does he come by car?" Bobby asked.

"Most of our tenants do," said the porter proudly, for one of the chief attractions of Chief Building was its private car park for the use of tenants alone, thus sparing them the trouble, indeed the impossibility, of finding parking space in the maze of small, narrow, and twisting streets that formed the centre of the town.

Bobby thanked the man and withdrew, nor had he long to wait before Mr Blythe drove up. At once Bobby noticed that he had on a very ordinary pair of driving gloves. Seeing Bobby approaching, Blythe said at once:

"Any news? Heard anything?"

Bobby shook his head.

"I was hoping perhaps you had had word," he said. "You knew his car was still at the hotel? He was using it that Tuesday night, so someone must have brought it back. If it was Anderson himself, how is it no one saw him, and what did he do afterwards? If it was someone else, who and why?"

"I don't see how anyone else could get hold of Anderson's car," Blythe said thoughtfully. "Anyhow, why should they trouble to take it back to the hotel? If there has been foul play, what good would it do to have it found there rather than anywhere else?"

"Delayed discovery a bit perhaps," Bobby said. "Difficult to say though till we know more."

"I suppose the idea might be to cause delay," Mr Blythe agreed. "I didn't think of that. Yes, that's possible. Do you think there is any reason to suspect foul play?"

"It's always a possibility in these cases," Bobby answered. "Only one possibility in many, but it has to be considered. Clearly it will be necessary to go on with the investigation. I wanted to make sure first that you had heard nothing. Oh, there's something else I wanted to ask you. You remember you showed me once a very swell pair of motoring gauntlets your Hopewell House boys gave you?"

"Good lord, have you got it back already?" Blythe cried, looking quite excited. "Quick work. Very smart indeed."

"You mean you have lost them?" Bobby asked.

"Not them," Blythe answered. "One of them, the right-hand one." He jerked open a locker. Within lay a solitary fur-lined gauntlet. He took it out. "One of them was stolen," he said. "If you've got it back, I shall be more than a bit relieved."

"Odd to steal an odd glove," Bobby remarked.

"I took it the thief had been interrupted," Blythe said.

"You've reported the loss, I suppose?" Bobby asked.

Mr Blythe shook his head.

"I only found it out last night for one thing," he said. He added with a faint smile: "I wasn't very keen on saying anything. I didn't want my boys to think I was careless with their presents. I was really thinking I would say nothing and get it matched in town. But if you've found it—?"

"I can't say for certain," Bobby told him. "There is an odd glove reported found. We'll have to show it you to see if you can identify it. You can't be sure when you lost it? Or where?"

"I only missed it last night," Blythe repeated, "but I am sure it was stolen, not lost. I shall be very relieved to get it back. The lads saved up a good many of their pennies to buy those gloves for me and I don't want them to think I don't value them. I hardly ever put them on except when I'm going to Hopewell House and then I always do."

"You leave your car in the car park here during the day, I suppose? You have your own garage at home?"

"No, no space," Blythe answered. "I garage at a place in the main road, only a few minutes away. Farquhar's. Very trustworthy people. Never lost anything before."

Bobby made a note of the address and then said:

"There's one thing more. Can you give me some sort of rough idea of Mr Anderson's financial position?"

"I'm afraid I can't," Blythe answered. "It's all very difficult. Of course, the war's hit us hard, like everyone else. Practice ruined. No clients, no new business. We're just living on our fat. And all expenses up. We have been trying to carry on much as usual in the hope that the war wouldn't be a long one. Doesn't look like it now, though. Mind you, I don't want you to think we are on the point of filing our petition. Nothing of the sort. We are hard hit, but we are still on our feet and we mean to stay there. But drawings by partners will have to be on a very limited scale for the present."

"You can't give me any details about Mr Anderson's financial position?"

"No. Not more than I've said. I believe I'm his executor, but that doesn't come into question yet and I hope to God it never will. Naturally, his disappearance is going to make things awkward."

"I suppose so," agreed Bobby. "Would it surprise you to know he had recently disposed of a sum of five thousand pounds?"

Mr Blythe gave Bobby a quick and doubtful glance.

"It would, very much," he said. "I shouldn't have thought Anderson had five thousand pennies at his disposal at present. I know I haven't."

Bobby thanked him and turned away. Blythe, still looking very puzzled and worried, drove his car into the car park provided for tenants. Bobby noted that he did not re-appear, so that presumably there was a way from the car park into the building. After a minute or two Bobby went back to speak to the porter again.

"Ever have any cases of pilfering from the cars parked here?" he asked.

"Never," declared the porter quite indignantly. "There's always an attendant on duty and I keep my own eyes open. We know our tenants and anyone else would be asked at once what he wanted. No sneak thief would stand a chance and it's never been tried on, either."

"I take it there's a way into the building from the car park?" Bobby asked.

"What about it?" the porter demanded. "The car attendant's always there, isn't he? And I've got eyes in my head."

Bobby admitted this undeniable fact, but reflected also that 'always' is a word that is not always used in its exact and literal meaning. Negatives are 'always'—in the full sense of the word—difficult to prove, and Blythe's story had in it nothing inherently improbable. The glove might easily have been stolen. The fact that only one of a pair had been taken was open to the explanation already given of haste or interruption. But other explanations were equally possible; and it seemed an unsatisfactory coincidence that the disappearance of the glove should coincide with the disappearance of Mr Anderson, and then that it should have reappeared so near the road the missing man must have traversed. But for all that, theft at Farquhar's garage, theft in the Chief Building car park, remained as a possible and even plausible explanation.

Bobby walked back to his office deep in thought. Difficult to believe, he decided, that there was no connection between the lost glove and the disappearance of Mr Anderson. Hard to suppose that a casual sneak thief would take only an odd glove, and even more difficult to suppose that such a sneak thief finding himself in possession of unwanted booty, would dispose of it on that one particular spot where the missing man must have passed. Noticeable, too, that Blythe had not reported its loss, though once again the reason he gave was plausible. Yet apparently the disappearance of the glove would never have been mentioned but for Bobby's questioning. It didn't seem, Bobby thought, to add up very satisfactorily.

Only, where did the hatless young man come in? Was he the hypothetical sneak thief, or merely someone who, having more or less by accident come into possession of the thing, wanted to be rid of it? If so, why? Because it was dangerous or embarrassing for some reason or another? If so, surely that meant that it had been recognized as George Blythe's property. That seemed reasoning both sound and simple. In and by itself an odd glove can be an embarrassment to no one. But then who could have recognised it? One of the Hopewell House lads? A possibility to be remembered. A personal friend? If so, a wide field was opened. Or one of the office staff? The personal friend theory would be difficult, indeed impossible, to investigate without Mr Blythe's own co-operation, and that Bobby felt he did not wish to invoke for the present. One has to be on firm ground before taking steps that might seem to indicate suspicions, especially suspicions of a well-known solicitor of good reputation like George Blythe. The Hopewell House lads during the day were all scattered at work. One evening the youthful discoverer of the glove might be taken there to see if he could recognize the young man he said he had seen. There remained the staff of Messrs Castles, and Bobby had it in his mind that the unknown young man had been described as hatless and that the only time he had seen Roy Green in the street he had been bareheaded.

A slender clue enough in days when half the young men in the country have given up hats, but even the most slender clue may prove of value and in default of a better be well worth following up.

Bobby went back to his office and found a brief report from Sergeant Wright to say there was no trace of the missing man or of anyone resembling him having travelled by any late train from any one of the three Midwych stations. As a matter of routine the police at all places where such trains stopped were being communicated with and asked to make the necessary inquiries. Secondly, it seemed fairly certain no one of the name of Earle had ever lived in Durban Street. The Art Gallery caretaker had held his present post for thirty years. He had kept a diary all that time and had shown Sergeant Wright the entry regarding the discovery of a child in one of the warehouse doorways, wrapped in a pyjama jacket and an old blanket, neither of which had afforded any clue to the child's identity.

"Well, that shows Mrs Jordan lied in part at least," Bobby reflected, and wondered why she had thought it worth while to lie. Certainly an explanation suggested itself to him, but he did not think that any purpose would be served by attempting to follow it up.

As well to remember it perhaps, but at present he knew of nothing to suggest that there could be any connection between the abandonment of a baby nearly a generation ago and Nathaniel Anderson's disappearance.

The third part of the report stated that there were only two cottages actually on the road between Rose Briar Cottage and the Upper Forest Hotel and one of them was unoccupied. Of the other, the inhabitants went to bed regularly at nine, slept all night as soundly as generally do hard-working farm labourers and their families, and had no recollection of hearing a car pass on any recent night. The only other residence anywhere near was Roman Ends farm; and as that stood some half mile back from the road, with which it was connected only by a narrow lane, Wright had not thought there was any need to make inquiries there.

Bobby supposed not. All the same he found it interesting that Osman Ford should chance to live so near. Another of the disconnected and isolated facts, entirely without significance in themselves, which seemed to be turning up in a way to suggest that in their totality some significance did in fact lie hid.

Another report from another of his assistants told Bobby that there would be duly carried out his request for an appeal to be made to any motorist using the road on the relevant night to come forward. But that was a slender hope. Motorists, unless exceptionally conscientious, are apt to dislike answering police appeals that may involve them in long drawn out and troublesome police proceedings.

Nor for that matter was it very likely that any motorist knew anything. If there had been foul play, no more fitting spot could have been selected than that stretch of lonely road, of which Ends Bridge, crossing the dark and slow-moving waters of the canal, was almost the centre.

He picked up the 'phone, got in touch with Long Barsley and asked the sergeant in charge to find the youngster who had rescued the motoring gauntlet, promise him a reward of half a crown, and bring him along at once.

In a very short time sergeant and boy arrived. Bobby handed over the promised half-crown at once so as to avoid any risk of a too great eagerness to earn it rendering the lad too eager to oblige his questioners, and then told him he was wanted to identify, if possible, the young man of the glove incident.

"It won't matter if you can't," Bobby explained. "Suit us just as well one way as another, only if you do happen to see him, we should like to know. Do you think you would know him again?"

"Oh, yes," declared the boy with great confidence, but when Bobby tried to get a description, the attempt was a complete failure.

Apparently the youngster combined a clear picture in his mind with a complete inability to translate that mental impression into spoken words.

"Well, never mind," Bobby said, anxious to avoid making the lad nervous or self-conscious, anxious indeed to treat it all as a quite ordinary and commonplace affair, without any real importance. "Doesn't really matter much, only I would like to see if you can spot the chap again."

They set out accordingly, Bobby, the boy, Sergeant Wright, and near Chief Building they gathered round an itinerant ice-cream merchant. Bobby was not sure how the dignity of an inspector of police and a private secretary to a chief constable consorted with eating ice-cream sandwiches in the street. But then he liked ice-cream, even if a city constable across the street did seem to be grinning a bit. Sergeant Wright was quite sure that eating ice-cream from a street barrow was very much 'infra dig', for sergeants and inspectors, too. Besides he had a sore tooth with an exposed nerve, but not for him, a sergeant, to draw back where his inspector led. So he accepted his two pennorth without protest, though gloomily aware that that grinning ape of a city constable across the road would spread the story all through the city force, which, knowing well its essential inferiority to the county men, simply loved to tell silly stories about them. But the ice-cream merchant told himself happily that day by day in every way the world, including the world of grown-ups, was growing more and more ice-cream-minded, and the Long Barsley youngster combined luscious enjoyment of the horn he had asked for with a bright-eyed attention to all passers-by.

"That's him," he said suddenly, giving his 'horn' a final lick, as there emerged from Chief Building a hatless young man evidently on his way to lunch.

Bobby recognized Roy Green. Sergeant Wright said:

"Sure?"

"Yes, that's the bloke without a hat, same as he was," answered the boy, and then, transferring his attention to the ice-cream barrow, decided not to spend any of his half-crown yet, since there was always the chance that if he looked long enough and hard enough, another horn might come his way.

It did, for Bobby thought he deserved it, and then he was returned to the care of the Long Barsley sergeant for safe redelivery. Sergeant Wright, now suffering in heroic silence from a violently protesting tooth waked to anguish by the sudden impact of ice-cream, was instructed to get hold unobtrusively of Roy Green when he was leaving the office that evening and bring him to headquarters. Thither Bobby himself repaired to get on with his other work; and later in the afternoon came a report that in the canal, below Ends Bridge, had been found a dead body, identified by papers on it as that of Nathaniel Anderson, the cause of death being first a bullet wound in the back and then drowning, since apparently life had not been extinct at the moment of immersion.

CHAPTER X
URSULA'S TEARS

HARDLY HAD THIS news been received, Bobby in fact was still occupied with routine instructions of one kind and another concerning the discovery, when there appeared a somewhat worried Sergeant Wright.

"I've brought Mr Green along, sir," he reported, "but his young lady has come along, too, no stopping her, sir. There wasn't anything I could say made any difference."

"If you were a married man, Wright," Bobby pointed out, "you would know it never does. Where is she?"

"Having hysterics on the charge-room floor," answered the sergeant gloomily. "And half a dozen of 'em fussing round her, all just about going to have hysterics their own selves."

For one brief moment Bobby allowed his imagination to dwell, not without awe, on the thought of half a dozen stout policemen all having hysterics on the charge-room floor.

But then he remembered his rank and office.

"Tell them," he said sternly, "not on duty. Er—why hysterics?"

"Seems to think her young man's going to be hanged right away," the sergeant explained. "Says he never did, and never had anything to do with it—at least, that's what it sounds like in between squeals and such."

"Curious," Bobby said. "Very. Why should she think he may be hanged? People are only hanged for murder. Did they know it was murder? We didn't—till this report came in. You've heard about that, Wright?"

"Yes, sir," Wright answered. "They told me outside. It does seem a bit like guilty knowledge, doesn't it?"

"I think I had better see her first," Bobby said slowly. "I've sent Inspector Blane to examine body and clothing. I don't suppose it'll tell us much—not after so long in the water. Make the girl a cup of tea, will you? And when she quietens down a bit ask her if she will be good enough to spare a few moments from hysterics for me. Where's Mr Green?"

"In the duty inspector's room, sir, with Robins keeping an eye on him and taking notes of such language as you don't often hear. It's along of his being a legal gentleman most like and knowing more words than most."

"Shouldn't wonder," agreed Bobby. "Well, tell Robins to go on watching and note taking—so long as his notes are for private use only. Because, Wright," said Bobby, very earnestly, "on duty no policeman must ever say anything except please and thank you— especially thank you."

"No, sir, I know, sir," answered the sergeant. "I'll remind Robins."

"Good," said Bobby. "Well, bring the young lady in when she's finished her hysterics—not before," he added warningly.

He had not long to wait before there appeared a small procession of first Sergeant Wright, then the flushed, tear-stained, slightly dishevelled Ursula Harris, and finally a very large policeman carrying with great care a tray, on it a large cup of tea and two biscuits; untouched, for they had been refused with contumely.

"Oh, yes, just put that down here, will you?" Bobby said, guessing that the offer of tea had not been received by Ursula with any gratitude. "Do take a chair, Miss Harris," he added in his friendliest tones, at the same time pushing forward the arm-chair Colonel Glynne had provided for his more important visitors. "We are very pleased to see you, of course, but I am wondering just a little why you came along."

"You've arrested Roy, haven't you?" she demanded. "You've got to arrest me, too, because it's all my fault, and even if Mr Anderson was going to write to Roy's father about us, he wouldn't murder him for that, would he? And he never did, either."

"One moment, please, please," Bobby said, throwing up his hands in an effort to stem this torrent. "What makes you think Mr Anderson has been murdered?"

"Well, he has, hasn't he?"

"Why should you think so?"

"Well, what's happened to him?"

"I am asking you a question," Bobby said. "You don't answer it. Let me repeat it. What makes you think Mr Anderson has been murdered?"

"Well, Anne thinks so—Miss Earle. He isn't ill or anything. There hasn't been an accident or we should have heard; or if he had committed suicide, someone would know, and besides he never would. Why should he? He's just disappeared."

"People who disappear aren't necessarily murdered," Bobby pointed out. "Sometimes they go away of their own accord."

"Mr Anderson wouldn't," she said confidently. "Why should he? Miss Earle thinks so, too."

"You can give me no other reason?" Bobby asked. "It's rather important, because, you see, Miss Harris, you happen to be right. Mr Anderson's body has been found and it is a case of murder."

He paused and she gave a little gasp and went very pale, but yet retained her self-control better than had been the case previously.

The news had certainly been a shock to her and yet a shock for which to some degree she was prepared. Bobby was watching her intently. He said:

"You see, you were right. Miss Harris, I want to be quite frank with you. I would like you to understand our position. You evidently suspected what has in fact happened. Unless you can explain, it must seem that you knew something."

She was thoroughly frightened now. She began to cry. Through her sobs she protested that everyone in the office had been wondering and guessing. She did not know who first suggested 'murder', but more and more often had the word got itself whispered, muttered, spoken more and more freely, loudly. They all knew about Roy. Of course, Roy had been silly to talk as he had done, but equally of course, he hadn't meant anything. Besides, it was Mr Blythe who had been so Beastly about it, not Mr Anderson. Of course, it was Mr Anderson who had said he would have to write to Roy's father, but it was all Mr Blythe really.

She began to cry again. Bobby waited patiently, indifferently, referring now and again to papers on his table. Tears may be a woman's best weapon. Indifference is a good defence when they are so used. When the tears began to flow less freely, Bobby said:

"Miss Harris, do please try to control yourself. You say all the office knew about you and Roy Green. Your private affairs have nothing to do with us, of course, but what does that mean? What did the office know about you two?"

"They knew Roy wouldn't ever give me up," she answered simply, "I told him he must but I knew he never would. You see, we love each other."

She said this with a simple pride that Bobby found all the more touching because it was so evident how wonderful she thought it, wonderful that she alone out of all alive should have been chosen for an experience she clearly believed unique in the world's history.

"He's my boy," she said suddenly and as simply as before.

"I'm sure a very lucky boy," said Bobby, but she shook her head.

"Oh, no," she said, still with the same simple, quiet conviction, as of one with absolute knowledge, "it's me that's lucky."

"Perhaps both of you," Bobby suggested smilingly. "I suppose you mean Mr Green's father was likely to object?"

"Oh, yes. He wants Roy to marry the daughter of one of his partners, because then Roy would have two shares, if you see what I mean, and then his father would have control of the practice; and that's rather important, because there's another partner Mr Green doesn't get on with very well. It's only a small practice, Roy says, but it brings in a lot of money, because they are trustees and executors for two different big estates. Only the other partner wants to do things Roy's father doesn't approve of and he thinks if Roy married the first partner's daughter, then the two of them would work together and old Mr Green would get his own way. You do understand, don't you?"

"I think so," Bobby answered. "A bit complicated, but the essential part is that Mr Green's father thinks it very important for business reasons that Roy should marry the daughter of one of his partners and that he is likely to object very strongly indeed to any idea of marriage between you two."

"That's right," Ursula agreed. "Of course, I told Roy at once he must give me up but he won't. He just laughed at me. So I said I would go away and he said if I did he would, too, and that would make everything worse all round, and so it would, wouldn't it?"

"Mr Anderson told you he was intending to let the elder Mr Green know?"

"Yes. He told Roy. He said Roy and I must promise not to have anything to do with each other. It wasn't Mr Anderson really. I don't believe he would ever have cared a scrap. Besides, if it's true about him and Anne, we could have told about him, too, couldn't we?"

"I suppose so," Bobby agreed, and thought to himself that the girl was either extraordinarily naive or even more extraordinarily cunning. He was not sure which. He said: "Is it true, do you think?"

"Oh yes, I usen't to but I do now. You've only to look at Anne to see how she feels. They kept most awfully quiet about it. I suppose they had to. A solicitor has to be careful. I didn't think Anne was that sort of girl," she added primly.

"Perhaps she isn't," Bobby remarked. "I understand you and Mr Roy Green thought it was Mr Blythe, not Mr Anderson, who wanted the elder Mr Green told?"

"Mr Anderson would never have known a thing about us if Mr Blythe hadn't told him. He happened to see us meeting where we generally did. Our trysting place," she explained, using a word that evidently for her was all compact of wonder and romance. "He saw us. Then he saw us saying good-bye, because we always went home separately. There's nothing wrong in meeting but he has a beastly mind and he was sure there was. He's like that. It's why he's so keen on Hopewell House because they're all boys. I expect a girl turned him down once and a jolly good thing, too, only that's why he hates it so, if a boy looks at you. Or perhaps it's something else, something inside him, his own self." She paused and looked puzzled as if she had said something she herself did not fully understand. "I believe it's that," she said.

Bobby did not ask what she meant, for he felt that here were strange depths of psychology that neither he nor she, nor perhaps any human being, fully understood. He said:

"What you mean is that Mr Blythe objected to you and Roy Green being too friendly, and that he was pressing Mr Anderson to warn the elder Mr Green so as to put an end to it—perhaps by calling his son home?"

Ursula nodded.

"Roy said he wouldn't go," she declared. "He said he would get another job if he had to, and anyhow it wouldn't matter, because very soon he'll be joining the Royal Air Force, only they won't have him just yet. He knows how to fly already and he's got a certificate to say so, too, only they told him he would have to forget all about that when he joined up. I think it's rather silly to tell him that, don't you? Because flying is just flying, isn't it? And if you can, you can, can't you?"

Bobby made no comment. He was wondering if all this artless chatter held any significant clue. He thought perhaps it did. Then he wondered if it was all quite as artless as it seemed, and even Ursula's round, innocent face and wide, guileless eyes did not entirely reassure him. Too well did he know how different may be the inner spirit from the outward show; how man, and woman, too, may smile and smile and be a villain still.

Ursula was talking again, more nervously now. She said:

"I expect you've heard about some of the things Roy said, but of course he didn't really mean them—not about murdering him. It was just because he was so awfully furious."

"Was it?" Bobby said, and told himself again that talk of murder seemed to have been just a little too prevalent in what should have been the calm, peaceful, everyday atmosphere of a busy solicitor's office.

"It was always Mr Blythe he meant, not Mr Anderson," Ursula insisted. "So it doesn't matter about his having said things, does it?"

"Such things are better not said," Bobby told her. "Where is this place you say you used to meet?"

Her reply was hardly unexpected.

"Near Ends Bridge," she explained. "There's an empty cottage where nobody lives and just behind is ever such an old apple tree. It makes a sort of shelter, no one can see you unless they look. It was there we found Mr Blythe's glove, so we knew he had been snooping around again, trying to catch us."

"What day was that?"

"Thursday evening. We made it up always to be there Mondays and Thursdays, even if we hadn't been able to arrange it. As soon as Roy saw the glove we knew who it belonged to, and Roy said that showed Mr Blythe had been snooping again, and I said to give it back to him, because then he would know we knew and he would be ashamed of himself. But Roy said, no, nothing would make him ashamed, and he threw it in the canal."

"How long do you think the glove could have been lying there?" Bobby asked.

Ursula was sure it hadn't been there on the Monday but could not be more definite. They hadn't given that point a thought. They had simply picked the glove up, recognized it, and thrown it at once into the canal with the feeling that it served Mr Blythe right to lose his expensive gauntlet.

That seemed the whole of her story, so Bobby took her to another room, promised that if she would wait there he would send Roy Green to join her presently, and then went back to interview Roy, who had, however, very little to add to Ursula's story. He agreed that he had been deeply disturbed by Mr Anderson's threat to write to his father, but insisted that nothing would induce him to give up Ursula. If old Mr Green disowned him, it couldn't be helped. He had a right to choose his own girl. As for the money aspect—well, so far he had been dependent on his father. But they could manage well enough until he joined the Air Force and then of course it would be all right.

"I don't know if you really think I did in poor old Anderson," he said, "and I don't know how you got on to that glove business. I suppose perhaps it does sound a bit funny, though it seemed all right at the time. It was only when one of the chaps at the office asked me if it was me, because of the things I had been saying, that I saw it was going to be awkward. Only it was always Blythe I meant. It was all through him. It was Blythe who saw us together near where we used to meet, and it was Blythe who chose to think what he did about us, the dirty-minded swine. I told Anderson it was all a filthy lie of Blythe's. I think he believed me, too. Perhaps I wouldn't have minded murdering Blythe if I had got the chance. I know I felt like it. After the things he hinted about Ursula. But it isn't Blythe that's got done in, it's Anderson."

"Yes, of course, there's that," agreed Bobby absently.

He was deep in thought. Plain enough that this young man hid strong, even violent passions behind his somewhat commonplace exterior. That much he had made clear by the intensity with which he had spoken, by the evident sincerity with which he had expressed his willingness to break with his family and his prospects for the sake of the girl he loved. Ursula, too, for all her round, baby face, her innocent-sounding chatter, had shown the strength and resolution of her spirit by the way in which she had insisted in sharing in what she had believed to be his arrest and danger. Were these two young people, Bobby wondered, as candid and as simple as they appeared? On the face of it, there seemed a marked contrast between their open, natural, innocent love affair, and the dark and hidden passion that had drawn together Anne Earle and the murdered man. But could one be sure? There were so many possibilities. One possibility—a possibility supported by one phrase Ursula had used—was that they knew of Mr Anderson's visits to Rose Briar Cottage, knew that he must return to his hotel by way of Ends Bridge, had almost certainly seen him doing so, had decided to stop him with the object of blackmailing him into silence about themselves by threatening to make public his own intrigue, and that as a result there had ensued a quarrel, shooting, murder.

"Where were you Tuesday night?" Bobby asked.

"We went to the pictures, the Regent in St. Peter's Square," Roy answered, and when he saw that Bobby looked doubtful, he added: "I've got the ticket stubs still, I expect."

He duly produced them. But it is perfectly easy to buy tickets, present them, walk out again immediately by a different door. No one will notice, or, if they do, remember the incident for five minutes. When Bobby pressed the point, Roy admitted that he could produce no independent evidence. So far as he knew, no one had seen them and certainly the attendants would not remember them.

"We don't often go there," he explained. "Generally we go to the Palace. Only the Regent had a picture Ursula wanted to see, so we went there that night. I expect they know us all right at the Palace but not at the Regent."

"It's a bit unlucky," Bobby remarked. "But there's no need for you to worry, that is, if you are innocent. Though it would have been a lot better if you had taken that glove to the nearest police-station instead of chucking it into the canal. Can't be helped now. There's nothing else you can tell me?"

"Well, I don't know that it matters," Roy answered slowly. "I don't know if I ought to say anything. There's a chap called Osman Ford. He had a most frightful row with Anderson a little while ago. It was only when Anderson said to ring up the police that Osman Ford cleared out; and he was muttering about what he would do and getting his own back and all that sort of thing, all the time he was going. He thought he had been done out of some money, thought Anderson had embezzled his wife's trust fund. Well, Ursula and I have seen him hanging around by Ends Bridge and you could tell he was up to no good by the way he sneaked along, keeping out of sight as much as he could, behind hedges and that sort of thing. I said at once he was up to mischief, and so did Ursula, too. You could tell, the way he crept along. I don't know if I ought to have told you, because of course it may have been nothing."

"I'm glad you did mention it," Bobby said. "Everything has to be considered in a case like this."

As he seemed to have nothing more to say, Bobby sent him off to join Ursula and then, though by now it was growing late, he managed to secure a search warrant. With it and Sergeant Wright he set off for Rose Briar Cottage. Not that he thought the search warrant was likely to be of any practical use, it was chiefly for psychological effect. He had much too high an opinion of Mrs Jordan's abilities and probable experience to suppose that, if she had any pistol hidden, it would be easy to find. Not for her the usual feminine top of a wardrobe. When they arrived, Mrs Jordan, who was sitting in the garden, greeted them without cordiality.

"Back again, are you?" she said. "What is it this time?"

"Have you heard about Mr Anderson?" Bobby asked.

"You've found him?" she asked and then quickly: "Is he dead? Murdered?" She seemed to read the answer in their eyes as she looked quickly from one to the other. "Anne was right, then," she muttered, more to herself than to them. "She knew. She said she did."

"How did she know?" Bobby asked.

Mrs Jordan seemed to miss the significance of this question. She answered slowly:

"Anne's a queer girl. From the very beginning she said it would end badly. She said it had to. She's like that. I don't know where she gets it from. Not from my side. Was he shot?"

"Why do you ask that?" Bobby said. "Why shot?"

"You come along and I'll show you," she answered.

The garden was surrounded by a high, close grown, quickset hedge on which the blossom of May still lingered. It was closely trimmed, it had an impenetrable air. Mrs Jordan paused when they had gone a short distance along the path it bordered and pointed to where a loose end of string dangled.

"I wrapped the pistol, that young fellow Dwight, or some such name, left behind him, in a bit of old mack and pushed it way down there in the hedge with a bit of string tied to it to pull it up by if I wanted. Well, now it's gone. Someone's taken it. Someone must have known."

"Have you any idea who it could be?" Bobby asked.

She shook her head.

"Did Miss Anne Earle know where it was?" he asked.

"No," she answered, and then turned round and stared at him. "You aren't such a fool," she asked, "as to think she killed the man she loved?"

Bobby did not answer, but a familiar line of poetry came into his mind: 'Each man kills the thing he loves.' Perhaps each woman, too. Mrs Jordan was speaking again. She said:

"He was shot, wasn't he?"

Bobby nodded. She said:

"I suppose next you'll be thinking I did it. Well, I didn't. Why should I?"

There might be many possible reasons, Bobby thought. But he did not say so. Instead he remarked:

"We have information that you and some unknown man were heard quarrelling one night. Apparently something was said about someone being pushed into the canal. Mr Anderson's body was found in the canal. Is there anything you would like to say about that? Would you care to say who the man was you were talking to?"

"No," she answered angrily. "It's all a blasted lie. That copper of yours again, sneaking and snooping and listening. It's all a lie."

"Well, think it over," Bobby said. "If you remember anything and like to tell us, it might help."

"Help who?" she sneered.

"You," he answered, "you, or even Miss Anne Earle."

CHAPTER XI
MRS FORD'S ANGER

IT WAS TOO late for anything more to be done that night; but as early as might be, telling himself that a farmer would probably be an early riser, Bobby appeared at Roman Ends farm. He was still in the act of alighting from his car when he saw Osman Ford standing at the door of the house, looking at him gloomily.

"I thought you would be around," he said as Bobby came up. "I saw in the paper that Anderson's dead. Foul play, it says. A bullet in the back. That spells murder. You can't shoot yourself in the back. Been swindling someone else as well as us, had he?"

"So far as is known at present," Bobby answered, "there is nothing to suggest that. Yours is the only suggestion of the kind that I've heard of."

"You had better come in," Osman said. He led the way into a sitting room, a bright cheerful apartment, with a pleasant outlook over the garden. "I reckon we shall know all about that soon," he went on. "His affairs will have to be gone into. If my missus's money is still there, I shan't have to wait any longer for my rights. That's one good thing. Blythe's straight. He won't hang on to other people's money, pretending it's for their good when all he wants is to keep it in his own clutches. Blythe promised me."

"Promised you what?" Bobby asked.

"Promised that if he ever became trustee as the deed provided if anything happened to prevent Anderson acting, I should have my money. Blythe's straight. He won't stand between me and my rights. He told me as much himself."

Bobby was watching him closely and with curiosity. The man seemed quite unaware of how strong a motive he was giving himself for desiring Anderson's death. But he might have realized that the facts would soon be known and that it would be more prudent to make a display of an innocent frankness. As easy for guilt to take on the semblance of innocence as for innocence to find itself caught in dark clouds of suspicion. Bobby said:

"What I am trying to establish is when and where Mr Anderson was last seen alive."

"I can't tell you that," Osman answered instantly. "I haven't seen him since that day I came to you and you wouldn't do anything because I didn't know it all already. Evidence you wanted, you said. I always thought that's what police were for, to get evidence. What you meant was you didn't believe me. Well, now we'll know all about it, when his affairs are gone into, and we'll see whether I was right or whether I wasn't."

"I suppose so," agreed Bobby. "Did you know he often drove along the road that skirts your land by the canal?"

"No, I didn't. Why should I?" retorted Osman. "You can get to Midwych that way, though it's round about. Not many do, but you can."

"Mr Anderson used it frequently."

"What about it?" Osman asked, but with uneasiness in his voice now. "Suppose he did, how should I know? Nothing to do with me."

Before Bobby could reply the door opened and Mrs Ford came in. Bobby remembered her as a small, shrinking, insignificant sort of person with a trick of slipping away unseen and unnoticed. 'Suppressed' was the word that had occurred to him. Now she had an altogether different air. She gave rather the impression that it was the other fellow who would want to slip away, unnoticed and if possible unseen. She even looked taller, as if somehow she had added several inches to her height. One of the aggressor class now apparently, and her voice was vibrant with the energy of attack as she snapped out:

"What's all this? Who is this man? What's he want?"

"Well, you see, my dear," Osman began, "it's about Mr Anderson—"

"Rubbish," interposed Mrs Ford, though what she meant was 'rubbish' did not clearly appear, even if it seemed probable she meant the word to include her husband. She gave Bobby a look indicating that in her opinion to call him 'rubbish' would be to pay him a high but totally undeserved compliment. "If it's true Anderson's been murdered," she said, "what's that to do with us?"

"Apparently a good deal," Bobby pointed out, "if one result is to release your capital he was holding up."

"Rubbish," said Mrs Ford, still more loudly and fiercely.

"Do you mean that is not the case?" Bobby asked.

"Rubbish," she repeated.

It seemed her favourite remark, Bobby thought, but reflected also that this was not a case in which repetition increased conviction. Nor did he find it enlightening. Abruptly she turned upon her husband.

"You great empty-head," she demanded, "what have you been telling him?"

Osman shuffled his feet uneasily, and Bobby was aware of an impression that he often did so when his wife addressed him. He made no effort to reply, and Bobby said:

"Mr Ford has very wisely been quite frank in explaining about the trust fund that Mr Anderson was holding up and that his death may release. Of course, we should soon have learned the facts, but it was much better, more satisfactory in every way, to hear them from Mr Ford himself."

"Why?" demanded Mrs Ford truculently. "It's nothing to do with you or anyone else."

"Now, now, my dear," began Osman Ford hesitatingly.

"You keep quiet," Mrs Ford ordered. "Talk, talk, talk, that's you all over."

Osman Ford shuffled his feet again. Bobby remembered bewilderedly that once he had believed Osman Ford was a bully who by threats and violence had forced a timid little woman into marrying him and who had continued to bully her ever since. He even remembered how concerned he had once felt for her. He still felt concerned but not for her. He even began to have an uneasy feeling that he might be feeling concerned for himself before this interview was over. He said:

"I was explaining to your husband, Mrs Ford, that I am anxious to establish when and where Mr Anderson was last seen alive. Our information is that he often used the canal road skirting your land. We have received further information that Mr Ford was seen near an empty cottage on that road and that he appeared to be trying to avoid observation."

"Just like him," said Mrs Ford, withering her unlucky husband with a glance.

He shuffled his feet uneasily under her glare. Then he said protestingly:

"Well, what about it? Our land, isn't it? Can't I go for a stroll at night on our own land? Anything wrong about that?"

"Mr Ford," Bobby said gravely, "I am carrying out preliminary inquiries. Certain facts seem to be established. The death of Mr Anderson probably releases your capital. The last known of him is that he was driving along the road between your land and the canal in which his body was found. So it is at least a possibility that the murder was committed on that road, somewhere near the Ends Bridge. You do not deny—"

"How dare you—?" interrupted Mrs Ford furiously.

"Now, now, my dear," her husband interrupted in his turn.

"You keep quiet," commanded Mrs Ford, whirling round on him. "Talk, talk, talk, that's you."

"You do not deny," Bobby continued, "that you were seen near the unoccupied cottage on that road, not far from the bridge. You say that it is your own land, which is perfectly true, but hardly explains why you chose that particular part of it for an evening stroll or why you appeared to be anxious to avoid being seen."

"If you want to know," Osman grumbled, "some of 'em told me there was a lot of canoodling going on down there towards park and I don't want that sort of thing on my land."

Mrs Ford made sounds expressive of extreme disapproval, though whether of the 'canoodling', or of her husband's dislike of it, was not quite clear. Her wrathful glances were being pretty equally divided between Osman and Bobby. Osman, still apt to shuffle his feet whenever his eye caught hers, kept an apprehensive watch on her. Bobby was apprehensive himself, he felt by no means sure that the little woman's anger would not presently find physical expression. There was an ominous, occasional curving of her fingers for instance, and Bobby observed, still apprehensively, that she appeared to cultivate particularly long and sharp nails. He said to Osman:

"Did you see anyone?"

"No. I went down there to look round two or three evenings but I didn't see anyone."

"Which evenings were they?"

"I go out most evenings, just for a look round and smoke a pipe before turning in. It was the early part of the week I went down by there."

Mrs Ford interposed.

"Why don't you say right out what you mean?" she demanded fiercely of Bobby. "Trying to make out Osman stopped Anderson and murdered him?"

"Now, now, my dear," said Osman.

"Talk, talk, talk," cried Mrs. Ford despairingly. "Nothing will stop a man's tongue."

Osman shuffled his feet and looked depressed.

Bobby said:

"I am, if you like, trying to establish whether that is a possibility to take into account, and if in Mr Ford's case—"

Mrs Ford interrupted him with what seemed almost a crow of delight.

"Now you've said it, young man," she cried, shaking a finger in his face. "I'll have the law on you for that. Scandal and libel and all. I'll see if just because you're a policeman you can go about saying things like that about respectable folk."

"Now, now, my dear," murmured Osman once again.

"Talk, talk, talk," said his wife mechanically, but hardly giving him a glance, so intent was she on watching Bobby to see how her threat affected him.

"But, you see, I haven't said anything 'like that'," Bobby told her with a smile which evidently irritated her greatly. "Police never do. When we do feel able to, we don't. We make an arrest instead. Fortunately in this case there's no question of that—yet. I am trying to get information. In any case my questions are what lawyers call privileged."

"Well, then, I'll give you some more information," she snapped. "I followed him." She flung out a hand to point at Osman who at once shuffled his feet again, and murmured "Now, now, my dear". "I followed him," she repeated loudly, ignoring his faint protest. "I thought I had best know what he was up to."

"Now, now, my dear," protested Osman, looking very surprised.

"Can't you hold your tongue just half a minute?" demanded his wife fiercely. "Talk. Talk. Talk. That's you all the time. I heard that story about the canoodling that was going on down by the canal road and when Osman went sneaking off with that disgusting pipe of his, I just thought I would like to see who was doing the canoodling. You can't trust a man any further than you can see him and there's that hussy he's got to keep his accounts for him."

"Now, now, my dear," said Osman, this time a trifle more loudly and firmly than usual.

"If you can't keep quiet for just one moment," Mrs Ford told him in a blaze of concentrated fury, "I'll . . . I'll . . . " Her curved, threatening fingers with the pointed nails flew up so near to Osman's face that he hurriedly jumped back. She gave him another fiercely warning glance and then turned towards Bobby, who was prudently edging towards the door. "Talk, talk. Chatter, chatter," she said. "That's a man all over; and if you've got a man, you've got to watch him, haven't you?"

"I expect it's just as well," agreed Bobby.

"That's why I thought I had better keep an eye on him Tuesday night, prowling round at that time of night," she went on, indicating with a gesture the wretched Osman who almost automatically responded by a fresh shuffling of his feet, "and I did, too, and I can take my oath he never saw a soul or spoke a word to anyone or did a thing except potter about like a great booby, and then go back to the house, smelling of—tobacco," and what a world of scorn she flung into that last word. "There was no Mr Anderson anywhere and what's more I don't believe he ever was by there. Just police talk. Talk, talk. Chatter, chatter," she repeated. "Police that is, all over."

"Well, that's evidence," Bobby agreed, remembering that if a wife cannot be made to testify against her husband, more than once her evidence in his favour has secured an acquittal. "That means there's evidence now that Mr Ford was in the vicinity of the scene of the murder that Tuesday night but that he did nothing except stroll, smoke a pipe, go back home."

She looked at him gloomily and for the first time with doubt.

"Think you are smart, don't you?" she said. Then she added with conviction: "You are smart, too." With a sudden and total change of manner, of voice, of everything, so that she almost became a different woman, she said gently: "But you aren't smart if you think Osman would murder anyone. He won't even swat a wasp. If it's pig killing, he's always something to do as far away as he can get."

"See here now, Violet," interrupted Osman, really roused this time, "you know that's not true. It's only just happened once or twice that way when there was pig-sticking. I—"

"You're a great softy," she interrupted in her turn and she made the last word sound like a caress, so full was it of a deep affection. Embarrassed, Osman went very red. In fact, he blushed like a school-girl. To Bobby, she went on: "I'll tell you something he doesn't know. There was someone hanging about near the empty cottage. It was Mr Castles. He looked as if he was waiting for someone. I thought perhaps it was a girl. Not that I cared. So long as it wasn't Osman. Osman was going back towards the house and I slipped round ahead so I could get in first. That's all."

"Are you sure it was Mr Castles?" Bobby asked.

"Well, I didn't see anyone," interposed Osman. "I don't see why I didn't if he was there."

"I suppose you couldn't hold your tongue for two minutes, even if your life depended on it, could you?" asked Mrs Ford wearily, in the manner of one whose patience was at last utterly exhausted. "I tell you I saw him if you didn't and it was him right enough."

"Well, I won't bother you any longer," Bobby said. "Thank you very much for what you've told me. I may have to ask you both to make a statement in writing, but I hardly think that's necessary yet. We don't know enough."

With that he took himself off. He was not much inclined to believe Mrs Ford's tale. He did not believe she had secretly followed her husband when he went out to smoke the pipe Bobby suspected he was not allowed in the house. He did not believe, therefore, that she had seen Castles. But he could not be sure. And she might have seen Castles in the neighbourhood some other time or possibly she had heard that someone else had seen him.

"A puzzling woman," he told himself, unconscious of the tautology, "but I doubt if she's quite the virago she makes herself out. Bullies her man a bit just by way of discipline but would probably lie, steal or murder for him without a moment's hesitation."

He paused abruptly. A memory of one of the words he had used stirred uneasily in his mind. 'Murder' he had said. Murder had been done in fact. He tried to put the idea out of his mind. Not very successfully. Not too willingly he decided it would have to be taken into consideration. Knowing her husband's need of her money there was the possibility that she might have been willing to go even to the extremity of murder in order to bring him help. Perhaps his need of that money had been desperate and she had known it.

"A clever woman, a resolute woman," he reflected, and then he reflected, too, that equally possibly her story might have been quite true, that she might have been watching her husband and so might have seen Castles on the canal road—waiting.

He wondered, too, if she knew about the circumstances that might perhaps be thought to give Castles cause of deep resentment against Anderson who had been chief partner in the firm that still practised under the name of Castles. If she knew, that might explain why she had chosen his name to give Bobby. Bobby supposed it was altogether likely that she did know. Many people in the Midwych neighbourhood must be acquainted with the circumstances.

It was still so early that Bobby was able to reach Midwych and his office about his usual time. Almost the first thing he did was to ring the office of Messrs Castles and ask if Mr Castles had arrived. If not, could he be asked to come round to the county police headquarters as soon as convenient? There were various points on which, said Bobby over the 'phone, he might be able to help.

It was not long before Castles made his appearance, obviously nervous. Greeting exchanged, Bobby asked one or two unimportant questions and then said:

"What I really wished to ask you about, Mr Castles, is that it seems probable, though we can't be absolutely sure, that Mr Anderson was murdered on the canal road near Ends Bridge. Also we have information that you were seen near there that Tuesday night. Is that true?"

"It's a dirty lie," Castles declared instantly and angrily. "Who told you that?"

"Well, of course, I can't tell you that just now, can I?" Bobby said. "If it turns out to be correct and we act on it, naturally you'll have to know. At present we have no idea whether it's of any importance. You know, if we told everybody all the things people tell us about each other—well, there would be quite a lot of fat in a good many different fires. All you've got to do is to let us know where you really were, Tuesday night. Playing bridge with friends or at home having your supper or whatever it is. Then that'll show we've been misinformed and that'll be all right."

"I wasn't anywhere near Ends Bridge anyhow," Castles said gloomily. "I don't suppose I could even have told you where the beastly place was before this happened."

"I see," said Bobby. "Where exactly were you, then?"

"I went for a walk."

"Alone?"

"Yes."

"Often do that?"

"No."

"Any special reason for taking a walk that evening?"

"I felt like it."

"Which way did you go?"

"I just wandered around. I didn't notice much."

"Meet anyone you knew? Call anywhere?"

"No. I wanted to be alone. That's why. I mean, that's why I went for a walk. To be alone and have a think. Business problems," he added, but so plainly as an afterthought that Bobby almost smiled.

"A bit of bad luck," he said dryly, "that you should choose to go for a solitary walk on the very night Mr Anderson was murdered. Are you sure you are being quite frank with me?"

"I've no proof to give," Castles admitted. "It happens to be true but I can't prove it. I hardly know myself where I went exactly. I just wandered around. I wanted to think things out."

"Was it only business?" Bobby asked.

Castles did not answer. He sat there, his eyes on the ground, silent and frowning. After waiting a little, Bobby said:

"Would you say your feelings towards Mr Anderson were always friendly?"

Castles leaned forward now, staring straight at Bobby.

"I knew you would ask that," he said. Then he said: "I don't know."

"You don't know how you felt towards Mr Anderson?"

"No," said Castles. After a pause he repeated: "No, I don't."

"But surely—" began Bobby, puzzled.

"Sometimes I think I hated him," Castles said. "There he was every day where my grandfather sat and my father. Even his chair was the one grandfather used. He used to call it his lucky chair, because the first day he bought it and sat in it, he brought off his first big case. And Anderson sat there every day. That was when I hated him, because it was where I ought to have been sitting. I couldn't help remembering how dad used to leave everything in the practice to him, how easy it would have been for Anderson to trip dad up, to give him the final push downhill. Mother always said that was what happened." He lifted tortured eyes to Bobby. "Sometimes I thought it was driving me mad. The doubt. Not knowing. Not being sure. Because, you see, there was nothing certain. It was only suspicion, doubt and suspicion. But what was certain, what I knew for fact was that I should have gone to the workhouse when mother died and been thrown out at twelve or thirteen to be an errand boy or something like that, only for Anderson. It was Anderson paid for everything, paid for my education, gave me my articles, promised me a partnership. All that was clear and known and certain. All the other was doubt and wonder and suspicion—and the memory of what my mother said when she was dying, the last words she ever spoke."

"What were they?" Bobby asked gently.

"She told me to—remember," Castles said, and the word hung strangely in the quiet and still air.

CHAPTER XII
CASTLES' STORY

It was Castleswho broke the silence first.

He said, a tiny pause between each word:

"I suppose you think that's as good as a confession."

Bobby said:

"No."

They remained looking at each other silently for some moments. Then Bobby said:

"It gives you a motive. Other people have motives too."

Castles got up and went to the window. He stood there, staring down at the busy street without, but seeing nothing save the dead face of his mother, of Anderson. He said without turning round:

"I don't know. I don't know if I had a motive." Then he turned quickly and angrily and stood facing Bobby. "You won't believe me," he said. "You won't understand. No one could. I don't myself. I don't know whether it was hate I felt or—or liking, gratitude, friendship. Something stronger than that even. Sometimes I lay awake at night and wondered."

"He had promised you a partnership, hadn't he?"

Castles nodded.

"You haven't got it, have you?"

"No." He went to his chair and sat down. "That was me," he said. "I mean, I could have had it. I made excuses. More experience. Less responsibility. That sort of thing. Anderson couldn't make it out. I wanted to be sure. I didn't want to take anything more from him till—"

"Till—?" Bobby hinted when he paused.

"Till I was sure," Castles said in a low voice.

They were both silent again. Castles seemed almost to have forgotten his surroundings. He sat there, Bobby thought, almost like a man in a trance. It seemed as if the doubt tearing at his mind made him insensitive to everything else, as a man stretched upon the rack would know only his own agony. Bobby, deeply puzzled, was asking himself if these tormenting doubts were not likely to have had issue in action; in action that would give relief by making decision certain—certain and irrevocable. He said presently:

"You can't tell me more precisely where you went for your walk that Tuesday evening?"

Castles shook his head.

"You won't believe me, you won't understand," he said again. "No one could. But sometimes when I've been going over it in my mind, what Anderson did for me when I was a child, what perhaps he did to my father, how it killed my mother, I sometimes haven't known what I was doing or remembered it when I had done it. I've found myself in different places and not known how I got there. I've seen a client and advised him—good sound advice, too—and afterwards I haven't had an idea who it was or what I had said. It was as if my mind were split in two—one half wondering about Anderson, one half on our clients' affairs." He looked up and his anguished and questioning eyes stared at Bobby, stared beyond him as though there were far distant things he saw more plainly. With an obvious effort, in thick, half strangled tones, he muttered: "It used to go round and round in my head, round and round. I thought sometimes it was driving me mad."

He paused. He appeared to expect some comment. Bobby remained silent, waiting. In tones now so low and hoarse Bobby could hardly distinguish the words, he muttered:

"Perhaps it has."

Bobby shivered a little. Strange and dreadful was it to hear a man thus question his own sanity. Not without some cause, Bobby thought, for evidently Castles had brooded on the dreadful problem tormenting him to a degree incompatible with perfect mental health. But then Bobby reflected, too, that a police officer must accept nothing without evidence and confirmation. He remembered that it was not unknown for a pretence of insanity to be assumed as a kind of protective armour.

"It's a pity you can't say exactly where you went for your walk," Bobby repeated. "It would help both of us if you could. You say that it wasn't so very often that you went for long solitary walks?"

"No. Only when I wanted to think—or to stop thinking."

"Which was it this time?"

"Both, I expect."

"Any special reason why you should want to think—or not to think—that Tuesday evening? You see, on the face of it, it does look as if there might be some connection. With Anderson's murder, I mean."

For the first time in the interview Castles smiled faintly, and oddly enough that faint smile made Bobby feel more uncomfortable than anything else that had passed during their talk.

"I am quite lawyer enough to appreciate that," Castles said. "I've felt that from the first, as soon as I knew."

"Was there any such special reason?" Bobby persisted.

"Yes."

"Are you willing to tell me what it was?"

"No."

"That will make things much more difficult, if you won't answer," Bobby pointed out gravely.

Castles, by his silence, seemed to accept this.

Bobby still persisted.

"Was it anything new you had heard or found out about Anderson?"

"He is dead now," Castles said.

"I don't think I see what you mean," Bobby remarked.

Castles made no effort to explain.

"It stands like this," Bobby went on, watching the other closely. "Sometimes you felt very friendly to Anderson—friendly and grateful for what he had done. Sometimes you felt doubtful and suspicious. You wondered what was really the truth about your father's ruin. You wondered if Anderson had had a hand in it. You remembered your mother's last words. There was perpetual doubt and worry in your mind. A divided mind. That's always dangerous. Then in some way, just recently, you came to know some new fact. Whatever it was, it increased your trouble."

"I don't admit that," Castles interrupted sharply. "I didn't say that."

"No. But it is the explanation I shall accept unless and until I get some other. You went for a long walk to think over this new fact. It is almost certain that during that time, during your walk, Mr Anderson was murdered."

For the second time during this strange interview, in which Castles had shown himself both so frank and so reticent, at one moment laying bare his inmost soul, at another refusing all explanation, Castles smiled; and again his smile had an oddly disturbing effect on Bobby, though why he did not know. Castles said:

"Pretty damning put like that. You would make a good prosecuting counsel. Well, are you going to charge me?"

Bobby shook his head.

"I am sure," he said, "that as a lawyer you know well enough there is no more than ground for further inquiry. Besides, if I had meant to charge you, I should have had to warn you, shouldn't I? You've been extremely frank with me, Mr Castles, and for that I thank you. You have also refused to answer the most important of my questions—about the new fact you came to know and that you seem to have felt affected your attitude towards Anderson. Are you sure it is wise to keep that to yourself?"

"I'm sure it isn't. But I'm going to. Also I have not admitted that there is any such new fact." Then once more he smiled, but this time a boyish, mischievous smile, as he added: "If you were half as clever as people say, you would know without being told."

"If I were half as clever as people say," retorted Bobby tartly, "I expect I should be at least twice as clever as I am. One more question: Does Mr Blythe know this new fact you've discovered?"

"Well, that's a clever question, anyhow. I wonder if it means you do know without being told? Anyhow, I'll answer it. He hasn't the remotest idea."

"Did you ever tell anyone else what you've told me? I mean about how you felt towards Anderson, sometimes friendly and sometimes—well, not so friendly?"

"Never. Not likely. I suppose you think I've been blabbing to you and I suppose I have, and so I dare say you think it's a habit of mine. It isn't. I can hold my tongue. Only it's been a bit of a shock. About Anderson being murdered. That's why it all came out. It—it's freed me." He drew a long breath. "I haven't got to think about it any more. I needn't—remember." He said this with an intensity that showed how deeply the last words spoken by his mother on her death bed had graven themselves on his memory. "It's all different now," he said with evident relief.

"No one had any idea of how you felt towards Anderson?"

"I think perhaps Blythe guessed," Castles admitted, "I don't know. I never said anything. Once or twice he told me I worried too much. Perhaps he only meant about business. Once or twice he rather stressed how decent Anderson had been in helping me. Then, too, once or twice he said something about people brooding too much and dwelling on the past. And about its being better to put the best interpretation possible on things instead of suspecting the worst. It was always quite general, just general talk. But sometimes it made me think he had an idea of how I felt. He told me once he always knew when one of his Hopewell House boys had something on his mind. Perhaps it was like that with me."

"Perhaps it was," agreed Bobby thoughtfully, and Castles said:

"You've asked me a good many questions. I would like to ask you one. Is it true Anderson was shot in the back?"

"Yes. Why?"

"It rules out suicide," Castles answered. "Another thing is that I've never touched a revolver in my life—or seen one. Except the one young Dwight brought to the office once. I remember I asked him if he had a licence and he said he had. I never thought of it again till now."

"Was that long ago?" Bobby asked.

"Oh, yes, a year or two back. I don't know exactly. Soon after he was articled, I think." Castles paused and looked uncomfortable. "I suppose you aren't going to suspect Dwight on the strength of his having had a revolver months ago?"

"Not much in itself," Bobby agreed, but he was thinking of what had happened at Rose Briar Cottage and of what Mrs Jordan had told him.

Castles plainly found something disturbing in Bobby's voice.

"Articled clerks don't go murdering their principal, even if they generally feel like it," he said, half uneasily, half jokingly. "Dwight had nothing against Anderson. No earthly reason why he should do such a thing."

"Is that quite certain?" Bobby asked.

"Of course. What do you mean?"

"In some offices," Bobby reminded him, "there are dislikes, strong dislikes, jealousies. Hatreds even."

"Not in ours," said Castles seriously. "I mean, not like that." He emphasized the last two words with a vague gesture. "Blythe and young Green don't get on, I know. But that's no reason why Dwight should murder Anderson, is it?"

"No," agreed Bobby. "Only sometimes there are love affairs in offices. Where there's love, there may be hate as well. Have you ever heard anything about Miss Anne Earle? In connection with either of your partners?"

Castles seemed genuinely surprised.

"Good lord, no," he said. "Anderson's married, you know, though his wife's left him. He has his reputation to think of. Wouldn't do for a well-known solicitor to get mixed up in a scandal. That's why he never got a divorce. You can't imagine a man in his position carrying on an intrigue with one of his own staff."

"Not even if he fell in love with her? Love's a queer thing. It just happens."

"Not to Anderson, it wouldn't," Castles said, "not at his age. And Blythe simply isn't interested in women. Too taken up with his Hopewell House boys. It means more to him than the practice, if you ask me. I don't know if you've heard any gossip, but if you have you can take it from me, there's nothing in it. Not Anderson, at his age, his temperament, his experience—and a wife."

He paused. Bobby reflected, but did not say, that none of these things gave absolute protection—neither age nor experience nor anything else. Certainly not age. Sometimes it was the elderly man, suddenly left desolate by death or desertion, who felt more strongly the urge to re-make his life, the dread of loneliness, the desire for an intimate companionship.

"And certainly not Blythe," Castles went on. "I don't know if I ought to tell you. I believe he has a sort of horror of women. Psychological. He had rather an awful experience when he was a child. When he was about eight or nine he somehow got into his mother's bedroom and his mother was there with a strange man in what is called a compromising situation. There was a divorce and I think the child was called to give evidence. Rather a beastly affair and he has never got over it. Warped in that way. I've always thought it was partly why he's so keen on Hopewell House. Keeps it as clear of women as the monks do at Mount Athos. Of course, that's confidential. I'm only telling you to make you see it's quite out of the question to suppose that either Anderson or Blythe could have had anything to do like that with any of the girls on our staff."

"What about the clerks?" Bobby asked.

Castles shook his head.

"I never heard of anything of the sort," he declared. "If there had been, I should have been sure to know."

Bobby was not of that opinion. He was inclined to believe that Castles was so absorbed by his own tormenting doubts that he saw and knew very little of what went on around him.

"Can you give me any information about the financial side of the firm?" he asked. "Especially as it affected Mr Anderson."

"No, and I don't know that I would if I could," Castles answered quickly. "I think that's going a little far, isn't it? I could understand it in a case of suicide. As it is, I don't see what the firm's finances could have to do with it."

"Just possibly," Bobby murmured, "everything."

"I don't see how. A man isn't murdered because he is hard up. The war has hit all solicitors pretty hard. I suppose we are a luxury trade. Litigation is, anyhow. All law business has gone west. I don't mean we are bankrupt, you know. Besides, I couldn't give you details, even if I wanted to. I'm a salaried clerk, not a partner. I don't see the private balance sheet. Blythe draws that up and he and Anderson keep it to themselves. Naturally. Equally naturally, everyone in the office has an idea how things are going. But not the actual figures."

"I think I remember that the first time I saw you you were looking at Mr Anderson's private ledger?"

"So I was. Nothing to do with what's happened. Something else altogether."

"Mr Blythe was rather surprised, wasn't he? I remember he looked taken aback."

"I daresay he was. I had my reasons. Good reasons. I don't intend to tell you—or anyone else—what they were. They're entirely irrelevant."

"Won't you let me judge that?"

"No."

"Would Mr Anderson have been pleased to find you looking at his private ledger?"

"It's no good going on asking questions," Castles retorted. "Irrelevant," he repeated. Then he said: "I should have known what to say."

"You force me to ask you this. Did you know there would be no need to answer him because you did not mean to give him the chance to question you?"

"That's a prosecuting counsel's question," Castles said angrily. "I think you are twisting things. Blythe saw me. He could have told Anderson. He never did. At least, if he did, Anderson must have told him it was all right. Anyhow, Anderson never said a word to me about it." He added once again, frowning heavily as he spoke: "If he had, I should have known what to say."

"But you won't tell me what you would have said?" Bobby asked; and when Castles shook his head again, Bobby said slowly: "Well, you know, that's almost as interesting as if you did."

"I don't know what you mean," Castles muttered uneasily.

"Well, of course, I don't mean you to," Bobby retorted with a faint smile. "A fair bargain—quid pro quo. You tell me why you wanted a look at Anderson's ledger when he wasn't there and I'll tell you why I think it's so interesting that you won't."

Castles got to his feet.

"If you've quite finished," he said, "I would like to be going. We aren't busy, but we have some work to do apart from trying to guess conundrums."

"One moment," Bobby said as Castles began to move towards the door. "From information received, I understand that Mr Anderson recently disposed of a sum of £5,000."

Castles, with his hand already outstretched towards the door, swung round as if he had received a sudden blow. Only by a visible effort did he recover himself and he still looked very disturbed.

"You do know a lot, don't you?" he said with what was evidently intended for a withering sneer. "Well, as you know it all already, there's no need for me to tell you anything more, is there? Good day."

"Good day," Bobby answered, "and thanks very much for what you've told me and still more for what you haven't. Should you mind asking Mr Dwight to come along to see me, just for a little chat. Got to make some inquiries about his revolver, you know. Police have to do that sort of thing. Oh, by the way, if it's worrying you at all, I might as well tell you we knew about it before—from information received, as we like to say. You can spare Dwight from the office for a bit?"

"I suppose we'll have to," Castles answered grumblingly. He opened the door and went out and then turned back and stared at Bobby. "I wonder what I have told you," he said doubtfully and went away, and Bobby, as he looked at the closed door, wondered, too.

CHAPTER XIII
QUESTION OF ALIBI

IT WAS SOME time, nearly the lunch hour in fact, before Dwight made his appearance. But for the fact that lunch, for Bobby, in these days of war, consisted generally of a sandwich or two sent in from a neighbouring ham and beef shop, he would probably, when Dwight did arrive, have been out getting his meal either at home or at a restaurant. Nor was Bobby entirely without suspicion that Dwight had hoped that might still be the case and so the interview be delayed a while. But Bobby was careful to make no reference to the delay nor did he take any notice of the young man's sullen and reluctant air.

"Very good of you to come along, Mr Dwight," he said pleasantly. "Do sit down, won't you? Have a cigarette?"

Dwight ignored the offer of the cigarette and though he did sit down he still maintained his air of sullen resentment.

"Castles been saying things about me?" he asked angrily. "Just like him. Trying to get me in to get himself out."

"Is he in? Is there any need for him to get out?" Bobby asked.

"How should I know?"

"If you don't, why suggest it?"

"It's pretty clear you think someone in the office killed Anderson, and it's as likely to be Castles as anyone. I don't suppose he liked knowing Anderson had got hold of the practice. After all, his grandfather made it and it was his father's, too."

"Old story that, isn't it? Any other reason?"

"No. I don't know anything about it. I don't know what you want to ask me. Suppose I had a revolver a couple of years ago, what about it?"

"For one thing, you don't seem to have had a licence. At least, I haven't been able to find an entry in the Firearms Register. I believe you told Castles you had one?"

"No. I didn't. I may have said I was going to get one. I don't remember. I didn't bother about a licence. I thought it wasn't worth while. I chucked the thing away instead. In the canal somewhere."

"How did you get hold of a revolver?" Bobby asked. "You can't buy one like a packet of cigarettes."

"I gave a chap in a pub ten bob for it. Somewhere by the canal docks. A sailor. He was tight. He said every time his ship got in he smuggled in a revolver. You can buy them easily enough anywhere on the Continent."

Bobby was inclined to believe this story. It is, of course, the fact that a small trade in smuggled revolvers goes on in all the ports. There are always people—sometimes criminals, sometimes merely those who like the feeling of hidden power the possession of a weapon gives them, or again those who have been refused or have not wished to apply for a licence—who are willing to give a good price for such things. The only doubtful point in Dwight's story was the modest amount he said he had paid, but if the sailor had had too much to drink that would be accounted for.

"What ammunition had you?" he asked.

"I hadn't any," Dwight answered. "It was loaded but that was all."

"Mr Dwight," Bobby said, "I don't want you to think that I am asking you these questions because of anything Mr Castles told me. He did admit he had seen you in possession of a pistol. He couldn't very well deny it. But he was quick to point out that it was a long time ago and he expressed a very strong opinion that it was absurd to suppose any connection with Mr Anderson's death. We have received much later information and I may tell you quite frankly that I am fairly certain it was you who was seen at Rose Briar Cottage. That was when what was probably your own revolver was fired after you, though not, I think, with any intention of hitting you. The occupier of the cottage says it was only fired in the air."

"You needn't say 'occupier'," growled Dwight. "What's the sense of being so damn official? You might as well say it was Mrs Jordan. She's telling a pack of lies."

"I can only tell you," Bobby said slowly, "that at present I am inclined to accept her story, not yours."

"Meaning I'm a liar?" asked Dwight truculently.

"You've made that accusation against Mrs Jordan, haven't you?" Bobby reminded him. "'Liar' is your word, not mine. And I think I must remind you that in a murder inquiry a witness not entirely frank comes automatically under suspicion. Would you care to reconsider what you've said? People do often find second thoughts best and we are always ready to hear them."

Dwight hesitated. He was plainly uneasy. Then he seemed to make up his mind.

"No," he said. "It's only Mrs Jordan's word against mine. She couldn't possibly have been sure it was—" He had evidently been about to say 'me', but stopped just in time. Instead he said: "She can't be really certain or you would have had her along to identify me."

"Hardly necessary when she mentioned your name," Bobby said. "It isn't only her word. Our man confirms to some extent."

"Some extent isn't good enough," retorted Dwight. "Neither Mrs Jordan nor your copper would stand up to cross-examination for two minutes. And when a witness breaks down in cross-examination, it's a big score to the other side."

"I can see you haven't studied law for nothing," Bobby said with a smile. "I agree. That is so. I can assure you that when we send papers to the public prosecutor, that's the first point checked. If they think we've put forward evidence that won't stand up, well, we get it in the neck good and hard. You ought to hear a K.C. explaining exactly what he thinks of us for expecting him to put a witness like that in the box. A study in language. Interesting but painful. I've seen strong men reduced to tears—or very nearly. When I say strong men I mean tough cops of twenty years' service. Pale and trembling as they creep away after listening to that K.C. So you may be sure we are pretty careful. Now let us suppose just for the sake of supposing that it actually was you at Rose Briar Cottage, what do you suppose might have been your motive?"

"I've told you it wasn't me," Dwight repeated, scowling more furiously than ever.

"It's only supposing," Bobby repeated, smiling more amiably than ever. "For instance, could your motive have been jealousy?"

"I don't know what you mean."

"I think you do. Mr Anderson was living with Miss Anne Earle."

Dwight jumped to his feet, pale with anger. His anger nearly choking him, he stuttered:

"Leave her alone, leave her name out of it."

"Mr Dwight," Bobby said with sudden sternness, "murder has been done, and in murder no one can be left alone, no one's name can be left out. Before to-day women have done murder—what's the matter?"

For quite suddenly the hot anger faded from Dwight's expression. He looked suddenly small and stricken and very white. He sat down quickly, so quickly that it almost seemed he had been afraid of falling. As though to hide what he feared might be written there, he put his hand up to his face.

When he did not speak, Bobby, slightly puzzled, repeated:

"What's the matter?" When there was still no answer, he said as gently as he could: "Won't you tell me what's the trouble? You've just thought of something, haven't you? You know, it's only guilty people who have anything to be afraid of. Innocent people are always safe."

But still Dwight would not answer, still he remained huddled in his chair in the same stricken attitude and Bobby thought:

"He's telling himself that perhaps Anne Earle did it. He's almost sure she did."

He waited silently till Dwight looked up and said:

"I'm sorry. It's nothing. It was just that I got scared all of a sudden. You are doing your best to make out it was me and I saw all at once that you might bring it off and then I should be hanged and it scared me stiff. I'm all right now. You'll have a job, you know, proving it was me, when it wasn't."

"I don't think it was that at all," Bobby told him quietly. "I think it is something quite different you are afraid of. I wish you would be a bit more open. It would be a lot better all round, much better than keeping your suspicions to yourself."

"I haven't any suspicions," Dwight asserted. "Why should I? I don't know anything about it." But his voice was so unsteady, he showed himself still so pale and shaken, that his words managed to convey almost the exact opposite of their literal meaning. "None," he repeated, staring defiantly at Bobby.

"I can't make you tell us if you won't," Bobby said. "I can only advise you to think it over very carefully. I will put this to you. It is the fact that Anderson and Miss Earle were living together. Police have nothing to do with private morals, only with public order, and in this case, as Anderson's wife had left him, and he and Miss Earle seem to have honestly cared for each other, I daresay some people would hold them justified. I'm glad I haven't to express any opinion one way or the other. They thought it necessary to keep their connection quiet. No doubt the practice would have suffered if it had been generally known that Anderson was living with one of his girl typists. To a great extent, they did manage to keep their secret to themselves. But some people knew. I think you had some idea, even if you weren't sure. I think also you were deeply in love with Miss Earle yourself. I think your jealousy drove you to break into Rose Briar Cottage to make sure of the truth. I think you took your revolver with you. I think it is even possible you took it with some mad idea of shooting Anderson if you found him there."

"Meaning you think I've shot him now?"

"If I did think so," Bobby said gravely, "I should not be questioning you. I should be charging you. You notice I have not given you the usual warning. That's because at present I see no substantial evidence against you."

"Thank you," said Dwight, with a feeble attempt at irony.

"But I do think there are grounds for asking you some direct and personal questions. I will ask you this: 'Are you in love with Miss Earle?'"

"I am not saying anything about her," Dwight replied with renewed sullenness.

"Did you suspect her connection with Mr Anderson?"

"What's the good of going on? I tell you I won't answer anything about her."

"Were you in fact jealous, even passionately jealous?"

This time Dwight made no answer at all, unless an even deeper scowl could be taken for reply.

Bobby went on:

"Will you tell me where you were Tuesday evening, the evening, that is, when we believe Mr Anderson was murdered?"

"If you like. I've an alibi all right, if that's what you are after. Tuesday evening I was playing billiards at the St Peter's Square billiard hall. I didn't leave till ten. Then I went straight back to where I hang out—the Welsdon Private Hotel. My people pay my bill there."

"That's very satisfactory," Bobby said. "You can give me the name of the person you played with?"

"It was Billy Swift, he's with Morgan's, the Beak Street solicitors. He'll remember because it happens he won—by a beastly fluke."

"That's all right," said Bobby. "I expect someone saw you when you got back to your hotel?"

"Oh, yes," answered Dwight confidently. "Mrs Hillman, she runs the place, was in the hall, and I said good night to her, and then there's always someone at the desk to spot who comes in, and it happens I ran into old Watkins. He'll remember, because I ran into him literally, at the foot of the stairs, and knocked his book out of his hands and he was awfully mad. I should think that's enough?"

"It certainly sounds like it," agreed Bobby.

"And if you think Billy Swift's telling lies to help a pal, which you can be jolly sure he wouldn't, more likely to tell 'em to down a pal, you can ask the attendants at the billiard hall. They all know me, and I remember speaking to the chap at the door, thinking I would book a table for another night, and then I thought I wouldn't."

"Sounds all right," Bobby repeated. "I don't think I need bother you any longer. You know, of course, we shall check up on your alibi, just as a matter of form."

Dwight nodded, though with a touch of uneasiness. But that was to be expected. Then Dwight said:

"There's just one little point I would like you to notice. It wasn't me at Rose Briar Cottage, but if you choose to believe it was, then it follows you believe I left the revolver behind, as Mrs Jordan is supposed to have fired it after the chap. So you can't very well believe, too, that I used it to shoot Anderson on Tuesday, when, by your own theory, I hadn't got it any longer. I suppose though that isn't the sort of thing you bother about thinking up, only points against a chap, not for him?"

"If we didn't think up points like that, for as well as against," Bobby answered, "we should soon be in pretty deep water. In this case it doesn't apply, because Mrs Jordan's evidence is that she tried to hide the revolver, but that someone found the hiding-place and took the revolver away. She says she doesn't know who or when."

Dwight stared at Bobby, looking both surprised and suspicious.

"Is this a trap?" he demanded.

Bobby sighed.

"If you are going to be a lawyer," he said, "you ought to know by now that traps are God's own gift to the defence. Defending counsel would talk of nothing else till he had the jury believe there was nothing else—why, laying a trap simply shouts that the evidence isn't good enough. Besides, traps are useless if the murderer has any sense. He spots them at once. And if the murderer is a fool, then they aren't required. Well, I think that's all. I'm sorry if you think I've bothered you unnecessarily, but it's important to be sure how many people knew of Rose Briar Cottage. They seem to have managed to keep it very fairly quiet. Mr Castles seems to have been ignorant. I imagine Mr Blythe knew?"

"I haven't an idea," answered Dwight cautiously, possibly seeing the little hidden snare, since, if he had known that Blythe knew he must have known himself. "If he had done he would have hated it. I mean, he always does, people being in love with each other. It's a sort of complex with him."

"Must be a complex he has to control pretty often."

"Oh, he knows it happens. It's not that, it's just that he can't stand any show of it. If you want the sack from our office, just let him see there's a spot of flirting going on. If he had suspected anything of the sort between Anderson and one of the staff, he would have gone right in off the deep end." He paused and added with a half smile: "There's a motive for you, as you're so jolly keen on finding one. Perhaps it was Blythe that cop of yours spotted climbing out of Rose Briar Cottage."

With a triumphant nod, as if he felt he had given Bobby something to think about, though something he himself did not take very seriously, Dwight retired; and Bobby put in some rapid and efficient work to test the alibi he had been given. He was not much surprised to find that the result was unsatisfactory in the extreme. At the Welsdon private hotel, Mrs Hillman, the proprietress and manager, agreed that it was quite likely she had seen and spoken to Mr Dwight on Tuesday evening, but it might have been Wednesday, it might have been Monday. There had been no reason to remember the incident exactly. When she saw any of her guests, she naturally said good night, and often chatted for a minute or two, if they seemed in the mood for it. She herself, she explained, had always to be in the mood for it. This information was imparted with the patient sigh of a martyr, but did not seem helpful as regarded Dwight's alibi. The girl at the reception desk was equally vague. She had certainly been on duty on Tuesday evening till eleven, when the hotel was supposed to close. But she would neither notice nor remember the return of any guest. A stranger, yes; but not a resident. Why should she? She would simply recognize him or her as a guest and forget it. Then there was Mr Watkins who did indeed remember very clearly the incident of the collision and how his book had been knocked out of his hand. He did not hide his unfavourable opinion of the younger generation in general and of Dwight in particular, but couldn't possibly say whether the incident had happened on Monday, Tuesday, or Wednesday. That sort of boorish behaviour was far too common for any one fresh demonstration of it to be remembered specially. But he had no doubt that it had occurred on whatever day the police thought likely. Sergeant Wright, who made the report, had equally no doubt that Mr Watkins was the sort of witness ready to commit stubborn, convincing, and unconscious perjury of the kind most dangerous to justice.

At the office of Messrs Morgan it was even worse. Mr Swift agreed he had played a match with Dwight and won it by a brilliant display of sheer skill—'shan't forget that game in a hurry. I put the balls just where I wanted—right on the top of my form'—but with some hesitation he admitted that the game, owing to the brilliance of his last break—'not a fluke in it, either'—had been over fairly early. He hadn't noticed when exactly, but 'definitely' early. He had then played another hundred up with another chap, and Dwight had hung about watching for a time, but Mr Swift had no idea how long or when Dwight had left. His attention had been on his game. He also admitted, though still with hesitation, when the question was put to him, that Dwight had rung up to ask him if he didn't remember that he, Dwight, had remained in the billiard hall till nearly closing time. But Mr Swift wasn't going to say he was sure when he wasn't, even if it did seem like letting down a pal.

The attendant at the billiard-hall door began, however, by being very positive. He was certain Mr Dwight, whom he knew well, had been almost the last to leave before closing time. But he could give no reason why he was so sure of this. It just happened that he remembered. Finally, sharp questioning by Sergeant Wright, and a vague hint about tracing 'phone calls, resulted in a scared admission that Dwight had rung him up, too, and had promised him a pound note if he could say he was sure Dwight had remained in the hall till late.

"Young fool's given himself away pretty thoroughly," opined Wright, making his report.

"I half expected he might do something of the sort," Bobby said. "His alibi's a wash-out."

"Looks to me as if it was him all right," declared Wright. "Faking alibis and all. It doesn't look too good."

"It doesn't follow because he tried to get faked confirmation that the alibi itself is faked," Bobby said thoughtfully. "It may have been just nervousness. He was pretty badly scared. All we are entitled to say is that his alibi isn't worth anything."

Wright looked unconvinced, but said 'Yes, sir,' in the way in which Bobby, when a sergeant, had been accustomed himself to say 'Yes, sir,' when he thoroughly disagreed with a superior. Then Wright retired and Bobby rang up Castles and asked if it would be possible for Mr Blythe to come round to see him. Mr Blythe promised to do so shortly, and in preparation for the interview Bobby unlocked a cupboard and got out the motoring gauntlet rescued from the canal. He meant it to be lying on his desk when Mr Blythe arrived.

CHAPTER XIV

ALIBI OF A GLOVE

IT HAS TO be confessed that Bobby, who had so recently expounded to young Dwight the futility of all traps, did experience a slight twinge of conscience as, awaiting the arrival of Mr Blythe, he placed the motoring gauntlet in its conspicuous position on his table. He comforted himself with the reflection that it wasn't really a trap, only a test, and at the moment the difference in the meaning of these two words seemed to him enormous. Then, too, all he meant to do was to notice if Blythe looked startled or uneasy on catching sight of the recovered glove. The test, however, that was so emphatically not a trap, was one that Blythe passed successfully, for when he entered the room and noticed the glove he merely looked mildly pleased.

"You've got it back for me then?" he said. "Quick work. Where was it?"

"I suppose it is the one you lost?" Bobby asked. "You can identify it positively?"

"Why, yes," Blythe answered. "Is there any doubt?" He picked it up and looked at it more closely. "Oh, it's mine all right," he said. "Where was it?" he asked again.

"In the canal," Bobby told him.

"In the canal?" repeated Blythe, looking even more surprised. "What on earth . . . how did it get there?"

"Our information," Bobby said, "is that it was thrown into the canal by a person who states it was found in an unoccupied cottage garden on the road near Ends Bridge."

"Near Ends Bridge," Blythe repeated. "I don't follow that. Ends Bridge? That's where you think Anderson may have been murdered. What was it doing there?"

"I am sure you will understand," Bobby said, "that that is what we very much want to know."

"So do I," Blythe told him. "I don't understand it at all. Are you sure? It seems so extraordinary. I thought you said the canal first?"

"Apparently it was thrown into the canal by the finder in order to get rid of it."

Blythe looked almost comically bewildered. Bobby, watching him closely, thought that if it was acting, it was very good acting. But there are some most excellent actors who yet have never trodden the boards. He thought he could detect, too, an undercurrent of discomfort and unease. Not that that was unnatural in the circumstances. He waited in silence for Blythe to speak. It was a minute or two before Blythe said:

"I lose my glove. It is taken from my car. It turns up in the canal, having been thrown in after being found close to where my partner was murdered."

Bobby still said nothing. There was again a pause till Blythe spoke, slowly and gravely.

"Does this mean," he asked, "that I—I'll put it plainly—that I am under suspicion of having murdered poor Anderson?"

"I think," Bobby said, "that at present it would be quite impossible to say anything more than that this business of your glove ought to be explained. We feel it is necessary to know how it got where our informant says it was found."

"Who is he? Your informant, I mean. Or don't you want to say?"

"At present I think we would rather not," Bobby answered. "Very likely all this will turn out to be entirely unimportant. Then we can forget it. And then it would be much better if no names had been mentioned. Make forgetting easier all round. Would you mind saying where you were that Tuesday evening?"

"The murder night? An alibi?" Blythe asked. "Oh, I'm not complaining. You're simply doing your duty, I can quite see that. Only you must admit, it's a bit startling for a respectable, middle-aged solicitor to find himself under suspicion of having murdered his own partner."

"Oh, we haven't got as far as suspicion—or anywhere near for that matter," Bobby protested.

"But you want an alibi all the same?" Blythe said, with a somewhat grim smile. "You know, I've heard of a solicitor murdering a rival solicitor or trying to, but never of one murdering his own partner. Partners may hate each other pretty cordially, but they are generally necessary to each other—necessary evils, I suppose, we call each other. Tuesday night—now, where was I? Good lord, I haven't one. An alibi, I mean. Of all the luck! That was the night I drove out to see old Sir Norris Langley. Every year he gives me a cheque for Hopewell House, but he likes to be asked for it, and it all depends on my putting him in a good humour whether it's in one or two figures—varies from £5 to £50 according to his mood. Generally nearer the £50 I'm glad to say."

"Well, then, if you saw Sir Norris—" began Bobby, but Blythe interrupted.

"Unluckily I didn't," he said. "That's the devil of it. When I was nearly at his place I remembered suddenly that he was in town, trying to get back into harness. Like all the rest of us, he wants a war job; and like all the rest of us who aren't as young as we were, he's finding he's not wanted. Too old at forty is the cry to-day when jobs are being handed out. So I turned round and drove back home again. And no alibi."

"You didn't meet anyone, speak to anyone, call anywhere?"

Blythe shook his head.

"No confirmation whatever," he admitted. "Only, oddly enough, if I can't give you an alibi for myself I can for my glove. It happens that I tore it slightly on the Sunday—you'll see where if you look at the tip of the thumb. One of my lads is a leather worker. I gave it him on Monday night to mend. It was in his possession all Tuesday and I only got it back on Wednesday morning. Lander, that's our Hopewell House porter, sent one of the lads round to my house with it. So, if I did murder Anderson, I certainly hadn't that glove with me at the time, and I suppose I would hardly take the trouble to go back to the scene of my crime to leave my glove there."

Bobby smiled faintly.

"Hardly," he agreed. "That clears it up in one sense. Makes it more difficult in another."

"You will want to get that confirmed, I suppose," Blythe said. "You can ask Lander. Lander will almost certainly have a note of it in his book. He's a very particular person. I'm pretty sure he'll be able to show you the entry, dated and initialled probably."

"That'll be more than good enough," Bobby said. "Do you mind if I send my sergeant?"

"I should much prefer it," said Blythe crisply.

Bobby asked to be excused for a moment and left Blythe alone in the room while he went to find Wright and give him the necessary instructions.

"There's something else I want you to do," Bobby added. "It's been worrying me all day but I've only just got it clear in my mind.

This morning when I went to see Osman Ford, Mrs Ford made a great fuss about not trusting him, about thinking he might be meeting some girl or another on the quiet. At the time I took it for eye-wash, but I've been thinking since that it may have been eye-wash and yet had something in it, too. There may be some reason why she thought of that particular excuse. So I want you to make a few discreet inquiries and try to find out if there is any gossip of that sort—either that Mrs Ford is jealous or that her husband gives her any reason for it." "Very good, sir," said Wright, and went off on his two errands; while Bobby went back to his room, apologising there for having left Blythe so long alone.

"Have you been long?" Blythe asked. "I hadn't noticed. Something else up your sleeve, I suppose. That's all right. No business of mine. You know, it's worrying. This glove business, I mean. I've been thinking. I can take it you are satisfied your informant is telling the truth and that the glove was really found where he says?"

"No," answered Bobby at once. "I'm not. There's no corroboration. The story may be an invention for all we can tell. The only thing certain—there is supporting evidence—is that it was thrown into the canal by the person who claims to have found it where I said. If that is false, if it is just a lie invented to throw suspicion on you, then we shall have to consider whether the finder of the glove isn't the actual murderer."

"That would mean a deliberate attempt to implicate me?"

"We thought of that possibility from the first," Bobby said.

"I'm glad to hear it," Blythe remarked. "Very glad. It's a disturbing idea all the same. If it's a deliberate attempt to make me seem guilty—"

He left the sentence unfinished. He looked extremely disturbed. Naturally so, Bobby supposed. Bobby said:

"It suggests you have an enemy. Do you know of one?"

"Not a pleasant thought," Blythe said. "No. Not that I know of. Not like that. Of course, I've had my little disagreements. And there are people I've had to press in the interests of our clients, who may have thought themselves badly treated. Disappointed clients of our own, too, for that matter, who thought we ought to have done better for them. But matter for a blackguardly trick like this—emphatically no."

"You can't make any suggestion, then?"

"No. It would mean there was someone deliberately trying to get me hanged. Good God. I just can't believe it."

Bobby did not speak. But he looked thoughtfully at the glove still lying on his table and Blythe saw the direction of his glance and nodded in agreement.

"Yes, there's always that, isn't there?" he said. After a pause he added: "I wonder if it was known that I was making a useless journey and so very likely wouldn't have an alibi for that particular evening?"

"Could anyone have known?" Bobby asked. "Did you mention it to anyone in the office or anywhere else?"

"Now, did I?" Blythe asked himself.

He wasn't sure, he said finally. He couldn't remember for certain. He had had the visit to Sir Norris in his mind for some time, but he had only decided to make it that Tuesday on the morning of the same day when he had had a letter putting off an appointment arranged for the evening. So, finding himself unexpectedly free, and as he had told the Hopewell House people not to expect his usual visit, he had thought the opportunity a good one for the contemplated visit to Sir Norris. He might, he thought, quite easily have mentioned that intention to almost any one. Quite possibly he might have said something to, or in the hearing of, Miss Harris, who took down his letters. If he had done so, she, in her turn, being a little chatterbox, might easily have mentioned it to any other of the staff. After all, there was nothing secret or confidential about his change of plan.

"What it comes to," said Bobby at last, for Blythe had rambled a little in these efforts at recollection, "is that almost anyone might have known, but there's no telling."

"I'm afraid that's about it," agreed Blythe. "Not much help, is it?"

Bobby agreed that in fact it was anything but helpful.

"It makes one feel very uncomfortable," Blythe said again. "It does seem someone is deliberately trying to make me look like poor Anderson's murderer. I don't see how else to explain the disappearance of my glove and its being found where you say. Planned and deliberate," he said, shaking his head. "Incredible. Only—there it is."

"I can quite see how you feel," Bobby said. "You are perfectly certain it was in the locker of your car when you parked it at Chief Building?"

"I remember it distinctly. I think you could probably get the evidence of the lad who brought it from Lander. Dickens his name is. I should think he probably remembers seeing me put it away in the locker. He might not, but I expect he would."

"I've made one or two inquiries," Bobby said, "and it seems it would be difficult for any stranger to get into the Chief Building car park without being seen. That seems to rule out any ordinary casual pilfering. Probably, therefore, the thief was someone known to the porter or the car attendant, someone neither of them would challenge if they saw him. That means someone working in the building."

"It's getting more and more unpleasant," Blythe said. "What you mean is that the thief was probably someone belonging to our own staff?"

"I think we must begin by working on those lines."

"It's incredible," declared Blythe with energy. "Why should they? I'm sure there's not one of them would do such a thing."

"Nevertheless it was done—by someone."

"It means one of our staff is trying to get me hanged. I refuse." said Blythe, still more energetically, "to consider such an idea."

"It may not be that so much," Bobby suggested, "as someone very anxious to escape a hanging. We have two concrete facts to start from. First: The murder. Second: Your glove, not in your possession at the time of the murder, was found near the spot where we believe the murder took place. The murderer may be merely trying to confuse us. Or the idea may be that if someone else is hanged for the crime, so much the better. That would mean safety."

"One partner murdered, the other hanged," Mr Blythe murmured. "A drastic sort of clearance."

Bobby looked up sharply. Blythe had not mentioned any name, but it seemed fairly evident he was thinking of Castles.

"If that did occur," Bobby said, "what would happen to the business?"

"To the practice," Mr Blythe corrected him gently. "Upon my soul, I don't know. It's a contingency I have never contemplated. I should imagine it would collapse pretty completely. I suppose Castles might try to carry on."

"He could start afresh under the same name, as it is his own name, I suppose?"

"Why not? Nothing to prevent him. A curious situation. It cuts a little too near the bone for my taste—as an interested party. I have felt at times that Castles was inclined to brood too much on the past. He was in a very unusual and difficult position. There he was, only a clerk in the practice his grandfather had built up, that his father had inherited. It's no wonder if he let it prey on his mind rather too much. But that's all. I don't believe there was anything more. I can't."

There was again a silence. Blythe, a little pale now, was evidently very deeply disturbed. Bobby felt that was not surprising. He himself was remembering how Castles had told of his strange, divided thoughts, how at times he had seemed even to doubt his own sanity, how on one point he had shown so strange and obstinate a reticence. Was it possible, Bobby wondered, that that tortured mind of his had really given birth to so diabolical a scheme—the wrecking by the murder of one partner, the hanging for the crime of the other, of the practice that his grandfather had made and his father lost, so that a new Castles might be built up from the ruins?

Grimly Bobby reflected that here was his job—to find out.

"Do you think there is anyone else on your staff likely to bear a grudge against you?" he asked.

Blythe made a faintly deprecatory gesture.

"Before this," he said, "I should have answered that we all got along exceedingly well together. Now I simply don't know what to say."

"I think you told me you had noticed that Mr Anderson seemed to be on friendly terms with Miss Earle?"

"Hardly that," Blythe protested. "I noticed—I thought—well, as I told you, I ventured to drop a discreet hint that it wasn't very wise to show any partiality for any member of the staff. What I said wasn't very well received. I never returned to the subject."

"I think you knew that they had been living together for some time?"

Mr Blythe protested it was a great shock to him to find how far matters had gone. He had never dreamed it was so serious an affair. Enough to ruin the firm, if it had come out. He repeated that he could hardly believe it.

"I'll pack the girl off at once," he protested, flushed with indignation. "I have always very much disliked this mixing of the sexes in offices, but I never thought it could be so bad as that. Never. I'll get rid of her at once."

Bobby begged him very earnestly to do no such thing. It would, he said, hinder, disturb, and complicate matters very seriously. Blythe, though reluctantly, promised to do nothing for the time.

"Though I dislike it intensely," he said; and with almost passionate intensity, so that Bobby remembered what he had been told about Blythe's unhappy childhood experience and the 'complex', to use the now common expression, it had left him with, he brought out the one word: "Disgusting."

"There are Mr Green and Miss Harris, too," Bobby said. "Do you know if there is anything between them? Should you object, if there were?"

"In office hours, most decidedly," Blythe answered, with something of the—repugnance, is hardly too strong a word—of the emotional repugnance he had just displayed. More mildly he added: "But then, that is so well known that I expect I should be the last person in the office to hear about it. Engaged couples, thinking themselves in love, as they call it, are apt to be very difficult in offices. Outside, of course—" He seemed to wave outside away with an uninterested gesture, and Bobby wondered if it was only the outward and visible signs, so to say, of courtship that troubled him and renewed those old, deeply seated, morbid memories of his childhood. "I hope," he went on, "I'm not unduly severe, but on that point I am strict and everyone knows it. But surely you don't mean either Green or Miss Harris would try to get me hanged so that they could flirt more comfortably in office hours. Preposterous."

"Murder is always preposterous, don't you think?" Bobby remarked. "Yet it happens. Do you think Mr Anderson had any knowledge of any attraction Green may have felt for Miss Harris?"

"Now you mention it," Blythe answered slowly, "I do remember Anderson saying something about having to write to Green's father. I didn't pay much attention. I thought it was because we were both inclined to think Green wasn't working quite hard enough at his studies. We shouldn't have been pleased if he had failed to get through his exams. Naturally, one likes one's articled pupils to make a good showing. Just possibly, if what you say is correct, Anderson knew about Miss Harris and meant to drop a hint to Green's father. Hardly a principal's fault if a pupil gets mixed up with the office typist. But an angry parent might think it was, and the elder Mr Green has a good deal of influence." He paused again and looked hard at Bobby: "You haven't got in your mind," he said, "that the boy might be so angry and upset at the, threat, and so anxious to prevent his father knowing, that he would go to such extremes as murder?"

"One has to consider everything," Bobby said. "People in love get into highly emotional states in which almost anything can happen."

"Yes, I expect that's true," Blythe agreed. "You seem very certain it must be someone in our office. Frankly, I find that quite incredible. Quite."

"I can understand that," Bobby said. "Can you give me any information now about Mr Anderson's estate?"

"So far as I can ascertain at present," Blythe said slowly, "it will be very small. Recently he sold out a good many of his holdings. Up to now I've found nothing to show what he did with the money. I doubt if the total value, all debts cleared, will be more than a couple of hundred or so, taking into account everything. At the present moment, the value of the practice is almost nominal. There are one or two small bequests, including £50 to myself as executor and the residue to his wife. I don't think there will be any residue. Beyond a hundred or so."

"At any rate," Bobby said, "he wasn't in difficulties or anything like that."

"Oh, no. There will certainly be a margin left after everything has been paid up. The surprise is that the residue will be so small. I know for a fact that quite a short time ago, it would have touched five figures or thereabouts. Now it won't be much over the three figure mark. And nothing to show why, or what has become of the rest of the estate. Possibly he has been speculating on the Stock Exchange."

"Did he speculate?"

"I've never known him to, though he said himself he always had the itch. As a young man he had an object lesson in the losses incurred by Castles' father. That served as a warning, he used to say. If he gave in to the temptation at last, that would explain where the money went."

"I ask," Bobby explained, "because Mr Osman Ford seems to be nervous about the safety of a trust fund."

"Oh, I know," Blythe said, smiling. "He's convinced that Anderson embezzled it, isn't he? It's quite safe. You can assure him of that. Anderson had to give him a serious warning—point out the penalties attached to libel and slander and so on. I know Anderson took a strict view of his duties as trustee—unnecessarily strict, perhaps. But that was no excuse for the attitude Mr Ford chose to take up."

"I understand you become trustee now," Bobby said. "Shall you be guided by Mr Anderson's views?"

"No, I don't think so. No. I shall take advice. Get an agricultural expert's opinion. If it's favourable, as it will be most likely, I shall consent to the release of the fund, I think. But, of course, I shall have to go into it carefully. From the national point of view, I suppose the more capital put into the land just now, the better. I shan't act in a hurry though. Legal caution, you know."

"One result of Anderson's murder, then," Bobby remarked, "is that Osman Ford gets possession of £5,000 would otherwise not have been able to touch."

Mr Blythe stared open-mouthed.

"I never thought of that," he said.

Bobby reflected that an experienced lawyer might well have thought of 'that' very quickly; and perhaps Blythe guessed Bobby was thinking this, for he said apologetically:

"All this is so bewildering—so utterly bewildering, so incredible indeed—that I can't realize it, can't take it in. My mind seems almost paralysed when I try to. It—well, it doesn't seem real."

Bobby said he could well understand that, and then Blythe went away and presently Wright appeared with his report. As regarded what might be called the alibi of the glove, the report was thoroughly satisfactory. The glove had undoubtedly been in the possession of Landon, the Hopewell House porter, from six o'clock on the Tuesday evening till seven the following morning, when it had been handed to the boy, Dickens, to be left at Mr Blythe's private residence. It must, therefore, have been placed where Roy Green said he had found it well after the commission of the murder, and in any case could not have been in Blythe's possession at the time.

"Means," said Wright, "someone is trying to frame Mr Blythe, and once we know who that is, we shan't have to look any further."

"Not much help, though," Bobby remarked, "till we do know. What about Mr Ford and Rose Briar Cottage?"

On that, Wright had secured some interesting and puzzling information. Osman had been seen once or twice entering or leaving the cottage, apparently trying to avoid observation while doing so. Also, when something had been said in his wife's presence about these visits, he had denied them angrily and emphatically, protesting that he had never been near the place and that he had no knowledge whatever of Mrs Jordan, whom he had never seen, with whom he said he had never exchanged a word.

CHAPTER XV
VARIOUS POSSIBILITIES

THOUGH WITH SOME hesitation, the doctor attending Colonel Glynne, chief constable of the Midwych county police, had at last given permission for his patient, recovering from a severe attack of pleurisy, to receive Bobby's report. So now Bobby, seated by the colonel's bed, was giving a very detailed and careful account of the Anderson case and also explaining in full the various steps he had taken.

"It's difficult to get a complete grasp of it all," he said finally, "because so much of it seems to have its roots in the past. I try to find out what's going on today and I'm always getting referred to past happenings. Babies found on doorsteps a quarter of a century ago. Bankruptcies nearly as far back. Wives leaving their husbands years since. Divorces further back still and children, mixed up in them. Unexplained drowning in the canal of a young man who would be middle-aged today. And so on."

"It does seem like that," agreed the Colonel, "As if everything went back to the way in which Anderson got possession of the Castles practice when the Mr Castles of that day came to grief with his speculations."

"I am wondering, sir, if there is any real reason to think Anderson was in any way responsible?" Bobby remarked.

The colonel hesitated before he answered.

"There was a lot of gossip," he said. "I remember thinking at the time it was rather a case of 'Thou shalt not kill, but need not strive officiously to keep alive.' Gossip never quite died down. No one knows the truth—except Anderson. And he's dead. It must have been a big temptation to get hold of what then was the leading firm of solicitors in the town. Though probably it didn't turn quite as well as expected. People are nervous about solicitors who speculate, even if it is only the solicitor's own money he loses. Not a penny of clients' money had been used, but the idea was there. It might have been. That made some clients leave. Then, there was the gossip about Anderson having—well, not tried very hard to put the brake on. That made other clients leave or prevented new ones from coming in. Of course, a good many clients remained. You can't change your solicitor quite as easily as you can your grocer. Solicitors often have too many threads between their fingers for them to be disentangled very easily. I've always thought," the colonel added hesitatingly, "that the old scandal was really the cause of Anderson's wife leaving him. I think she knew of the talk that went on, and it led to distrust and quarrelling between them. She suspected. He knew and resented it. In the end, she left him."

"Perhaps," mused Bobby, "that accounts for the feeling that grew up between Miss Earle and Anderson. They both felt in a way separated from other people—she because she was a foundling, and he because of this talk and gossip that was still going on. Do you know, sir, how Blythe came to join the firm?"

"Anderson wanted a partner—above all, a partner in good standing in what you may call philanthropic and religious circles. Not that Blythe has ever stressed the religious side of his work. You might call him merely a social worker. He was prominent at the time in the Old Street Settlement, which has always been purely humanitarian and ethical—it was founded by an ethical society. He left that though to give all his time to Hopewell House. And he has done very good work there on extremely slender resources. Hopewell House is quite famous, and how he has managed to keep it going is a miracle of finance. If he had given as much care and attention to his own business he would have done a good deal better for himself—and for the firm."

"I haven't come across any suggestion that Anderson resented that," Bobby said.

"I was only giving you my own opinion," the colonel explained. "Anderson may not have felt like that at all. Quite probably he felt the Hopewell House connection helped the firm—publicity for one thing, very creditable publicity, too."

"Yes, I see that," Bobby agreed. He went on, "Mr Blythe seems to have very strict ideas about any sign of flirtation in the office. A kind of left-over apparently of the scandal when he was a child."

"An unpleasant affair," agreed the colonel. "I remember it very well. I suppose Blythe never quite managed to get free from that memory—left him with what they call a complex today."

"It's that sort of background which makes it so difficult to understand motives and actions in this case," Bobby said. "Everyone concerned seems to be a sort of different mental study. Difficult even to make up your mind about Anderson. There's his rather doubtful record, complicated by his relations with the son of the man he supplanted. There's his connection with Miss Earle, Mrs Jordan looking on, and his gift of £5,000 to her—a large sum, especially when it seems it was almost all he had. At any rate, Blythe says there's nothing much left. And then there's his uncompromising attitude towards the Ford money he was trustee for."

"What that means," the colonel said meditatively, "is that the motive for his murder may be either revenge, or jealousy, or money. Three of the chief motives for murder, I suppose."

"Yes, sir," agreed Bobby, "and it makes this case stand out— three separate and distinct possible motives and nothing to show which was active. Generally you can ask 'Who benefits?' and get a pointer like that. Even Blythe benefits. He is left sole partner in the practice. If he wants to buy Anderson's share he'll probably get it at his own price. There'll be no need for him to carry out Anderson's promise to Castles. And he was apparently afraid of the results of the scandal if Anderson's connection with Miss Earle got known. He was certainly morbidly sensitive to anything of the sort, as a result of what happened to him as a child."

"You are making out a strong case against him—in the way of possibilities," the colonel said, "but you are forgetting his glove alibi, aren't you? Someone evidently trying to fake evidence to bring him in and you don't fake evidence against the guilty.

"Why not, sir?" Bobby asked quietly. "I think that is conceivable. If X believes Y to be guilty but thinks there's no proof, X might make an effort to supply the proof required and think himself justified."

"Oh, well," said the colonel doubtfully. "Hum…yes…perhaps."

"For that matter," Bobby continued, "Blythe might be guilty, and might fake evidence against himself with the idea that the fake, when discovered, would establish his innocence, since it is only against the innocent that faked evidence is required."

The colonel blinked.

"Oh, well," he said. Then, clutching at common sense, he said: "You couldn't persuade counsel to put forward theories like that in court."

"No, sir," agreed Bobby. "Juries want evidence, not theories. I quite see that, but I don't think we can regard Blythe as entirely outside suspicion. We could reconstruct the crime like this. I think it possible he knew more of his partner's affairs than he admitted to me. Anyhow, he did admit to a quarrel with Anderson about Miss Earle that may have been more serious than he says. There is the possibility that he tried to catch Anderson in the act, so to say. And that a quarrel resulted, ending in murder. If Blythe had been watching Anderson— and Rose Briar Cottage—he might have seen Mrs Jordan hiding Dwight's pistol and that would account for his possession of a weapon. And I think one has to remember his morbid, almost unbalanced attitude to such affairs."

"Working on these lines, do you mean you think you could establish a strong enough case to charge him on?" the colonel asked doubtfully.

"Well, sir," Bobby said, "shall we go on to consider other possibilities? Castles, for instance."

"Yes, Castles," agreed the colonel. "Yes. That story of his about his mother's last word to him on her death bed—'Remember'. It does rather stick in your mind, doesn't it? Only he told you about it himself."

"He did seem to go very near to accusing himself," Bobby said thoughtfully. "He was certainly in a very queer state, mentally. Brooding on the past. Obsessed by it. Torn between doubt and suspicion and gratitude. That sort of inner conflict might easily lead to a kind of divided personality resulting in very queer actions only half realized at the time. He has no alibi and he refuses to give any explanation of the long solitary walk he took that evening, though he admits something fresh had come to his knowledge. That fresh fact may have clinched his suspicions. It may have been some sort of proof that Anderson had, in fact, betrayed old Mr Castles. If it wasn't something of that sort, why won't he say?"

"Exactly," said the colonel. "Working on those lines you could get up a strong case against Castles, a very strong case indeed."

"Yes, sir," agreed Bobby. "He was at that time in this abnormal state mentally, and it is very noticeable that now he is, as he says himself, much calmer. A great burden lifted. That's how he feels, he says. The question is, was it by his own action that that burden was lifted?"

"A very strong case," the colonel repeated. "But what about young Dwight? Jealousy is one of the strongest of motives for murder."

"There's no doubt he was desperately jealous and very bitterly resented the liaison between Anderson and Miss Earle," Bobby said slowly. "I think, too, from one or two things he let drop that he may have had some sort of romantic notion of avenging a girl's honour on her elderly seducer. He is the only one we know to have visited the cottage—we have Mrs Jordan's evidence for that—and the only one we know to have been in possession of a revolver. We have his own admission on that point. He may easily have recovered it from the hedge where Mrs Jordan hid it. Quite a good hiding place so far as searching the cottage went, which is what she was chiefly afraid of. But it had the disadvantage that anyone keeping a watch on the place might see her and guess what she was doing. That applies to everyone, including Dwight. The alibi he put forward is quite useless."

"Jealousy—that's a motive," the colonel repeated. "Strikes me, we need hardly look any further. Dwight is the most likely person, and after all the most likely person—well, the most likely person is the most likely person."

"I've been thinking that, too," Bobby said.

"Working on those lines," said the colonel, "I should say we ought soon to have a good enough case."

"Yes, sir," agreed Bobby. "There's Roy Green, too. And Miss Harris. After all, they are the only ones we can say definitely were in the habit of meeting near Ends Bridge. They admit that. They say they were in a cinema on the Tuesday night, but a cinema alibi is worth nothing. Unless it's confirmed, which this one isn't. They seem to be passionately in love with each other. Anderson was threatening to inform the elder Mr Green of his son's infatuation. As a result Roy would have been removed and the lovers separated. It is extremely likely as they were in the habit of meeting pretty frequently near the bridge that they had seen Anderson there. If Anderson happened himself to see young Green and the girl together and stopped to ask them what they were up to, and if he renewed his threat to tell the boy's father, a quarrel might easily have developed— with fatal results. Or the same thing might have happened if Green had recognized Anderson's car and stopped it with the idea that it would be easier to have things out there rather than at the office."

"One can believe anything of a boy in love," agreed the colonel. "Anything at all. Yes, it's possible. Threatened with what he would think an unfair attempt to separate him from the girl he loved— well, there it is."

"There is also," said Bobby, "the fact that it was Green who found Anderson's glove or says he did. He would have been able to go into the car park at Chief Building since he was known as employed there, and so would have had a chance to get hold of the glove."

"He tried to get rid of it though by throwing it into the canal. If he hadn't been seen, we should have known nothing about it."

"Perhaps," said Bobby quietly, "he took care that he was seen. Those who are guilty themselves do sometimes try to divert suspicion to others. On the principle that if someone else is hanged, they become safe."

"Yes, I know," sighed the colonel. "Yes. That's so. It's getting very complicated, isn't it? But hang it, Owen, you are making out an almost equally strong case against them all."

"There is still Miss Earle," Bobby said quietly.

The colonel fairly jumped in the bed.

"You aren't going to make out a case against her now, are you?" he cried. "Hang it all, man, didn't you tell me you thought she and Anderson were really fond of each other?"

"They gave me that impression, certainly," Bobby admitted. "Only there's always the old saying, isn't there? 'Where love is, hate's close by.' In these outside the law affairs, there's often, always perhaps, a sense of insecurity that doubles the risk of jealousy— and its dangers. Another thing, Anderson seems to have made her a present of a large sum of money. A kind of settlement. At least, that's her story. But there seems no trace of any such gift at the office or among Anderson's papers. Only the fact that his estate is unexpectedly small. I am wondering if Anderson gave Miss Earle the money in notes or bearer securities, or something like that."

"In which case," observed the colonel, "she might have been afraid he would take it back. Dead, he couldn't. Five thousand pounds. It might be a big temptation."

"I think it must be remembered," Bobby said. "There's another thing. If Roy Green is telling the truth, someone deliberately used Blythe's glove to draw suspicion to him. Miss Earle is one of the people who work at Chief Building and are known there. She could have gone to the car park without attracting attention and taken the glove from Blythe's car."

"All right, all right," said the colonel gloomily. "She is a possibility, too. I hope to goodness, Owen, you've got to the end of your suspects."

"There's still another who on the face of it is perhaps the most likely of all," Bobby said. "Osman Ford. When he came to see me and wanted us to take steps about the trust fund he looked murderous enough. Anyhow, it is clear that he very strongly resented Anderson's attitude and that he had no hope of getting the trust fund released while Anderson was alive. In the event of Anderson's death he knew he was pretty sure to get it. He admits he was often near the locus of the crime and his story of wanting to know if what he called 'canoodling' was going on may be true or may be just an excuse. It's not too strong. Apparently he has the reputation of being a man of violent temper, and already he has come under suspicion of murder. A rival suitor of Mrs Ford's—Miss Vigor she was then—was found drowned in the canal in circumstances that seem to have given rise to some gossip. There is also the very odd fact that he seems to have been visiting Rose Briar Cottage."

"Do you think," the colonel asked, "that there can have been anything between him and Anne Earle and that Anderson found it out and that is why he was murdered?"

"Well, sir, I had considered that," Bobby answered, "but there doesn't seem any evidence, any suggestion indeed, that Miss Earle and Ford ever met. His visits seem to have been only occasional, and usually when Miss Earle was away and only Mrs Jordan was there. You remember, sir, there's the story the Long Barsley constable told of hearing a quarrel going on between Mrs Jordan and some unknown man. The only two men known to have visited the cottage are Anderson and Ford, and the reference overheard to pushing someone into the canal does rather point to Ford. Though I don't see at present any other link with the murder."

"No," agreed the colonel. "Hand me that pad, will you?" He began to write. "It stands like this then," he said, reading aloud when he had finished writing.

(1) George Blythe.

Motive. Resentment at intrigue Anderson was carrying on. Fear of resultant scandal. Desire to secure control of the practice. Implicated by discovery of glove near the locus of crime. Known to have very strong emotional reactions to irregular relationships outside marriage. No alibi and doubtful explanation offered.

(2) Arthur Castles.

Motive. Revenge. Admits to strongly divided feelings towards Anderson. Mental state not fully normal. Admits to having chosen that evening for a long solitary walk and refuses to explain why.

(3) William Dwight.

Motive. Jealousy. Evidence he visited Rose Briar Cottage once before, taking a loaded revolver with him. Is the only one of those under suspicion definitely known to have been in possession of a pistol. Puts forward thoroughly unsatisfactory alibi.

(4) Roy Green.

Motive. Fear of being separated from Miss Harris. Admits to having been frequently near the scene of the crime. Claims to have found Blythe's glove, but instead of reporting the discovery, threw it into the canal. No satisfactory alibi.

(5) Anne Earle.

Motive. Jealousy, complicated by desire to make sure of the money Anderson had apparently not so much settled on her, as placed in her charge. Consequently he could have claimed its return. Noted that she is the last person known to have seen him alive and that she is one of those with access to the car park at Chief Building and so to Blythe's car from which his glove was taken.

(6) Osman Ford.

Motive. Desire to secure release of the trust fund and resentment at Anderson's refusal to let it go. Threats made by him against Anderson, and admitted presence near locus of crime.

The colonel ceased reading and shook his head doubtfully.

"What a list," he commented. "And what's the good of concentrating on motive, when everyone had a strong motive and all of them different? Anyhow, I take it that's the lot?"

"Well, sir," Bobby said hesitatingly, "there's still Mrs Jordan. She may have been afraid the liaison between Anderson and her niece wouldn't last and decided to make sure of the money while it was still there. She may have seen Anderson after Miss Earle left him. Miss Earle says Mrs Jordan had gone to bed when she got back from saying good-night to Anderson, but she didn't actually see her. It's possible Mrs Jordan was in fact waiting outside for a chance to speak to Anderson, and she is the last person known to have been in possession of the revolver. Also one has to remember that she has behaved rather oddly. She certainly told lies about how she identified Miss Earle as her niece. Though I don't see quite how that can link up with the murder. But then there's so much unexplained or that we don't understand."

Colonel Glynne took up his pad again and wrote diligently for some moments.

"No. 7, Mrs Jordan, and I hope that completes the list," he said. "And hardly a bit of solid evidence in all of it. How on earth are we to decide where to make a start?"

"There's one thing that seems to me important," Bobby said. "If you notice, £5,000 is always turning up. Mr Blythe guaranteed new buildings at Hopewell House to that extent. £5,000 is the amount of the Mrs Ford trust fund. £5,000 is the amount apparently placed by Anderson in Miss Earle's charge. And Mr Blythe says that though the Anderson estate will only be a hundred or two, he fully expected it would be about £10,000, which is twice £5,000."

"Well, I did notice that £5,000 was always being mentioned in one way or another," the colonel said. "But isn't it a little fanciful to extend that to Blythe's expectation that Anderson's estate would be £10,000 because that is twice £5,000?"

"I'm not sure, sir," Bobby answered thoughtfully, "that there we haven't the most significant factor of all. I'm not sure, I don't see very clearly yet, but I feel it may turn out that way. If you put that with one other incident, I think it suggests the very starting point we need."

"What do you mean?" the colonel asked. "What incident?"

Bobby pointed it out, and the colonel nodded his head thoughtfully.

"Yes," he agreed, "yes. It's only a trifle. It may mean nothing. But you think it may be what you want?"

"I should like to take it as our starting point and see where it gets us," Bobby said. "That is, sir, if you agree."

"Very well," said the colonel briefly.

CHAPTER XVI
MRS JORDAN UNEASY

IN EVERY CASE of serious crime, a tremendous amount of work is done of which no one ever hears save those engaged in the investigation. Innumerable statements are taken, countless witnesses are questioned, clue after clue followed up, all with no other result than that the statements are seen to be worthless, the witnesses are found to have nothing to say, the clues to be without significance. Yet in their totality all this apparent waste of time and energy does serve the negative purpose of closing the blind alleys and so allowing attention to be concentrated on the possibly correct path.

So it had been with the inquiry into the death of Mr Anderson. Various lines of investigation had been followed up without result. The inquest, a purely formal affair, had been adjourned 'to enable the police to complete their inquiries'. The newspapers, occupied with the war situation, gave but small attention to the death of an elderly solicitor. Bobby, seated in his office, glancing once again over the pile of accumulated papers, wondered a little gloomily if the truth would ever be known.

"Not much hope," he told himself; and then through the open window came a sudden gust of wind, fluttering the papers before him, stirring them and lifting them, as with an invisible hand, bringing to the top of the pile those that had been at the bottom, scattering others on the floor. Sergeant Wright was in the room. He had spent a good deal of valuable time following up a report that a revolver had been found in a lonely spot on the banks of the canal some distance below Ends Bridge. In the end the sergeant had found that the revolver was not a revolver but a child's pop-gun, probably, since it really was a lonely spot, flung by some child in a temper, or by its mother for a punishment, from a passing barge. In the story told in the nearest public house, the 'pop' had first been omitted from 'pop-gun', and then the resultant 'gun' turned into 'revolver', with a few other details added to suggest that it must be the one used by Mr Anderson's murderer. Just one of those things that are continually turning up in police work, but it had cost valuable time and had a good deal ruffled the temper of Sergeant Wright, now helping Bobby to collect and re-arrange his scattered papers.

Now, too, in some odd way that stirring, that consequent necessary re-arrangement of his papers had brought to the surface of Bobby's mind a thought that had been half consciously present in it for some time.

"Wright," he said, "I suppose you haven't come across anything to make you think that ... that ..."

He paused and Wright, not quite sure what his chief was driving at, said interrogatively:

"Yes, sir?"

For that matter, Bobby himself was not quite sure what he meant. Yet somehow or another, from indications too vague to put into words but that had followed the plainer hint of Mr Blythe's glove, he had formed the impression that someone else was at work, some 'hidden hand' to use the old catch-phrase. But with what object, whether to discover the truth or to conceal it, he was not at all sure. Yet he was sure that someone else was actively at work, quietly and in secret. Possibly, he supposed, with indifference to the solution of the mystery, with some entirely different object in view. Who this could be, or what the object, it was, he felt, important to know. When, however, he tried to explain all this to Wright, he did not succeed in making himself very clear—probably because his own mind was not very clear on the point.

"Yes, sir, I quite understand," Wright assured him in the manner of those who do not understand in the least. "I'll watch out; and if there's any amateur messing things up, or any smart Aleck of a reporter trying to hold out on us, I'll attend to him all right."

That wasn't at all what Bobby meant. It was a more secret and a more formidable influence that he vaguely felt to be in action. For still it seemed to him that what had happened so far was but the first act of the tragedy, and that now the play had passed into the control of an unknown producer who meant that henceforth it should develop in his way and not another.

"I just have the idea," Bobby continued now, "that there's something else going on we haven't quite got the hang of. If it breaks, it may help us—or it may not. Only at present you know, Wright, even if I am correct in thinking I know who killed Anderson, I haven't a notion how it's going to be proved."

"No, sir," agreed Wright, who knew Bobby's theory and was not inclined to attach much importance either to it or to the incident on which it was founded.

"Besides, of course, I may be entirely wrong," added Bobby.

"Yes, sir," agreed Wright again, more heartily than he intended.

"Motive generally gives a lead," Bobby went on, "but here there are half a dozen different people, with half a dozen different motives, and nothing to suggest which one was operative—revenge, greed, hate, love, jealousy, they all come into it."

"So they do, sir," said Wright, still in agreement and now beginning to scratch his head, which was the gesture natural to him when he was puzzled, and then instead rubbing the tip of his nose, since that, since Bobby's arrival, had become the fashionable sign of bewilderment in the Wychshire county force.

"As for identity of time and place," Bobby continued, still thinking aloud, "that possibility can be established for every one of our suspects."

"Not a single sound alibi," sighed Wright, "in the whole boiling."

"As for the famous 'principle of exchange'," Bobby went on, "it's a wash-out. Even if, as very likely happened, the contact of murderer and victim did leave signs in the way of exchange of traces of some sort—well, the murderer had plenty of time to get rid of them before anyone knew there had been a murder. Anderson's car was carefully cleaned before we got to it. So was Blythe's glove. Examination of the body has been no help and wasn't likely to be after a couple of days in the canal. The weapon used may be anywhere. Very likely at the bottom of the canal and nothing to show where within ten miles or so, so it's hopeless to drag for it."

"If we drained off the water we could make sure," suggested Wright, who had large ideas.

"Mean another ha'penny on the rates probably," Bobby pointed out; "and what would the Watch Committee have to say to that?"

Wright turned pale at the thought and offered no reply. Bobby went on:

"Besides, with the pressure on transport what it is, can you see our getting permission to hold up canal traffic for lord knows how long just on the off chance?"

Wright agreed meekly that he certainly couldn't 'see' it.

"Not a hope," he admitted. Then he said: "That Miss Earle, she's feeling it. Did you notice her at the inquest?"

Bobby nodded. The memory indeed was clear in his mind of her dark and passionate restraint as she stood, immobile and silent, at the back of the room during the brief formal inquest proceedings; looking, as one of the reporters present had remarked, 'like the wrath of God'. A little strange, Bobby remembered thinking at the time, that one who had never spoken, scarcely moved, had yet been able so to impress her personality on others, even on a newspaper man, who, as a class, are not as a rule too easily impressed. The memory of her still and sombre figure had remained with Bobby ever since. So apparently had it with Sergeant Wright, who said now:

"There's plenty round about Long Barsley think she did it herself. So she would all right, if you ask me, if she thought Mr Anderson was going to give her the go by."

"Nothing to suggest that," Bobby said.

"You never know," Wright answered. "Outside marriage, you can chuck 'em when you want." He added thoughtfully: "And nothing they can do except perhaps what this one did." He paused again and once more added: "There's that £5,000 we've heard about, and what I say is—where is it?"

"Yes, I know," Bobby agreed. "I expect that comes into the story somewhere, but nothing we can lay hold of—yet."

"No, sir," said Wright, but a little doubtfully, and then withdrew to spend most of the rest of the day following up yet another illusive and finally worthless clue, while Bobby went back to his pile of statements and other papers, to re-read them all with the melancholy thought in his mind that probably it would soon be necessary to put them away, marked:

"Inquiry closed temporarily, in default of further information."

That it is always the unexpected that happens is, however, as true of the work of the detective as of anything else, and the next day, in the afternoon, Mrs Jordan came to see Bobby. The Government reports he was busy with he put aside at once, for he hoped she might have information of importance to give him. To his surprise he found that what she seemed chiefly concerned about was a rumour she said she had heard that the arrest of Mr Blythe was contemplated. It puzzled Bobby, for in the first place he did not know that any such rumour was in circulation, and secondly he did not see why, if it were, it should trouble Mrs Jordan.

"Why should anyone think Mr Blythe is under suspicion?" he asked.

"Don't come the innocent over me, young man," she retorted. "It's all over Long Barsley and everywhere else about his glove."

"Curious," commented Bobby. "Nothing has been said about that or about whom it belonged to, and I've heard nothing about any talk going round."

"More's said than police ever know," declared Mrs Jordan, and Bobby admitted sadly to himself that this was only too true.

"Do you mean people are saying that Mr Blythe is the murderer?" he asked.

"I mean people are putting two and two together and making five, same as they generally do," she answered. "If a man gets done in and something belonging to someone else is found on the spot, aren't people going to talk?"

"Well, they shouldn't," Bobby told her.

"I know," she said. "Don't I know? But they do all right. No stopping them. They're wrong of course. It wasn't Blythe.'

"What makes you say that?"

"Because it was someone else."

"Who?"

"Billy Dwight."

"Why do you say that?"

"The way he keeps hanging around, watching Anne. It's her next."

Bobby sat upright with a jerk. This was unexpected, unpleasant, and disturbing. He had been wondering what lay behind Mrs Jordan's visit, and here it was and sufficiently alarming, too. One murder may well lead to another, and Mrs Jordan seemed very much in earnest.

"What grounds—?" he began, and his visitor interrupted him sharply.

"Plain as the nose on your face," she snapped. "He's off his head with jealousy, same as they get sometimes. He's that type. He was keen on Anne from the start."

"Did she encourage him?" Bobby asked.

"Her being her was all the encouragement he wanted," she answered. "Her looks, the way she held herself, how she walked." She said this with a sort of vicarious pride that sat a little oddly on her now. Yet, Bobby supposed, in her lusty youth she, too, must have made a strong appeal. She went on: "The less Anne noticed him, the keener he got; and if she was rough with him, then she only put an edge to it, like a knife gets when it's put to a grindstone. She was the same to all boys and most of them were afraid of her."

"I can believe that," agreed Bobby, thinking to himself that indeed the average youngster would not much know what to make of Anne Earle's dark reserve. "She wasn't like that to Mr Anderson, though, was she?"

"No. He was older, he was alone, there was no family to meet. It was always that she couldn't face. A family when she had none herself. Morbid about it, she was. I mean, about being abandoned, as she called it; about being found on a doorstep. Morbid. Seemed to think that people knew it just by looking at her. Morbid. And hard. Hard. Hard as can be. That's her. Hard."

"Hard?" Bobby repeated, not quite understanding. "In what way?"

"She won't understand, she can't forgive or forget," Mrs Jordan muttered, and she spoke with an emotion Bobby had hardly thought her capable of. "It's hard to hear the things she says about her mother. That's my sister, you know. You don't like to hear your own sister ..."

She broke off abruptly and Bobby said:

"I suppose it's natural she should feel it. You can't think much of a mother who could treat her child like that."

"Do you suppose she wanted to?" Mrs Jordan asked passionately. "You're a man. You can't understand. A man always gets out of it. To hell with all men. She ought to understand. She could try. She won't. She said she might be brought to kill a baby she had borne, but never to put it down on a doorstep and go off herself all safe and comfortable. That's what she said—safe and comfortable. She's right about that though. She's different. Proud and bitter, hard, and keeps her rage within her. She told me once when she was still a child she got alone into a church and there before the altar she knelt down and put a curse upon her mother," and suddenly, and to Bobby's discomposure, Mrs Jordan burst into tears.

He waited a little. The violence of the storm of sobs that had shaken her, died down. She began to mop her face with her handkerchief. Opening her handbag she started to repair, though awkwardly and with a shaking hand, the ravages her storm of weeping had done to her complexion. She said:

"Wasn't that a dreadful thing to hear? I went upon my bended knees to her to take it back and she would not."

Bobby had a keen pictorial imagination. There was in fact a certain latent artistic ability in him, so that he always tended to see things as interpreted in line and form. But for a defective colour sense he might even have been tempted to become an art student in the hope of earning his living as a professional artist. Now he seemed to see the tableau clearly—the implacable young girl, the older woman crouching in vain at her feet. Such power has an evil deed, not only to injure another's body but to corrupt also that other's spirit.

"My own sister," Mrs Jordan said again and loudly, as if she wished him to realize that. "It was what cut so deep, to hear such things said of my own sister by her own girl."

"You hadn't seen your sister or been in touch with her for a very long time, though, had you?" Bobby asked.

"What's that to do with it?" she asked suspiciously. "I didn't ought to have told you, only so damn smooth you are you get it out of folk. It isn't what I came about. You want to know who killed Anderson? You can take it from me, it wasn't Mr Blythe, and his glove being there has just nothing to do with it. It was Billy Dwight did him in, and if you aren't careful, it'll be Anne next."

"Can't you give me something more definite?" Bobby asked. "You must see how difficult, impossible in fact, it is for us to take action without something definite to go on. Facts are what we want."

"It's a fact Billy Dwight was mad jealous," she told him. "You know yourself it's a fact he broke into Rose Briar Cottage."

"He denies it," Bobby said, "and though I'm inclined myself to believe you, there's no proof. It's your word against his, you see. Besides, if it ever came into court, you would have to admit that first you denied the whole thing."

"That was only because I didn't want any coppers snooping round and raising a stink," she explained. "It was only a stink I was afraid of then, I never dreamed it would come to murder. But it was him all right did it. If it isn't, what's he watching Anne for the way he is, and if it isn't murder in his mind, what's twisted his face the way it is, what's put the look in his eyes there's there now?"

"We can't take action on a look," Bobby told her. "Jealousy gives a possible motive, but that's all. If we could identify the pistol as his, that would be something." He said this because he thought there was just a chance that Mrs Jordan knew more about that pistol than she had so far revealed. But she gave no sign and he continued: "But we don't know what's become of the pistol and if we can't produce it we can't make any use of it. The only thing I can do at present is to put on a man to try to keep an eye on Miss Earle and see that nothing happens. And we'll try to keep an eye on Dwight, too."

"Well, that's something," she said ungraciously, getting to her feet. "If you lay off Blythe and attend to Dwight, you'll stand a better chance of getting your man. That glove didn't mean a thing."

"What makes you so sure of that?" Bobby asked; and as she merely shrugged her ample shoulders and moved towards the door he said, pleasantly but quite firmly: "No, don't go yet, please. Why are you so interested in that glove? And are you really sure there is any gossip going on about it—or about Mr Blythe?"

"Yes, I am," she answered defiantly.

"Well, it's curious," Bobby said, "because though the lad who found it or his mother may have talked about the glove, or it may have got out in some other way, Mr Blythe's name has never been mentioned."

"Don't talk silly," she retorted. "Everyone knew those swell gloves of his—at least, there's plenty did, and couldn't help, the way he liked to show them off because those lads of his at Hopewell House clubbed together to buy them for him."

"Well, there's that," Bobby admitted. "But I don't see that that explains your interest."

"My interest's Anne," she flashed out. "That's all. I don't want her murdered next."

"More do we," Bobby agreed, "and I can promise you we shall take every possible precaution, but at the moment we are talking about Mr Blythe and his glove."

She snarled an angry and somewhat blasphemous wish about both Mr Blythe and his glove and again she moved towards the door and again he stopped her.

"Have you any idea how the glove came to be where it was found?" he asked. "Someone must have put it there, you know, and you seem sure it wasn't Blythe himself. So who was it?"

"How should I know?" she snarled.

"Was it Miss Anne?"

"No, it wasn't, you leave my girl alone," Mrs Jordan almost screamed at him.

"No one can be left alone in a case of murder and you yourself have just this minute asked me to have her looked after," Bobby reminded her quietly. "The glove must have been put there by someone who knew Mr Blythe and who had access to his car at the Chief Building car park. There aren't so many people who come under that heading but Miss Earle is one. Do you think it likely or do you know anything to suggest?—"

"No, I don't," Mrs Jordan shouted, interrupting him, and this time banged open the door and rushed away, and Sergeant Wright, who had been in the passage outside, looked into the room and asked:

"Is anything wrong, sir? I mean that woman—she looked like murder, if ever woman did."

CHAPTER XVII
ANNE THREATENS

BOBBY WAS NOT much surprised when only a day or two later Anne Earle herself came to see him. He had expected her and had left instructions that she was to be shown to his room as soon as she arrived, for he thought it likely that anything she might wish to say would be of interest. When she entered he got up to put a chair for her, but she would not take it, waving it away with one of those slight, almost imperceptible and yet strangely dramatic gestures which seemed characteristic of her. Dark and secret with hidden passion, she stood with her heavy glance fixed on him, and yet not much as if she saw him, but only some reflection of her own brooding thoughts. He went back to his chair and said formally:

"What can we do for you, Miss Earle?"

"Why are you having me followed?" she asked, yet still as if speaking from some far-off loneliness.

"Oh, have you noticed that?" he asked in his turn and without surprise, for somehow he had always felt that for all her hidden manner of living in her own secret world, there was yet little of her immediate surroundings of which she was not aware. Now for answer she made another of her slow gestures that this time seemed deeply scornful of so unnecessary a question. She said again:

"Why are you having me followed?"

"From information received," Bobby said then, "there seems reason to believe that it may be advisable for your own safety."

"Why?" she asked, and then: "Nonsense," she said.

"Oh, very possibly," he agreed, "but we can't afford to run risks."

"Nonsense," she repeated. "What risks?"

"It would be easier if we knew," Bobby answered carefully and slowly. "It has been suggested to us that your life may be in danger. It was pointed out that one murder has been committed and that perhaps there might be another. I am very much inclined to agree with you that the idea may be nonsense. But as the suggestion has been made, we are bound to take notice of it. For your sake first of all, for your safety. For our own sake next. We should hate to have another murder on our hands. And if that did happen, and it came out, as it certainly would, that we had been asked to give you protection, and we had failed to take even ordinary precautions— well, you've simply no idea of the fuss there would be. You see, honestly, it's not only your life and safety I'm thinking of, but my own job as well."

As he had hoped she might, for he was beginning to have some knowledge of her strange and powerful personality, so warped and twisted by the circumstances of her birth, she rewarded this frankness with a faint smile, a smile that lightened wonder fully the habitual tragic intensity of her expression, that even touched it in passing with a fleeting and a momentary sweetness. Then it was gone, quickly as though she put such weakness from her, but Bobby took advantage of the moment to say:

"Won't you sit down? I wish you would. You see, if you won't, I shall have to stand, too."

She seemed to consider this gravely, to accept the argument. She seated herself, and in so doing became much more human, much less aloof.

"Who told you all that nonsense?" she asked.

"I'm afraid I can't tell you that," he explained. "Everything said to the police is under the seal of the confessional so to say, except of course, so far as the claims of justice are concerned."

"You mean," she flashed, "confidential when it suits you and not when it doesn't."

"Oh, well," said Bobby, not quite liking this, though admitting to himself that the remark did possess a certain fallacious plausibility.

"If you won't tell me," she went on quietly, "I'll tell you."

"Oh, well," said Bobby again, thinking it very likely she might guess correctly, but determined to do his best to prevent her seeing that her guess was correct—if in fact it were. "Well, who?" he challenged her.

"The murderer," she answered.

Once more Bobby sat upright with a jerk. Once more he found the suggestion unpleasant, unexpected, disturbing. And he was by no means sure that it might not also be accurate. The possibility of Mrs Jordan's guilt had indeed been considered, and in some odd way this apparently unknowing denunciation by her own niece seemed confirmation. It might be because she herself was guilty that she had tried to put them on a false trail. A more sinister thought still flashed abruptly into his mind. There was that £5,000. Mr Anderson, who alone knew the details of the gift or settlement, was no longer there to say anything about it. If anything happened to Anne, if she also were removed, there would presumably be no one else to claim it but Mrs Jordan herself.

Bobby seemed to see her making her careful plans; diverting suspicion from herself by this preliminary warning and demand for police protection; feeling sure, or making sure by some casual remark, that Anne should become aware of it; knowing her well enough to be well aware that once she did know she would demand its removal, and that then the contemplated deed could be carried out with an excellent chance of safety and success. Possibly this was in fact what really lay behind Mrs Jordan's recent visit. Grim thoughts and ugly, but then murder is a grim and ugly business. He wondered if Anne knew. No telling that, no telling what went on behind the dark, inscrutable loveliness that was hers. They were both silent for some moments. Bobby because he was deep in contemplation of this new and troubling possibility; Anne, because, as it seemed, she had again withdrawn from her immediate surroundings into that brooding world of her own in which she lived.

Bobby roused himself from his speculations. No use, he decided, indulging in them till there was more evidence one way or another.

"The murderer?" he said. "Oh, yes. Well, who is that?"

"You know," she told him, "if it's true what you say, that someone came to tell you I was in danger."

"Oh, that's true," he assured her, "but I don't see why you should think that it was necessarily the murderer who wanted us to give you protection."

"Because," she answered, as one who had it quite clear in her own mind, "the murderer calculates that any protection of yours won't amount to much—how can it? And the murderer knows, too, that I mean to see he hangs." She spoke simply and quietly, with less of that strong passionate resolve in her voice and manner than she often showed, and yet all the same, and perhaps the more because of that absence, conveying in her words an even greater impression of an implacable determination. "So there's this attempt to frighten me through you," she concluded, now with contempt.

"It's possible that's the idea," Bobby admitted thoughtfully, and again he wondered if by any chance the girl knew who it was of whom she spoke. She interrupted his thoughts, saying:

"So will you please tell your man to stop following me?"

Bobby shook his head.

"Sorry," he said. "I wish I could. Goodness knows, we are hard enough up for man power. The work doubled and the force halved. But there it is. I can't afford to disregard even an improbable story. Nonsense very likely, but it has to be treated seriously."

"If you don't," she told him calmly, "I shall buy a dog whip and thrash him with it, and I shall go on till he stops following me."

Bobby was a good deal taken aback. He knew her well enough by now to feel sure that she meant what she said.

"If you did, we should have to prosecute you for assault," he said weakly.

She did not answer. It was characteristic of her that having stated her intention she left it at that. Probably she knew the consequences as well as did Bobby himself. The country-wide sensation, the public interest, the sympathy for her, the general ridicule for the police, the complete upheaval and probable ruin of the whole conduct of the investigation.

"It is for your own safety," he urged.

"Never mind my safety," she said. "I will attend to that myself. But I don't want a policeman always at my heels. I couldn't do anything, I should never find out anything."

"That's our job," Bobby told her. "To find out."

"And all you do is to tell a man to follow me about," she said scornfully. She added: "Well, are you going to tell him to stop it?"

"I must if you insist," Bobby admitted, "but I think it very likely that if you do make any attempt to get at the truth by yourself, there may actually be an attempt on your life."

"It is what I am counting on," she told him calmly. "If that happens; then I shall know. Now I only suspect."

"If it happens and if it succeeds," Bobby pointed out grimly, "you may still not know. People have been murdered before now and never known who it was. Or if you did know, you would never have the chance to tell."

She looked at him very steadily and intently. It was with an almost dreadful intensity that she answered:

"If I knew I should tell, though I had to rise from the grave to speak."

And for the moment Bobby really believed that that power would be hers. Then he tried to bring the conversation back to a more ordinary level by saying:

"Well, you might tell me why you stole Mr Blythe's glove and put it where it was found?"

"Why should you say I did that?"

"Well, it's the fact, isn't it?"

"Isn't it a little childish," she retorted, "to try to trick an admission out of me like that?"

"You haven't answered my question yet," Bobby reminded her, though wincing a little at the rebuke.

"I do not mean to," she assured him calmly. "You can guess as much as you like. That's all you are doing—guessing. And then trying to trap me into an admission."

"Not necessary," he retorted. "Hardly guessing, either. It's plain enough. You had opportunity. You are the only person who knew where Roy Green and Miss Harris used to meet." "How do you know that?" she interrupted. "I don't believe you do know. You are only guessing again."

"No," he answered. "Deduction from the facts. It was their secret. But Miss Harris is a romantic little person. She called it their trysting place. She was sure to confide such a lovely secret to you, you the only person who saw them together. You used it to throw suspicion on Mr Blythe. That tends to exonerate him—and to direct suspicion somewhere else, to you."

She was silent for a moment, looking at him with a new interest, almost as if seeing him clearly for the first time.

"Have you made all that up merely because Ursula talked about her trysting place?" she asked.

"A detective has to notice small things," Bobby told her. "Small things sometimes lead to big. Won't you tell me what your reason was?"

She seemed to consider this gravely and then said:

"There's nothing to prevent your guessing that perhaps someone or another felt your official routine wasn't getting anywhere and that something had to be done to quicken it."

"I thought perhaps that was the idea," Bobby agreed, and he remembered again that sudden breath of wind through the open window which had stirred and disarranged and moved all the papers in the case. The glove incident had been designed, to serve the same purpose of making him re-arrange his thoughts and plans. He said: "I wish I could make you understand how foolish and how dangerous that sort of thing is. It only confuses. It is much more likely to help the murderer than anything else. Did it ever strike you that the consequences for Mr Blythe might be serious? Rather a stab in the back for him, an assassin's stab in the back, wasn't it?"

"No," she answered, "because it couldn't have been him. He was quite safe. Everyone knew he was visiting one of his rich subscribers that night. That made him all right. But you were doing nothing. It was all nothing to you. Just routine. What you call your duty. Like stopping motorists from going too fast. It couldn't hurt Mr Blythe, but it might make him see you did something."

"As a matter of fact," Bobby told her, "it could have hurt Mr Blythe very seriously, because it happens he didn't make the visit you say everyone knew he intended. He is by no means free from suspicion and the glove incident might have been very serious for him, only for something else we discovered."

"What was that?" she asked.

"I haven't the least intention of telling you," he answered, and she broke out passionately:

"I don't believe you. I don't believe you are even trying- just routine and your duty and you don't really care."

"I would ask you to believe," Bobby said with some anger, "that we take our duty seriously."

"Very likely you do," she retorted with all her old scorn, "but it's more than duty to me. He and I. We were alone. We only had each other. My mother deserted me. On a doorstep. Nothing could make that up to me—but he tried. His wife deserted him. Nothing could make that up to him. But I tried. We were like each other. We knew. There was a great gulf between us and the others—we were on one side and they on the other with, their own, their wives, their families. There had always been a great gulf between me and everyone else. Now it was there for him, too. He had come to my side of the gulf. That's over now. Finished. Done with. But whoever ended it, shan't escape. Not while I live."

"Miss Earle—" Bobby began, but she was on her feet now, ready to go.

She said:

"You told me just now you suspected me. I don't know if you meant it or if you were only trying to frighten me. Well, I suspect someone, too. I won't tell you who it is. But perhaps something may happen soon and then you'll know."

She turned towards the door, and Bobby, startled and alarmed, jumped to his feet, meaning to stop her.

"For heaven's sake—" he began.

His voice died away. She had turned again to face him and there was that about her, in her manner, in her direct and sombre gaze, in her whole aspect, that convinced him words were useless.

"I've a good mind to arrest you on suspicion," he told her angrily.

She paid no attention to the threat. Probably she knew it was futile. No magistrate would have sanctioned her detention for a moment. She went away then and Bobby, gloomily watching her go, thought to himself that death walked with her, though whether to claim her or another, or both, he did not know. He went back to his desk and he found his hand shaking a little and his forehead a little damp.

"What a woman," he muttered, half aloud. "Judith and Holofernes, Sisera and Jael. All that. Capable of having done it herself, too, if she felt like it, if she felt she had reason."

A fresh, disturbing thought came to him. If she did believe she had discovered the truth, what action did she contemplate? Very uncomfortably he remembered the last look she had given him as she went away.

"Capable of anything, once she gets an idea in her head," he told himself.

Or worse still, suppose she found out, only found out wrong. What then? A contingency that had to be faced but of which he did not at all like the look. She was in no condition to form sound judgments. Any misunderstood detail might easily lead her to entirely wrong beliefs on which, again, she might easily take disastrous action.

He got to his feet and began to walk up and down the room, chilled with fear of coming developments, in the grip of something not far from panic. He made a grab for the telephone, meaning to consult the chief constable, and then remembered that Colonel Glynne had suffered a relapse and that the doctor had said he was not to be disturbed. He sent for Sergeant Wright instead, and learned from him that one of the best men in the force had been entrusted with the task of watching Miss Earle and that he had been very careful, as instructed, to make sure that she should have no suspicion she was being followed. He was confident that in this he had succeeded. He had also discovered that it was true that Dwight was, if not exactly following her, at any rate prowling about in the vicinity of Rose Briar Cottage in a highly suspicious manner.

"Can't say I like it, sir," Wright added uneasily. "He's up to something."

"We'll wait a bit and then perhaps we might bring him in for questioning, to try to find out what he is up to," Bobby decided. "Meanwhile, take your man off Miss Earle and put him on Dwight instead."

"Sir?" said Wright, very much surprised.

"She's spotted him," Bobby explained, "she's been here to complain. She says she'll go for him with a dog whip if it goes on. We don't want that."

"No, sir," agreed Wright, "wouldn't do at all, that wouldn't. Be in all the papers at once." After a pause, he added: "A formidable young party, sir."

He retired then, and Bobby reflected moodily that now he was face to face with two apparently insoluble problems, first, how to secure enough evidence to justify him in making an arrest of the person he so strongly suspected, and, secondly, the problem of discovering what it was Anne Earle intended, in time, if possible, to forestall it.

"What ever she has in mind," he found himself saying aloud, "it's going to be pretty drastic, and only God knows what will come of it."

CHAPTER XVIII
HER OWN FATHER

SO STRONG INDEED were Bobby's misgivings that he even took the trouble, which he did not grudge, or at least not much, and the time, which he did grudge, for in these days he had none to spare, to travel up to London to consult the office of the public prosecutor.

He got small comfort. He was told that on the evidence he could produce, it was hopeless to expect a conviction. Very likely, most likely indeed, his suspicions were well founded. The public prosecutor's office, placing the tips of its fingers together, leaning back in its chair, surveying gravely the ceiling through a pair of gold rimmed pince-nez, offered to bet half a dollar to a bad ha'penny that Bobby was quite right. But what, inquired the public prosecutor's office sadly, was the good of being right if one couldn't prove it? No use going into court to offer judge and jury a safe bet. One had to show them facts. Inspector Owen's powers of observation and deduction did him immense credit, but remained entirely useless without facts. Facts!

Bobby winced at this repetition to himself of what he himself had so often preached to others. He had not really known before how annoying, maddening indeed, it could be. Facts. Quite so. Certainly. Of course. Only where were they?

On that point the public prosecutor's office had nothing to say. Not their affair. Their business was not to find facts but to receive them from others, chew them, digest them, serve them up in a dainty dish fit to set before a jury and a judge.

Probably also, in the considered opinion of the public prosecutor's office, Bobby was right in his expectation of still more mischief to come. Miss Anne Earle—who was very likely guilty herself, for one never knew what these irregular unions might not lead to—was no doubt up to something. Tilting the chair still further back, fixing those gold rimmed pince-nez still more intently on the ceiling, the public prosecutor's office, increasing the odds, offered to bet a quid to a brass trouser button that Miss Anne Earle meant to make trouble, or, that if she didn't, then someone else did.

"Nothing you can do about it, though, inspector," observed the public prosecutor's office. "Not your move. You can't take action on intention."

"You mean we've just got to stand by till something fresh breaks?" Bobby asked gloomily.

The public prosecutor's office agreed genially that that was precisely what it did mean. If murderers, the public prosecutor's office pointed out, would just be content to go home and forget all about it, then it would almost always be impossible to get a conviction. But to go home and forget it, was exactly the one thing no murderer seemed able to do. The public prosecutor's office regarded this strange fact with great apparent interest. A murderer always did something, or else someone else did something, and then the murderer re-acted and then you got him. No doubt Inspector Owen would agree that the one safe thing for a murderer to do was to wash his hands and go home to tea; and yet, oddly enough, that was the one thing they never did seem capable of doing. The public prosecutor's office shook a mildly rebuking head over this quaint and puzzling fact, and then abruptly shook hands with Bobby and wished him the best of luck. Wherewith Bobby returned to Midwych, not greatly comforted, and found waiting for him little Ursula Harris in a very nervous and worried state of mind.

"You see," she explained, "Roy and me, we made it up never to meet again where we used to. I mean to say, not in that old empty cottage garden. It gives me the creeps and Roy said so, too. Only—"

"Only what?" Bobby asked when she paused.

"Only Roy and I—we had been out and we came back that way, along that road, I mean. And we thought we would just have a look again and we did and—and—"

"Well?" said Bobby patiently.

"I was never so frightened in my life," Ursula said, and looked it.

"What at?" asked Bobby.

"A—a grave," said Ursula and shuddered.

"A—what?" asked Bobby, puzzled.

"It's what it looked like," said Ursula and began to cry.

Bobby sighed and waited. He knew that when a woman begins to cry there is nothing else to do. When the sobs diminished a little in violence, he asked:

"What makes you say that?"

"Because we saw it."

"But why did you think it was a grave?"

"Because it looked like one."

"I see," said Bobby, baffled by replies at once so simple, so straightforward, and so unenlightening. "Well, I wish you would tell me exactly what it did look like."

Ursula pondered this question for a moment or two. Then she said:

"Like a grave."

"Oh, yes," said Bobby, just a trifle wildly. "Yes. Exactly. Well, you might tell me all about it?"

"But I have," Ursula protested.

"Was there," asked Bobby, trying to jolt her into greater clarity, "anyone in it?"

"Oh, no," said Ursula, and added: "Not yet," and somehow those last two words did more to startle and impress Bobby than anything said before.

He made one more effort.

He said:

"Don't you think it may have been merely a hole someone had been digging to bury rubbish?"

"It wouldn't have looked like a grave then," said Ursula simply. Then, apparently beginning to feel the need of further explanation, she added: "Between the pigsty and the hedge, and it's only by the merest chance we happened to see it." She paused, looked confused, explained hesitatingly. "Roy asked me to wait while he went away a minute or two, and, of course, he does sometimes when we are out, and he did, and I waited, and then he called out to me to come, and he sounded funny, and I did, and he showed me and he said: What does that look like? And I knew at once what he meant because it did. Have you ever seen a grave?"

"Yes," Bobby answered.

"Long and narrow and deep," Ursula said, "and so was this, and there was a spade, and the spade was marked 'Roman Ends Farm,' and that's where Mr Osman Ford lives, and why is he digging graves in that little old cottage garden, between the pigsty and the hedge, where no one ever looks?"

Bobby had no reply to make to that question. He sat, silent and uneasy, deep in thought. Some development he had certainly expected, but not this.

"Roy said not to tell anyone," Ursula burst out. "He said most likely it was nothing at all, and anyhow we were mixed up in it quite enough as it was. Only I think perhaps he means to go there by himself to-night just to see, only he wanted me kept away. Only if he goes all by himself like that, without telling anyone, then—then perhaps the grave will be for him," and as she said this her voice sank to a barely audible whisper.

"Oh, not it, even if it is a grave, which isn't a bit likely," declared Bobby, with a bright and cheerful confidence he was far from feeling. "Why should it be?"

"Because Osman Ford knows we saw him, and if anything happened to Roy, then he couldn't say so any more, could he? Roy says that's silly, but it isn't a bit. Osman Ford knows we were there, and he's only waiting till we go back, because he thinks we are sure to. And we did, too, and now Roy means to again to-night, I know he does, and please, you must see nothing happens to him."

"We'll take care of him," Bobby promised. "We'll try to find out what it's all about, and who has been digging holes there, and what for, and I'll send one of our men along to warn Mr Green to keep away."

"You can't."

"Can't what?"

"Can't warn Roy to keep away. That's why I came to tell you. Roy had a telegram to go to meet his father in London, and I expect it's about us, and they are going to motor back, and I daresay if they do Roy won't go home at all but straight on to the old cottage to see if anything happens, because I just know he means to."

"Awkward his going off like that," agreed Bobby. "Making things difficult, I call it. But don't you worry. The resources of civilization are not exhausted nor even those of the Wychshire county police. We'll catch him all right before he has any chance to get into mischief, and we'll find out who has been digging holes behind this pigsty of yours and what's the big idea."

He spoke more cheerfully and light-heartedly than he felt; but at any rate he succeeded in sending away the girl greatly comforted, and with, in addition, many assurances that she had acted very sensibly in coming to him to tell her story.

All the same Bobby was a good deal more worried than he had chosen to appear. The story puzzled him, alarmed him. Very likely it meant nothing. Someone employed about the farm had, for some perfectly natural and sensible reason, dug this hole between the pigsty and the hedge in the old abandoned garden, and little Ursula Harris's romantic imagination had done the rest.

But though Bobby thus tried to reassure himself as he had reassured the girl, he did not succeed very well, and in spite of all the work on his desk he would have either to neglect or entrust to someone else with a consequent loss of touch, he made up his mind to pay a visit that evening to Rose Briar Cottage. For he could not get it out of his mind that this tale of mysterious digging was in some way connected with Anne Earle.

"Odd's on she's up to something," he told himself moodily, "something she thinks will put us on the right lines—or off them perhaps," and he reflected that whichever alternative was true, or even if neither was true, it was advisable to make sure as quickly as possible.

The long summer's day was drawing to its close, however, before he was able to make a start, and as it happened, just as he was leaving, there came through a preliminary warning of a possible air raid—the first of many that Midwych was to receive in the coming days. He had to wait a little to make sure everything was in readiness; learned from the competent authority that there was no likelihood of any immediate development, though one or two enemy reconnaissance planes were in the neighbourhood, flying very high and probably taking photographs; issued orders that the black-out regulations were to be enforced with extra care; and so at last was able to get away.

Half a mile or so from his destination he was surprised to overtake Sergeant Wright, cycling in the same direction. He stopped the car and called to him, and Wright alighted and explained that Clayton, the man to whom had been entrusted the task of watching Dwight, had 'phoned in to say that he had been given the slip.

"Whereabouts?" Bobby asked.

"In town," Wright answered. "Dwight went in a pub, the White Lion, at the corner of Bliss Street and Barsley Road. It has doors in each street and what's more, there's an old skittle alley at the back with big windows it would be quite easy to drop out of. Clayton's a good man, sir," Wright added, a little anxiously, for failure is failure, even when success has been impossible, and sometimes superior officers do not choose to recognize that last fact.

"I know," Bobby said. "Tell him not to worry. It's easy enough to throw off a tail, especially if the chap has been tipped off beforehand. I shouldn't be a bit surprised if that hadn't happened. Just the sort of thing the Anne Earle girl would do—give Dwight a hint, I mean."

"She's capable of it," Wright agreed. "Capable of anything if you ask me. There's a way she has of looking at you as if you were on one side of a barrier and she on the other—and your side was the human side and hers was different." Then he said: "I told Clayton to try to pick Dwight up where he lives and I would come on here to see if he were hanging round Rose Briar Cottage. I thought that was the best way to get in touch with him again."

"I expect so," agreed Bobby, "but I think we'll lay off Dwight for the moment. Ursula Harris has come in with a queer tale about that unoccupied cottage near Ends Bridge. There may be nothing in it, but I want you to go along there and keep an eye open. I'll push on to Rose Briar Cottage. I want a talk with Miss Earle if I can find her and I'll keep a lookout for Dwight as well. You might stay around the Ends Bridge cottage till I can arrange for a relief. It may be an all night job. Had your supper yet?"

"Well, no, sir," Wright answered.

"Better not take the time to go home," Bobby said. "I have a feeling something may break to-night. Ring up Central, and tell them to let your wife know you may be late and get yourself something to eat at any pub you can find. I don't expect anything to happen till it's dark, so you have time, but get along as soon as you can. Try to keep out of sight. If there is going to be any dirty work we had better not risk giving warning till we've some idea what it's all about. We may get a lead to Anderson's murderer. At least, that's what I'm hoping."

Wright saluted and returned to his cycle. Bobby drove on and arrived soon at Rose Briar Cottage, where he found Mrs Jordan wandering up and down the garden path, between the garden gate and the cottage door. When she saw Bobby's car approaching she came out into the road, and as he alighted she said to him:

"Is anything wrong? Have you seen Anne?"

"Why should there be anything wrong?" he asked. "What makes you ask?"

"I'm uneasy, that's all," she answered, and with a flash of her old spirit: "There's always something wrong when cops come snooping." Then she asked again: "Have you seen Anne?"

"No. I came along in the hope of getting a word with her," Bobby answered, his own feeling of uneasiness increasing as he noticed how uneasy Mrs Jordan seemed. "Do you mean she hasn't returned from the office?" he asked.

"Oh, yes. She was back at the usual time. She had her supper. She went out again. I didn't know. She went out without a word to me."

"Haven't you any idea where she went?"

Mrs Jordan shook her head. She stood there, gross and vulgar and pathetic. Even beneath its make-up her face showed pale, and there was terror in her eyes as she said:

"I'm afraid."

"What of?" Bobby asked, and got no answer, nor expected one, for he, too, was afraid, and he, too, could have given no answer had he been asked why.

He stood hesitating, unable to decide whether to wait there on the chance of Anne's returning, or to try to find her, for he had an uncomfortable suspicion that her destination was that unoccupied cottage, where, between the pigsty and the hedge, Ursula had seen what she had taken for an open grave.

Mrs Jordan said, breaking in upon his thoughts:

"She left a letter for you on the mantelpiece, but I'm only to give it you in the morning if she hasn't got back."

"I think I had better have it now," Bobby said.

"Anne's written right across, not till the morning," Mrs Jordan objected, evidently torn between an instinct to obey Anne's injunction, that showed the strong influence and control exerted on her by the girl's powerful personality, and her own unexpressed and yet vividly felt apprehensions.

"She may be in danger. I think I had better see it," Bobby said. "On the mantelpiece, is it? In the sitting-room?"

The cottage door was still open as Mrs Jordan had left it. Bobby entered and went into the sitting-room. Mrs Jordan followed. She did not speak. She seemed relieved or at least acquiescent. The letter was there and Bobby picked it up. It was superscribed: "Give this to Mr Owen if I'm not back by morning." Bobby tore open the envelope. The letter within was brief. It ran:

DEAR MR OWEN:

I know the murderer. Osman Ford. He was seen near by just before, and it was the only way he could get hold of his wife's money he wanted to use for himself. I have made a plan to get a confession from him, and I am going to try, but perhaps he will murder me, too, instead. I shan't mind, because then you can have him hanged for that, even if you can't get the proof that he did the other.

ANNE EARLE.

"What does she say?" Mrs Jordan asked.

Bobby handed her the letter and she read it; and as she read it, so Bobby could almost see how horror and fear and dismay rose about her and enveloped her as it were in an aura of themselves that made itself felt like an actual presence.

He tried to take the letter back, but she held it, though unconsciously, in a grip of paralysed terror, as if she lacked the power to release it.

"She means she is going to risk being murdered herself so as to make sure Anderson's murderer doesn't escape," Bobby muttered.

"If it were only that," Mrs Jordan said hoarsely. "But Osman Ford's her father."

CHAPTER XIX
THE DARK GARDEN

IT WAS AN unexpected revelation. For just a moment Bobby even wondered if it were true. A glance at Mrs Jordan told him that at least she believed it, so plainly did mingled fear and dismay and horror show in her pallid looks.

"Her father," she stammered again, and then in a voice barely audible: "I never meant to tell—you or anyone."

"Are you sure?" Bobby asked, rather needlessly, but his mind was busy, trying to grasp this new fact and all that it implied and meant.

Mrs Jordan did not answer the question. She was still deep in the terror of her own thoughts, so deep that she was hardly conscious that he had spoken at all. In the same sort of whisper, as if to herself, she said:

"I never thought that was in her mind. How could I?" Suddenly remembering Bobby's presence, she looked up at him, one trembling hand uplifted as in unconscious appeal, and slowly she asked: "You see, he is her father, so what are we to do?"

"Does Osman Ford know?" Bobby asked.

"No one knew but me," Mrs Jordan answered. "You see, I never thought of anything like this. Is she right? I mean, is it true? Is it Osman who killed Anderson?"

"I don't know," Bobby answered. "Do you?"

"She's gone to find out," Mrs Jordan said. "He's her father and she wants to get him hanged, and perhaps she will, because she's like that. I mean, when she wants a thing to happen, often it does, when she wants it enough. What are you going to do?"

"Try to find her, I suppose. You are sure you can't give me any idea where she may have gone?"

Mrs Jordan shook her head.

"Are you sure she had no suspicion of the truth—about Osman Ford being her father?"

"No. How could she? No one knew but me," Mrs Jordan repeated. "Only for this, no one would ever have known, no one."

"Why did you keep it secret?" Bobby asked, anger in his voice. "They had a right to know, hadn't they? Both of them. Why didn't you tell them?"

"I never would have but for this," she repeated. "It's no good standing there, asking questions. Why don't you do something?"

"All I can do is to try to find her as soon as possible," Bobby said. "To find her and tell her. The sooner she knows the better."

"If he did it—if it's true he killed Anderson, if she's found out something to show it's him ... ?"

"Then he'll have to stand trial," Bobby answered grimly, "and the rest will be for the jury. But I would rather not lay the charge on evidence given us by his daughter."

"You couldn't do that, you never could," Mrs Jordan cried; but he did not answer as he turned and went away, for he knew that if evidence, proving the guilt of anyone, were brought to him, then it would have to be used, no matter from whom it came.

"All the same, his own daughter," he muttered. "His own daughter," and he seemed to have a vision of the girl, implacable in her pursuit, ignorant that it was her father she was attempting to hunt down. "Oh, my God, what a mess," he said under his breath.

One thing was clear in his mind. The moment he could find Anne, she should know the truth, even though that might mean the escape of the guilty. But then it by no means followed that her belief was actually correct. Only it might be. With a fresh dismay he remembered little Ursula's story of that hole, dug between pigsty and hedge, she thought had been dug by Osman Ford and that she had called a grave. An added horror there, for it might be if Osman Ford were guilty and if he knew that Anne suspected the truth, then possibly it was for her the pit had been dug—and by him. Father planning daughter's death, and daughter seeking proof of the father's dreadful guilt!

"A nightmare, what a nightmare," Bobby muttered, and for his part saw clearly there was nothing he could do, since the current of events had passed far beyond his control.

He found his car where he had left it parked by the roadside, and for a moment or two hesitated, trying to make up his mind whether to visit first Roman Ends farm to find Osman Ford, or to go first to the deserted cottage by the bridge over the canal. He decided finally in favour of the second course, both because he thought it possible he might find Anne had gone there in her effort to discover what she believed to be the truth, and also because he hoped to be able there to get in touch with Sergeant Wright. On the whole it seemed to him likely that Anne's plan, of which she spoke in her letter, would be in some way connected with the cottage or its neighbourhood.

Near the bridge he alighted. It was dark by now, a dark and silent night with heavy clouds overhead and an occasional slight splutter of rain. Near the canal and over the fields adjoining a thin damp, mist rose. He put his electric torch in his pocket and began to grope his way along the road. Till now he had hardly realized how intense was the darkness, a darkness that in the old phrase could almost be felt, that seemed to press down upon the earth like a palpable thing. The use of the torch only seemed to make the darkness more intense when its light was switched off again. Nor did he wish to keep it shining continuously, since that would proclaim his presence and his whereabouts, and he did not know who might not be watching. He had gone only a little way when a sound by the roadside attracted his attention. He listened. He heard it again. This time plainly, a kind of half-muffled groan. Switching on his torch he saw there, half in, half out of the ditch that bordered the road, the crumpled figure of a man. It was Wright, and when Bobby knelt by his side he opened his eyes and at once recognized him.

"Oh, it's you, sir," he muttered. "I've been coshed. From behind," he added defensively.

"That's all right," Bobby said. "Let me feel." He whistled softly. "Copped it all right, you have," he said. "Skin broken, bleeding a bit, no bone broken though, I think. My car's not far. Can you walk?"

"I'm O.K.," Wright declared. "Hit me from behind, he did. The murderer, I mean."

"Who's that?" Bobby asked.

"Dwight," the sergeant answered. "He said so ... he said he would out me ... but I'm O.K.," and proved his words by promptly losing consciousness.

Bobby knew how to make use of what is sometimes called the 'fireman's lift'. With some trouble, for Wright was a heavily-built man, Bobby got him hoisted into the correct position, and then was able to carry him easily enough to where he had left his car. He managed to get him inside and made him as comfortable and warm as possible with the rugs. There was a flask of brandy in one of the car lockers. With the contents, in default of clean boiled water, he bathed the wound gently, and then bandaged it as best he could with lint from a first-aid box there was also in the car. Wright opened his eyes and said:

"Don't bother about me, sir. I'm O.K. You go after Dwight, sir. He's your man, he's the murderer, he said so."

Again Bobby had a difficult choice to make. He did not like the idea of leaving the injured man alone in the car, and yet he felt, too, that he ought not to leave the vicinity, even temporarily, till he knew more of what was going on. He wondered if Dwight had really proclaimed himself the murderer, or whether that was merely an impression the injured sergeant had received, due perhaps in part to the injury itself. Safe neither to leave Wright alone nor to leave Dwight free to carry out possibly his further plans without let or hindrance. Only too likely that Dwight was here because he had known or suspected that Anne also would be here. He had apparently been watching her for some time past. For that matter it might well be Dwight who was responsible for the secret digging in the garden of the old deserted cottage. Swiftly these thoughts and considerations passed through Bobby's mind, swiftly he decided that Wright must take his chance till it was a little plainer what was happening or about to happen, and then Wright himself clenched the matter by muttering in an excited whisper:

"There he is, sir, there—over there, in the field there, I saw him shine his light. If you're quick, sir, you can catch him."

He tried to sit up in his excitement but collapsed with a groan; and Bobby, already half-way out of the car, hesitated and said:

"Sure you'll be all right?"

"If I keep still, if I don't sit up," Wright answered. "There, sir, look; there it is again, the light. You can catch him, sir, if you're quick. Don't mind me."

Losing no further time, Bobby jumped down and started at a run he had to change at once to a hesitating and uncertain stumbling walk, so dense was the all-pervading darkness. The light Wright had noticed first was still visible, apparently in the middle of the field that here was skirted by the canal road. To enter it Bobby had to force his way through a hedge, not without damage to his clothing and his hands, and when he had managed to get through, and was pushing on towards the still visible light, which by now he had recognized as the glow of a cigarette, he discovered that he had lost his torch, jerked either from his hand or from his pocket, he could not be sure which, as he had pushed and scrambled and struggled through the hedge. He half-turned, with some intention of going back to try to recover it, and then, recognizing the futility of such an attempt in that darkness, he turned again to discover now that the guiding light for which he had been making had vanished. Presumably the cigarette had either been extinguished or thrown away.

Only then did Bobby fully realize the immensity of the darkness in which he and all around were enveloped. A feeling of utter helplessness possessed him. He had even lost his sense of direction in that quick turn he had made with the idea of recovering his torch, and he was no longer certain in which direction lay the cottage, in which the spot where he had left his car, in which the light that was no longer visible. He lay down flat in the hope that some landmark he could recognize would show itself against the horizon, but the horizon showed only the same inky blackness that seemed to begin where he put out his hand and to continue without end. It was so intense he even had a feeling that he could gather it up in handfuls and hold it so. He cursed the haste that had brought him here into the middle of this utter blackness, with, for guidance, nothing but the light that now had vanished. Then he reflected that at any rate he was in a field, that the field would have a boundary, a hedge. If he could find it he could follow it round till he reached a gate; but when he did this, the gate he came to admitted only to another field, and he did not know whether to enter it would bring him nearer to or further away from the canal road he sought. He left it without passing through and continued with difficulty to grope his way by the hedge. Presently he became aware that he had lost it and in that all-enveloping darkness stood still, a helpless prisoner of the night.

He began to wonder whether he would not have to spend all the night there, unable to penetrate the encircling wall of blackness which was always all around him, which moved in unison with him as he moved, and then quite near at hand he heard a faint and tiny sound.

So small, faint, and remote it was, he could not be sure it was not merely a product of his own strained attention, imagining what was not there in fact at all. Then he heard it again, this time familiar and unmistakable, the striking of a match. The tiny flame appeared, shone out indeed like a beacon against the immense background of the night. It showed clearly for an instant the form of a man, standing sideways to Bobby, so that he could not distinguish the features, but holding in one hand something which, even in that momentary glimpse, Bobby recognized as a revolver with an unnaturally long barrel. That meant, he supposed, that it was fitted with a 'silencer', or rather a 'reducer' as it is more accurately called, since the thing does not silence, though it does greatly reduce, the sound of the explosion.

Bobby began to run towards the unknown. At once the match went out. He guessed what he had to expect and swerved sharply to one side, though that was useless enough since he was as likely to swerve into the path of the bullet as away from it. He heard the 'plop' to which the 'reducer' had diminished the normal report. He heard, too, and liked it less, the whine of a bullet passing overhead. Next came the sound of rapid footsteps. Whoever had fired at him was now in flight, endeavouring to escape. Bobby started to run in pursuit, but warily, for he did not know when he would not be fired upon again.

"Who was it?" he thought as he ran. "Dwight? Since Dwight apparently was or had been in the neighbourhood. Osman Ford? Since it was on his land all this was happening. Or someone else altogether? Young Roy Green, perhaps?"

His run slackened, became a walk. He stood still, once more baffled by the surrounding darkness into which the man of the revolver had fled as into a sure refuge. In vain he strained his ears, hoping to hear even the faintest sound that might direct him. But the silence was as vast, as universal as the darkness, and once more he felt himself held a prisoner and helpless in the night. He wondered if perhaps the fugitive was doing the same thing, standing still and quiet, secure in the cloak of invisibility the night provided. Intently Bobby listened, hoping for some faint sound to help. Gradually he began to distinguish one from other the different soft sounds, the flight of a beetle, the scurrying progress of a field mouse through the grass, the scratching of a mole busy underground, that taken together make up in their totality the enormous quietness of the night. But he heard nothing to show there was any other human presence near.

Then all at once, and not far away, there broke out a confused shouting, a sound of struggling, blows, a stamping to and fro.

Bobby shouted at the top of his voice and began to run in the direction whence the sounds came. But it is not easy to run fast in the pitchy darkness of a night without stars or moon, with heavy rain clouds low overhead, with a thin mist spreading on the surface of the ground. Again he heard the 'plop', something like the drawing of a cork from some giant bottle, that told once more of the discharge of a pistol fitted with a 'silencer' or, better, a 'reducer'. It was followed, not so much followed as echoed simultaneously, by a shrill, piercing scream and the noise of a body falling. Bobby tried to increase his speed, to run faster still in spite of that hampering, treacherous darkness. Quickly he paid the penalty, catching his foot in a tangle of grass and falling headlong. For a moment he lay half-stunned and breathless, for he had fallen heavily. He scrambled to his feet again and ran on, and almost instantly found himself grappled in a fierce and close embrace.

He had been taken by surprise and at a disadvantage. He felt a hand gripping at his throat. He retaliated with a blow that in the darkness missed entirely, but somehow he got free from the fingers clutching to strangle him. Confusedly they fought on. Once his unknown antagonist managed to wrench himself free, but before he could altogether escape once again Bobby gripped him, and once again they were struggling and wrestling together, Bobby trying to make his grasp secure, the other twisting and fighting to get loose. Neither of them spoke a word, their breath came heavily, their feet were loud in the night as they stamped to and fro, the blows they exchanged were ineffective, they lost their balance and rolled over on the ground and Bobby was undermost. His grip loosened for the fraction of a second so that with a sudden swift and violent effort the other was able to wrench himself free, to get to his feet. In another fraction of a second he would have melted away in that darkness which offered so secure a refuge. But Bobby was able just at the last to throw out a hand and grip the fugitive by the ankle and pluck him down. Instantly he was upon him, grinding him down with his knee in the small of his back.

"Had enough?" Bobby asked. By way of emphasis he took his prostrate prisoner ungently by both ears and made ready to bang his head on the ground if he still showed signs of resistance. "Had enough?" he repeated. "Coming quietly or do you want some more? Where's your pistol?"

A voice he had not expected, a voice he recognized for that of Roy Green, stammered:

"I haven't got one. You swine, let me up. You swine, if I had I would have potted you long ago."

"Oh, it's you, is it?" Bobby said.

"You're breaking my back," Roy panted. "Let me up. You're killing me."

"No great loss if I did," Bobby answered unsympathetically.

He twisted the boy's arms behind his back and held him helpless in a grip all policemen know. Roy said again:

"Let me go. You've no right. Where's the other cop?"

"What other cop?" Bobby asked. "What do you mean?"

"It was another chap just now," Roy answered sullenly. "Then it was you. What's the game?"

"Where's your pistol?" Bobby repeated. "The one you took a pot shot at me with just now."

"I tell you I haven't got one. He had one. The other chap I mean. He fired at me and I yelled and fell down to make him think I was hit and then I went for him and then it was you. I haven't any pistol. I've never had one. Why should I? I wish I had and I wish I had tried to shoot you and done it, too. Just now it was another chap and now it's you. What's it mean?"

"Have you any idea who it was, who you were scrapping with, I mean?"

"No. How could I tell, in this darkness? You can't see a thing. It's like—like a coal cellar. I don't know who it was. If it wasn't one of your cops, who was it? I ran right into him and before I could say a word or ask what it was all about, he fired at me. He called me a damn police spy. Perhaps he thought I was you. I don't know.

He hit me with something hard. I think it was a gun. It had a long barrel thing. I tried to hit back, and I think I landed one, but I don't know, and then he hit me again, and then it wasn't him any longer, it was you."

"Sounds a bit muddled," Bobby said. "If he called you a police spy, it's not likely he was a policeman himself, is it? You didn't recognize the voice?"

"No. No. It was all so sudden, I hadn't time to think even."

"You can't form any idea?"

"No. It wasn't natural. Not disguised, I don't mean, a sort of scream, only in a whisper, if you see what I mean. Not natural," he repeated, shuddering a little at the memory.

Bobby felt he knew what Roy meant. The killer's scream in a high-pitched whisper from which all trace of humanity had vanished in the beast-like urge to kill.

"Well, look here," he said. "Wait a minute though." He ran a practised hand up and down the boy's clothing and made sure that he had on him no weapon of any sort or kind. But he found something nearly as valuable at the moment—a small electric torch of which he took instant and probably unlawful possession.

"You're hurting, let me loose," Roy said again.

Bobby hesitated for a moment.

"All right," he said then, and let go the grip in which he had held Roy's arms uncomfortably twisted behind his back. But he still held him by one arm, having no mind to see him vanish suddenly into that black night, in which, once it was attained, it was as though a fugitive dematerialized. He said:

"What brought you here at this time of night?"

"It's not so late as all that," Roy answered sullenly. "There's been some funny work in that old cottage garden. I thought I would see if I could find out what was up. I meant to wait behind the hedge round the garden to try to spot what it was all about. I thought I would cut across the field so as to come up at the back, if you see what I mean, just in case there was anyone there already. But it's so blasted dark I got lost. I couldn't tell which way—where the cottage was, I mean. I was beginning to think I should never find it. Then I ran into that other bloke, whoever he was, and he fired at me and went for me like hell. I expect he thought I was you and then I thought at first you were him."

"Bit of a muddle," Bobby repeated thoughtfully. "What do you mean by 'funny work' in the cottage garden?"

"Someone's been digging a hole," Roy answered. "Behind the old pigsty—between the pigsty and the hedge. Ursula said it looked like a grave. It's just a hole, but that's what Ursula said."

"I think perhaps she is right and you've run a good chance of being its occupant," Bobby said grimly. "Why didn't you come and tell us?"

"I wanted to be sure, I wanted—"

He didn't complete the sentence, so Bobby finished it for him.

"You mean you wanted to be extra clever and find it all out for yourself," he said. "A fool's trick," he said dispassionately, and wondered if the boy's story were true or if there were another and more sinister explanation. Perhaps he had heard, through Ursula again, that Anne had some plan for discovering the truth. If that truth was that Roy himself was guilty, a possibility still, then it might be he himself had dug what he called a hole, though Ursula called it a grave, and that therefore it was he who had planned who was to be its occupant. "Did you hear anything else?" Bobby asked abruptly.

"You hear all sorts of funny noises at night," Roy answered. "There was something rummy about that pistol the chap fired at me. It was—sort of smothered, if you see what I mean. There was something like it before. I couldn't make out what it was. Just as I got back. Over there, in the cottage garden or somewhere near."

"Are you sure?" Bobby asked, startled and alarmed, for this meant that an earlier shot still had been fired.

Three then, it seemed. One at Bobby himself and one at Roy a moment ago, and now apparently a third as well. But at whom directed? And had it missed as had those other two or had it found its mark? Disturbing questions, and they brought to Bobby's mind a vision of digging, of digging that no longer resembled a grave because it had been completed, finished and smoothed over—a task that possibly, indeed, someone at that very moment was busy with.

"What's it all about?" Roy's voice broke in suddenly upon his troubled and uneasy thoughts. "What's it—mean?"

"I don't know," Bobby answered. "I wish I did. But I may as well tell you at once I am not altogether satisfied with your story. I hope it will stand up when we look into it. Anyhow, there's something very queer going on about here and I want help." Again he hesitated. He knew he was taking a risk, but he felt it was necessary to obtain help and the only way of getting it was through Roy. After all, his story hung together, and his appearance here was consistent with the story little Ursula Harris told. Bobby went on: "I took your torch. You had better have it back. Catch hold. I've lost mine, worse luck. I want you to go back to Ends Bridge, you know, where the road crosses the canal. You can drive a car, can't you? Good. You'll find my car there, by the roadside. One of my men is in it. He's been knocked out and he is in pretty bad shape. I want you to go for help. Stop at the first 'phone box you come to and dial the county police. The number is MID 1234, easy to remember. Tell them where I am and that I want help. One car with four men and two motor-cyclists. Tell them to turn out the police surgeon and fetch him along. There may be something for him; and if there isn't, he'll just have to curse. Then find the first doctor you can and get the chap in the car seen to. If the doctor thinks it'll be O.K., take him home and go home yourself. And stay there. Understand?"

"What are you going to do?"

"I shall be stopping around to see what else happens," Bobby answered. "It's been a bit lively so far and it may continue."

"All right," Roy said.

"Sure you understand?"

"Yes. One car. Four men. The police doctor. Two motor-cyclists. Why not mobilize the whole blessed police force at once? And get one of your men you've left in your car seen to by a doctor. Doesn't strike you you nearly killed me, I suppose?"

With this parting shot he turned and began to make his way back across the field, using the torch Bobby had returned to him with which to pick his way.

All the same, as he stood for a moment to watch Roy vanish into the darkness, and saw the light of the torch flash out and vanish and flash again, Bobby wondered if it was not the murderer himself whom thus he was permitting to make a safe departure, to whom he had entrusted the task of calling the aid needed so desperately, at whose mercy he had placed the life of Sergeant Wright.

A heavy responsibility indeed to have undertaken. Nor did he feel quite sure he could justify himself if it turned out ill.

The light, however, that the departing Roy switched on from time to time and that, though kept carefully on the ground, none the less shone out clearly against the immense background of that black night, served also to show Bobby the correct direction to follow. He knew now, provided, that is, Roy was taking the right path for Ends Bridge, where the deserted cottage must stand. Towards it, therefore, he began to make his way.

This time with success in spite of the ever-hampering darkness, for presently he found that he had reached that corner of the cottage garden hedge where it met the other hedge bordering the canal road. Treading very cautiously, he groped his way along, trying to find a gap, of which he remembered having noticed one or two, whereby he could penetrate into the garden. He stiffened to attention. There was a careful step approaching, slow and careful, and by the rustling of a skirt he knew the new-comer must be a woman.

CHAPTER XX
FROM OUT THE PIT

HE HAD AN impulse to call out, to ask who was there, even to make a guess and use Anne Earle's name. But between stood the strongly-grown hawthorn hedge that was the boundary of the garden of the deserted cottage. Probably, too, if he gave any such challenge, the woman, whoever she might be, would disappear into the darkness. Already he had had too much evidence of how easily in the shelter of that impenetrable night pursuit and recognition could be evaded.

As silently as might be he groped his way along the hedge, hoping to find a gap through which he could pass. He thought he remembered there was one such gap just behind where the old pigsty stood at the bottom of the garden. He remembered, too, that if he found it and got through there he must be careful to avoid that freshly-dug pit of which Ursula had spoken. He wondered again if it could be Anne he had heard pass by, and, if so, if she would have answered if he had risked calling her by name.

Probably it had been Anne, he told himself. He had felt all the time that the scheme she seemed to have formed for obtaining proof of the murderer's guilt, whatever that scheme might be, almost certainly had some connection with this garden. Of the other women in any way connected with recent events, nothing he was sure would induce Ursula to come near the place, and so far as he knew there was nothing to bring to this vicinity either Mrs Jordan or Mrs Osman Ford. The only persons he had expected to find were Anne and whoever it was against whom she expected to obtain proof. Dwight, perhaps, since Dwight apparently was in the neighbourhood, or young Roy Green, or possibly the person unidentified with whom Roy had wrestled and who might or might not be identical with Dwight.

His mind was busy with these thoughts as he came presently to the gap in the hedge he was searching for. Not without difficulty he crawled through, and almost at once he became certain that there was someone else there, not far away, like himself intent and listening and prepared. Almost at once, too, he heard another sound, a little further away. It was someone else approaching, stumbling and nearly falling, and then came a low exclamation in a voice Bobby knew at once for that of Roy Green.

Roy was back then in this garden of darkness and of doubt. Instead of carrying out the errands given him, instead of hurrying to bring help, he had returned. And what, Bobby asked himself with a cold chill at the heart, had happened to Wright, whose helplessness he had, too rashly he felt now, trusted to Roy's care. How easy to send car and unconscious man down the slope of the embankment into the canal, and how difficult afterwards to prove what had happened.

"If he has done that, I'll see he pays for it, proof or no proof," Bobby swore to himself.

Even, he told himself fiercely, at the cost of his own life, for if indeed that had happened, then it was through him that Wright had lost his life; and for a life, a life must pay.

But if this was Roy come back, who was it of whose presence so near by he was so certainly aware?

He remained motionless, thinking it best to wait what happened next. Abruptly, another voice that was not Roy's called out, shrill and startled:

"Who's there?"

No answer came. The silence that had been broken returned. It seemed that the whole garden waited, watchful and still and expectant. Bobby began to move forward, very slowly, very carefully, testing well each step before he took the next. A feeling of helplessness possessed him, enclosed as he was in this prison of unending night, so full of mystery and peril. Crowded the garden seemed to be. Dwight was here, he believed, and Roy Green certainly, and the unknown woman he had heard go by so recently, and that other to whose shrill challenge 'Who's there?' neither he himself nor anyone else had given any answer.

Another step forward Bobby took with the same caution and it brought him against a low wooden paling. It puzzled him for a moment, and then he realized that this was what, when the cottage had been occupied, had been the pigsty. Close by then must be the digging of which Ursula Harris had spoken. She had likened it to a grave Bobby remembered. He sank on his hands and knees and so made his way behind the sty, since between it and the hedge Ursula said the pit had been dug.

There had once been a kind of rough path here, so that the ground was comparatively smooth, and progress was easier and more silent. There came to him the smell of fresh-turned earth. He put out a hand and felt the edge of a pit. Fragments of earth his hand displaced crumbled and fell, and the sound of their fall was heavy and dull, and full of strange and ominous foreboding. Cautiously Bobby dragged himself nearer, nearer still. He hardly knew what he expected, but he did know it would be dreadful. Groping carefully with outstretched hand, he made out that the edge of the pit extended as far as he could reach, parallel with the pigsty. Towards the hedge it was narrow. Long and narrow, therefore, like a grave. He dragged himself nearer still and stared downwards into its interior, but he could distinguish nothing, nothing but a great blackness.

"The blackness of the pit," he found himself muttering.

Slowly, carefully, with dread, he leaned over further still, and groped with his hand to see if he could reach to the bottom. He was hardly surprised when his hand touched a face, a human face that was cold and still, and so he knew that what he had found was indeed a grave and that the grave had an occupant. Yet though it was hardly a surprise, though it was but what he had more than half expected, he gave a loud and sudden cry as his hand touched those cold features.

As if the note of terror and of urgency that, though without his knowledge, had informed his voice, had roused the garden to sudden action, had stripped from it all that dark secrecy and silence which before had seemed to fill it, abruptly it became full of a confusion of sounds, of voices crying, of a running to and fro, of angry, startled exclamations, of a woman's voice crying ceaselessly:

"Osman. Osman. Osman. Where are you?"

"So Osman Ford is here, why is he here?" Bobby muttered.

Abruptly, suddenly, unexpectedly, a light began to glow, somewhere half way between the empty cottage and the end of the garden where Bobby stood. At first a tiny light, a little glowing light that flickered humbly by the ground and did no more than make its own self visible. But swiftly, swiftly, it grew, increased, till it became a dancing flame, a high and ardent flame, a leaping pyramid of light before which the darkness of the night drew back and shrivelled utterly away, till cottage and garden and beyond were all lit up in a pattern of changing light and shade. Bobby remembered now having noticed a pile of brushwood, old hedge clippings, broken palings, other odd bits of wood, all thrown together in a pile. This it was that was now alight. Someone had put a match to it, and now it glowed, a pyramid of fire, and in its glow, as that increased, one thing after another grew into visibility and recognition.

One by one in quick succession, garden and cottage, out-buildings, the hedge, became as it were outlined against the hitherto all prevailing night as that rolled back before the mounting flame. Into that bright visibility there grew also one by one other human forms, startled or passive, alert or still, and nearest of them all, quite close to his right hand, stood Roy Green. Bobby said to him:

"So it's you."

Roy said quickly:

"Dwight's there. What's he here for?"

"Why have you come back?" Bobby asked.

Neither answered the other's question.

Close by, a little further back from where Bobby stood, Dwight was moving forward. He stopped and called out loudly:

"Where's Anne? I'm looking for Anne. What have you done to Anne?"

"Give me your torch," Bobby said to Roy.

Roy was still holding it in one hand. Bobby took it from him and ran back a step or two to that open pit he had found between the pigsty and the hedge. He bent over and flashed the light of the torch into its depths that still lay dark in heavy shadow. Nor was he surprised when he recognized the still, cold face of Anne Earle looking up at him. There was loose earth upon it, and more loose earth upon her body, as though already an effort had been made to complete the burial. Into the circle of light, from the direction of the cottage, came the sound of a man's steps. It was Osman Ford, and in one hand he held a spade. Bobby said to him:

"Did you do this?"

Osman did not answer. He came a little nearer and stood gazing down into the pit lit up by the beam of Bobby's torch. Osman said:—

"It's her I saw in Castles' office."

"Did you kill her?" Bobby asked.

"No. No. Why should I?" Osman said, and yet the question did not seem much to surprise him.

Unexpectedly he put out his hand and took the torch from Bobby and still kept the ray direct on the quiet and prostrate form, lying cold at the bottom of that narrow pit, loose earth staining face and clothing.

"What are you doing with that spade?" Bobby asked.

"I picked it up," Osman said abstractedly. "I picked it up. It was under my feet and so I picked it up."

"Why are you here?" Bobby asked.

"I had a letter," Osman said. "I think she wrote it," he said, though apparently now speaking more to himself. He knelt down by the edge of the pit. He continued to direct the ray from the torch so that it illumined the pit and the prostrate form within, while behind the flame from the burning pile leaped ever higher and threw ever further and wider the circle of light it made in the darkness. Till now Osman had seemed only half aware of Bobby's presence, of Bobby's questions, but now he looked up at him and said:

"I have only seen her once or twice and I never noticed her much, so why do I think now that I have always known—"

"Known what?"

"Known that she was my daughter."

"Is that why you killed her?" Bobby asked.

Osman said:

"I heard a shot. I remember now I heard a shot, a muffled shot."

"How long have you known she was your daughter?" Bobby asked.

"I only knew when I saw her there," Osman answered with a gesture towards the pit and the body. "Then I saw it was myself looking up at me. I do not understand. I had a letter and I think she wrote it."

"Where is it?" Bobby asked.

"I showed it to Blythe, I gave it to Blythe," Osman answered.

Roy Green touched Bobby on the arm.

"Mr Blythe's here, too," he said.

"Making it complete," Bobby muttered. "Anyone else?"

"There was a woman here just now," Dwight said. "I thought at first that it was Anne but it was not, for her step was different."

"Where is Mr Blythe?" Bobby asked, and the lawyer stepped forward from the further side of the burning pile of brushwood behind which he had been standing.

"I saw it all," he said, and from behind the hedge a voice said shrilly:

"That was uncommon clever of you in the dark."

"Who's that?" Bobby asked sharply, and Mrs Ford came forward, forcing her way through the hawthorn hedge of which a stray branch made an ugly scratch on one hand. Only then did Bobby notice a similar scratch on Blythe's face that had bled a little, that in fact was still bleeding, so that he had to dab at it occasionally with his hand.

"I followed my man," she said. "I saw there was something troubling him and I followed him. What's to do?"

"Murder," Bobby answered. "Anne Earle has been murdered and the murderer has tried to bury her in a pit he had dug before, and I think it must be one of you, but I do not know which."

None of them made any answer except, indeed, that from them all came much the same sharp intake of breath, the same stir and quick movement that might be either knowledge of guilt or the protest of innocence. Dwight was the first to speak. He said loudly:

"I was following her to look after her."

"You attacked Sergeant Wright," Bobby said to him. "Perhaps you tried to murder him. Perhaps you murdered Miss Earle, too." To Roy he said: "You've come back. Why did you come back? To commit a murder?" He swung round upon Osman. "You were standing there by her grave with a spade in your hand. Was that to cover up what you knew was there because it was you had put it there?" When Mrs Ford tried to speak he silenced her with a strong gesture: "You say you followed your husband," he said, "but perhaps you came with him to help him in what he had to do. Did you know she was his daughter?"

"I've thought that long enough," she answered composedly "How could I help when there was so much of him in her, of her in him? Both with the same slow anger to lead them anywhere. But not to murder." She went and stood by her husband's side. Then she said: "There's still someone else over there, watching by the corner of the cottage. Come out there," she called, "and let's see who you are."

It was Mrs Jordan who moved forward.

"Where is Anne?" she said. "I came for Anne because I thought she might be here. What has happened to Anne?"

But Bobby, at least, thought that she already knew or guessed, and then he found himself wondering how that could be, or if it was possible that for this knowledge so plainly visible in her eyes, there was good reason.

Mr Blythe began to speak. He said:

"I think I can tell you what happened because I saw it all. That unhappy man," he pointed to Osman Ford who stood still and silent, apparently only half conscious of what was going on around, though to his wife he had muttered in a murmur audible only to her: "Did you know? How strange you should know before me."

More loudly he said: "You shouldn't have come but I'm glad you're here." "That unhappy man," Mr Blythe continued, unheeding the interruption, still with one uplifted hand directed towards Osman, "came to see me this afternoon. I don't know anything about a letter, but he seemed in a very excited mood. I thought at first he had been drinking. Afterwards I felt it was something much more serious. I couldn't guess what. But I was very uneasy. He wanted to know if I thought he was suspected of the murder of my dear friend and partner. I told him I knew no reason to think so. He said he had been questioned and I reminded him others had been questioned too, including myself. He asserted that someone—he wouldn't give any name—was trying to make out he was guilty. I tried to persuade him he had nothing to fear if he were innocent. He left me in the same excited mood, and it made me so uneasy I decided after he had gone to have another talk with him and try to get him into a more reasonable mood. On my way to his house, as I was driving along the road by the canal, I saw a light in this garden. I knew the cottage was empty. I felt puzzled. Curious perhaps. Uneasy certainly. I drove on a short distance, and then I thought I would see if anyone was there and I stopped the car and got down and walked back. To see if anything was going on. I heard voices. It was Mr Ford talking to a woman. My first thought was that I had come upon some vulgar assignation. Disgusting enough but not my business. I turned back towards where I had left the car and then I heard—well, I can't quite describe it. It made me think of the report of a gun and yet it wasn't loud enough for that. But I remembered Ford told me once he was buying a silencer as they call it for his rook rifle, so that when he shot one bird the report should not alarm all the rest of them. I found myself asking if a silencer for a rook rifle could be adapted to a revolver, and if so why and for what purpose. I was thoroughly uneasy. There was a light in the garden again. It came from an electric torch on the ground. By its light I could distinguish Ford with a dead woman's body at his feet. I felt it was as much as my own life was worth to let him know I had seen him. Not very heroic perhaps, but middle-aged lawyers aren't always heroes. I tried to creep away without letting him hear me. I saw he was holding a spade, and then I heard footsteps and so did he, I think, for I saw him listen. He had switched off his torch before, but I heard plainly movements he had been making. Now they stopped. I suppose it was your footsteps, Inspector, we both heard. That is all I know."

"A pack of lies," Mrs Ford said. "I pray God never to forgive you them."

"All lies," Osman repeated. "Why are you telling lies like that about me? Did you kill her yourself?" he asked.

"Inspector," Mr Blythe said. "You can test for yourself whether one detail at least is true or a lie. There is something bulging in Mr Ford's coat pocket that looks to me like a pistol."

He had shot out his hand again as he spoke, and Bobby said:

"Your hand's bleeding. There's blood on your hand."

"I scratched my face scrambling away in the dark," Mr Blythe answered, slightly disconcerted. "That's all. Some blood must have got on my hand when I wiped it. It's nothing. Mrs Ford's hand is bleeding, too."

There was in fact a little blood oozing from a place where she had scratched herself forcing her way through the hedge. Apparently she had not known before for she looked surprised when she lifted her hand and saw it. Mr Blythe said:

"You see. Look there."

Osman had put his hand into his coat pocket and from it he drew a revolver at which he was looking with the same dazed expression he had worn before.

"I didn't know it was there," he said bewilderedly.

Mrs Ford took it from him.

"It's not yours," she said. "Someone's pushed it on you."

"Inspector," Mr Blythe said, "I think you should take possession of it. Because I should not be surprised if it doesn't turn out to be the weapon used to kill poor Anderson."

"No, I shouldn't either," Bobby said, and moved forward and took the pistol carefully from Mrs Ford, holding it in a clean handkerchief as he did so. "There may be finger-prints," he explained.

"There'll be mine," Mrs Ford said.

"There may be others, too," Bobby answered.

"I think we may be sure of that," said Mr Blythe.

Intent, listening, absorbed, as they all were, they all at once and simultaneously heard a strange, unexpected sound from close behind. When they turned and looked it was to see quite clearly a white hand lifted from the grave and feeling and groping on the earth by its edge.

In the flickering, changing, strong, uncertain light of the burning fire, they saw Anne, pale, living, earth-stained, rise up from the pit into which she had been laid. In horror, in wonder, in fear and in fascination, not able to speak or move, they saw her draw herself to the level ground, stand upright, come a step towards them and then another. She had one hand laid to her breast. She lifted the other. She said clearly and loudly:

"That's the man who killed Mr Anderson and to-night he killed me because he thought I knew."

CHAPTER XXI
ARREST

EVEN YET NOT one of those present had either moved or spoken. Stricken into immobility by the strangeness, the horror, the wonder of the scene, they stared bewildered and awe-stricken at the motionless, upright figure of the girl who thus had risen as it seemed from the dead to denounce her slayer. Only the circle of light in which they stood changed and altered, only the shadows came and went as the flame from the burning brushwood waxed and waned, only the crackling and spluttering of the fire broke that enormous silence. In their midst the girl who thus had risen alive from the living grave into which she had been thrown, from which one last effort of her fierce and passionate energy had enabled her to rise, still pointed an accusing hand, and yet at whom she pointed it not one of them could be sure.

Then, slowly, while they yet watched, she seemed to falter; that energy as from another world by which she had been upheld before, began to leave her; her pointing and accusing hand turned and was laid now upon her breast, where was growing steadily a faint stain of blood; she would have fallen had not with a swift, sudden rush Mrs Jordan run forward and gathered her in her arms.

It was as though the woman's action released them from the spell that had held them all so still and silent. There was among them a general stir and movement, a sharp indrawing of breath till then held suspended, a muttering of low whispered, awe-struck exclamations. In a loud, clear voice Mr Blythe called:

"Inspector. Arrest that man. Osman Ford. You heard. You saw."

"We all did," Bobby answered; and clear in his mind was the memory of how Anne had said to him that even from her grave she would rise to be certain that the murderer did not escape.

Mrs Ford cried:

"It was you she pointed at. It was you, George Blythe."

"A great shock for you, Mrs Ford," Blythe said, making his voice very gentle. "You can't believe it. Naturally. None of us can. Only, as Inspector Owen says, 'We all heard. We all saw.'"

"The first thing is get Miss Earle attended to," Bobby said.

He moved forward to where Mrs Jordan crouched with the girl held close in her arms. She looked up at him and said:

"Anne is dead. I think perhaps she was already dead when she spoke. Leave me alone with her, my Anne, my daughter, my child."

"Was she your daughter?" Bobby asked.

"Mine and Osman Ford's," Mrs Jordan answered. "I never dared tell her. I left her on a doorstep when she was a baby, and so I never dared tell her who I was because she never forgave it. She was hard, hard, but it was that made her so hard."

"A second murder," Mr Blythe's clear, loud voice broke in, authoritative and stern. "Inspector."

"A second murder. Yes," Bobby said and stood up.

"You'll find the same pistol has been used," Blythe went on. "First for Anderson. Now for Miss Earle. You saw yourself Ford take it from his pocket."

"I never saw it before," Osman said, but in a curiously aloof, almost disinterested voice. "I don't know how it got there." He moved nearer to Mrs Jordan. Looking down at her, he said: "You never told me. Why didn't you?"

"I meant to," she said slowly. "That's why I came back. To get money from you for holding my tongue. But that was before I knew what it was to have a daughter. I don't think I ever thought of her twice after I put her down there on that doorstep and left her. Now she's left me. That's fair does. God always plays fair in the end, don't he? You see," she went on, still speaking directly to Osman, "if I had told you, you would have told her, and then she would have known, and I couldn't risk that, knowing how she felt."

Mrs Ford was standing now by her husband's side.

"You were a great fool," she said dispassionately. "Hadn't you the sense to see what was making her hard as you call it, was just that she was alone, poor kid? She hated the mother who left her. That's why she took up with Anderson, because he had been deserted too. She hated the mother who left her. She would have loved the mother who came back."

"I suppose I've always done wrong," Mrs Jordan said, and bowed herself lower yet over the still body in her arms.

"Did you know?" Osman said slowly to his wife.

"I guessed," she answered. "It wasn't difficult. The first time I saw Anne I saw a look of you in the eyes. Then I saw her again and just the same slow fire in her there always is in you. I think I ought to have told you, but I didn't know what to do, and I knew, too, because I watched the cottage, that she had got herself mixed up with Anderson. Perhaps I shouldn't have guessed so soon if I hadn't recognized Mrs Jordan and known her again for the Edie Earle you carried on with before Youngman cut you out with her as he tried to cut you out with me. But I shouldn't have known her again so quick, only for you going to her cottage and my watching to find out why."

"You knew about that, too?" Osman asked her bewilderedly.

"Of course I did, you great goop," she told him. "Think I've no eyes in my head? I guessed it was money she wanted from you. I could see well enough there was nothing else she was like to ask for—or get. I expect you run straight, Osman Ford, because you haven't the wits to run crooked." With a gesture that took all sting from the words, she put up her hand to reach, not without difficulty, the big man's shoulder. "Or even maybe the wish," she said. "Of course, I always knew you had been tangled up with Edie, and when Youngman was found drowned and Edie ran away—"

"It was an accident," Mrs Jordan said. 'We were larking by the canal and he went a bit too far, so I gave him a push and he fell in the canal and I ran away. I never thought he would get more than a ducking. I never thought about his getting drowned. I thought he would just climb out. I suppose it was through his having had drink. When I heard he had been found drowned and the police asking questions, I got frightened and I left my baby on a doorstep because I didn't know then what it meant to have a daughter, and I went to London and then I got to Australia and then I came back thinking to get money out of Osman because if he didn't I would tell about Anne, but then I didn't dare, because I couldn't without Anne knowing I was the mother she had cursed in church before the altar when she was a kid. But all that's over now, for this is the end."

"Not the end, poor woman, I'm afraid," Blythe said in a low voice to Bobby. "I don't see how to keep her name out of it. Do you?"

There came a sudden interruption. A very loud, very angry voice bellowed:

"Put out that light. What's going on here? An air-raid warning on and you start a bonfire. I'll trouble you for your names and addresses, please."

There came into the light from the burning brushwood a constable in uniform, that Constable Smith who had made the first report on Rose Briar Cottage. He saw Bobby, recognized him and stopped dead, very much surprised. Mr Blythe said in that clear, authoritative voice of his:

"There has been murder done, constable. That man." He pointed to Osman Ford. "We are all witnesses of how he was denounced and the Inspector even has the murder weapon with his finger prints on it."

Bobby was still holding the revolver Osman Ford had taken from his pocket, saying as he did so that he did not know how it had got there. Mr Blythe pointed to it. Bobby said:

"There is a little blood on it, too."

"Well, it's not mine," Mr Blythe said quickly, instinctively putting up a hand to touch his cheek where the scratch across it had bled freely.

"Osman's not hurt, Osman's not bleeding anywhere," Mrs Ford interposed.

"Isn't he?" Mr Blythe said. "I think you are, though." He made a gesture towards her hand, where in fact the freshly-made scratch, inflicted recently as she scrambled through the hawthorn hedge around the garden, was bleeding slightly.

She looked at the small wound with a surprised air, as if aware of it for the first time, and Bobby said to Constable Smith:

"Never mind that now. I expect a test will show what group it belongs to and that may help."

"Mine's the rarest of all," Mrs Ford said. "Class 3 or something. A doctor told me once. That'll prove it isn't mine."

"Oh, nonsense," Blythe said, loudly and impatiently.

To the staring and still bewildered Constable Smith, Bobby said:

"Arrest Mr George Blythe. Take him to Long Barsley. I am charging him with the murder of Nathaniel Anderson, and the murder, to-night, of Anne Earle."

"Preposterous, preposterous," Mr Blythe almost shouted, but Constable Smith's hand was on his left shoulder and on his right stood Bobby. "You can't do this," Blythe said in a sort of hoarse whisper. "Think of what it'll mean to Hopewell House and all the lads there."

"Coming quietly, are you?" Constable Smith said.

CHAPTER XXII
CONCLUSION

BOBBY'S FIRST ANXIETY now was to make a full report to his chief, but only after a no doubt very proper display of professional hesitation did the doctor in attendance on Colonel Glynne agree that this might be done.

"An extraordinary story," the colonel commented when Bobby had finished. "You took rather a risk though in arresting Blythe on the spot. I think in your place I should have felt it more prudent to wait. Of course, it's all right now the accountants have found proof that it was Blythe who first embezzled the Osman Ford money for his beloved Hopewell House and then, when he knew Castles had discovered there was something wrong with the Ford account and was probably going to tax Anderson with it, embezzled Anderson's estate to make up the deficiency, after first killing Anderson to make sure there were no protests from that quarter. Odd that with so many motives for murder on the surface, the true murder motive should lie so deep. Though I don't suppose Blythe ever contemplated murder when he first began monkeying with the Ford trust fund."

"I daresay not," Bobby agreed. "I daresay Blythe was like the office boy who takes a shilling from the petty cash, meaning to put it back next day, only next day he hasn't got it, so he takes another shilling to hide the first deficiency and so gets deeper and deeper every day. But for Castles' discovery and Blythe's conviction that Castles meant to tax Anderson with it, when Blythe's own guilt was bound to come out, I don't suppose the murder would ever have been committed. An odd point is that it is quite possible Castles would never have said anything. One half of him felt deeply grateful to Anderson, even fond of Anderson, who had shown him a good deal of kindness. I quite believe him when he says that he had more than half made up his mind to hold his tongue and be content with the knowledge that he could ruin Anderson if he wished to. It put them on equal terms so to say. A complicated, confused state of mind, but I think I can understand it. If he struck, his blow was at the man to whom he owed everything and but for whom he would never have had the opportunity. But Blythe was not to know there was so good a chance that Castles would say nothing. All Blythe saw was that the truth was on the point of coming out and that he had to stop it. If he didn't there would be disaster both for himself and for Hopewell House—or at least he thought so because he had so thoroughly identified himself with the place. I honestly believe he had got himself into thinking that anything he did for the benefit of Hopewell House was justified. Since his arrest he has said in so many words that it was better to use the Mrs Osman Ford capital for Hopewell House than to leave it lying idle in investments. The annual interest payable to Mrs Ford he felt able to provide when it was wanted, and he was confident the capital would never have to be produced as he knew Anderson was fully determined not to let it be realized. Of course, the whole situation changed when it became clear that Castles suspected something was wrong. I fancy Blythe still felt justified. Anything was, if only it helped Hopewell House. A disinterested murderer, in fact."

"That is what helped to make it so difficult," the colonel remarked. "A disinterested motive is hard to discover. But you've felt sure he was your man for a long time, haven't you?"

"Well, sir, I would rather say it was only very strong suspicion. I only felt certain when he tried to rush me into arresting Osman Ford. I thought it quite clear he had a motive for showing such anxiety. Then he made such a point of Osman's finger prints being on the pistol when everybody had seen Osman take it out of his pocket. Besides, those bulging pockets in that loose sort of Norfolk jacket Osman Ford always wore were simply a gift to anyone wanting to plant anything on him—especially in that darkness and confusion and with the man himself in the sort of dazed muddled bewilderment he had fallen into. Then, too, I noticed there was blood on the pistol grip and that suggested Blythe had been handling it. His face was bleeding quite freely where he had managed to give it a bad scratch, bumping against something in the dark. He tried to turn that off by pointing out that Mrs Ford had cut her hand and saying she had had hold of the pistol. But I could see the blood on it wasn't so fresh as all that."

"It would only have been your word against his," the colonel remarked. "A jury might have hesitated. An element of doubt."

"Oh, yes, I know," Bobby agreed. "I expect it's just as well that the experts can prove that Mrs Ford's blood and Blythe's belong to different groups. Luckily hers belongs to group three, which is the rare one. His belongs to group two, which is much commoner. And as the blood on the pistol is group two, and no one else present had any scratch or wound, it seems pretty conclusive."

"Juries baulk at scientific evidence," observed the colonel, who was inclined to do so himself. "They don't like it. Too unfamiliar. Have you got your whole train of thought in order?"

"I think so, sir," Bobby said. "What first started me wondering was that incident when Blythe and I found Castles examining Anderson's private ledger. You remember I mentioned that to you the last time I saw you, when we had finished considering all the various possibilities."

"I remember," Colonel Glynne answered. "You mean that Blythe knew at once it was the Osman Ford account Castles was looking at, though the ledger was upside down to him and though he went out of his way to tell you he had never seen the book open before."

"Yes, sir," Bobby agreed. "I don't suppose I should have thought so much of it, if Osman Ford hadn't told me about his suspicions. The ledger incident didn't quite fit, and when there's even the smallest suggestion of crooked work it is as well to notice and remember every trifle. The truth may be incredible and often is, but it always hangs together and that is just what crooked work never does. Then I began to notice other things. I knew Blythe had shown uneasiness when Osman Ford questioned him about the money. That looked as if Blythe knew there was a good reason for uneasiness. The amount of the Ford fund—£5,000—was the exact amount presented to Hopewell House through Blythe by what Blythe called to me his very useful friend, 'Mr Anon'. There was a sort of odd—I hardly know what to call it—secret significance perhaps—in his voice when he said that. I wondered if 'Mr Anon' had been very useful some other way some other time. Then the first time I saw him he gave me the idea he would have liked to hear more about Miss Earle's visit and he seemed to be rather unnecessarily communicative. Nervous people often are and I wondered if he were nervous; and if so, why. And I didn't like the more than touch of fanaticism he seemed to show when he said, speaking of his work for Hopewell House: 'That Counts'. I thought it sounded very much as if for him nothing else counted; and in the end nothing else did count, neither theft nor murder nor the effort to send an innocent man to the gallows for his own crime. Or for that matter burying a victim alive, though possibly he did not realize Miss Earle was still living when he threw her body in the pit he had dug."

"A strange state of mind," Colonel Glynne commented. "He must really have managed to persuade himself that everything was permitted to him if it helped his Hopewell House. The Disinterested Murderer, as you called him."

"I think, too," Bobby went on, "that he was genuinely shocked by the connection between Anderson and Miss Earle. Yet he tried to persuade me that he took a very lenient view of it. That was another small inconsistency to remember, and every inconsistency may turn out important, however small and trivial it seems. What was certain was that if Osman Ford's suspicions were correct and the trust fund had been tampered with, then the person responsible must be one of the three—Anderson, Blythe, or Castles. When Anderson was murdered, it was only logical to assume some connection between that and the trust fund fraud. But that there had been such a fraud wasn't at all certain, and for a time it seemed as if no embezzlement could have actually taken place, since Blythe was promising full and immediate payment. But then it appeared that Anderson's estate was mysteriously small. It ought, Blythe admitted, I expect it was too obvious from the office accounts to be denied, to have been about £10,000. And £10,000 is twice £5,000. We knew one £5,000 had gone to Miss Earle. It seemed logical to suppose that the missing £5,000 Blythe had been able as executor to use to replace the missing trust fund, to satisfy Osman Ford. He hadn't much to fear from any inquiry by the wife absent in America. I couldn't help noticing £5,000 was the sum Blythe had guaranteed for the Hopewell House building extensions."

"Swimming bath and workshops, wasn't it?" the colonel asked.

"Yes, sir," agreed Bobby. "Incidentally there is evidence now that Blythe was seen adapting a 'reducer' he had bought so as to fit it to the barrel of Dwight's revolver he had taken from Mrs Jordan's hiding-place. I wondered about that after what he said about Osman Ford's buying one for his rook rifle. That was quite true. Ford did make such a purchase and he remembers mentioning it to Blythe. He says it struck him at the time that Blythe was rather oddly interested."

"Useful bit of evidence," interposed the colonel. "I mean, about Blythe's having been seen altering a reducer. Sort of detail that impresses a jury."

"It was a bit of luck Wright's inquiry I asked him to make, proved successful," Bobby observed. "A mere chance Blythe was seen. In any case, since Anderson couldn't be his own murderer he was cleared on that score, and therefore, on the theory that the two crimes were connected, he was innocent of the suspected embezzlement also. Castles' behaviour seemed to show him, too, as innocent of fraud. His whole attitude, his self-assurance when he was discovered in what on the face of it was a wholly indefensible proceeding—having a look at his chief's private ledger—made it clear he felt very sure of himself. Everything he said and did supported his claim that he had discovered some new fact but could not quite make up his mind what to do about it. The logical deduction was he had found out something gravely wrong, and it was fairly obvious he believed that in some way Anderson was involved. On the theory of the inter-connection of two separate crimes—embezzlement and murder—then if he were innocent of the one, he was also innocent of the other. Only Blythe was left, and if he were guilty of the embezzlement, then on the theory I was working on, he was probably the murderer as well. The great difficulty was that all this was mere reasoning. No concrete facts."

"Mere reasoning," grunted the colonel. "I like the 'mere'. Very carefully and logically thought out, I should say, with a very subtle appreciation of the interplay of character involved. Anderson's infatuation. Blythe's fanaticism. Castles' hesitation between gratitude and revenge. All pointing in the same direction."

"Well, sir," Bobby went on, "that's how it seemed to me, and yet I had to remember other possibilities. Right up to the end I couldn't help feeling that my reasoning might be wrong, that the trust fund had never been tampered with, that consequently my theory of two connected crimes had no foundation in fact. It was Castles' behaviour in the private ledger incident that my theory was built on, and yet I had to remember there might be some other explanation. The murder might have been a private act of vengeance on Castles' part. Or a result of Dwight's jealousy. One can never be sure how far jealousy will not drive a man. It's a kind of madness. Only it seemed clear Dwight himself was suspecting Anne. That is why he took to watching her, why he followed her to the cottage that night. He knew I was having her followed and he jumped to the conclusion that that meant we were going to arrest her. To prevent that he knocked out Sergeant Wright so that he could warn Anne of what he believed to be her danger and persuade her to escape with him. Wright told me when I found him that night that Dwight had confessed to being the murderer. Dwight explains now that what he really said was that Anne was not the murderer. Wright apparently heard 'Anne', and took it for 'am', and also heard 'murderer'. He retorted with something about 'arrest'. Dwight took that to refer to Anne, got into a panic, and proceeded to knock Wright out. I must admit I was a bit shaken in believing him innocent, though, when Wright told me he had confessed."

"If we didn't want him for a witness," grumbled the colonel, "I would insist on a prosecution—deserves six weeks' hard labour."

"Yes, sir," agreed Bobby, who knew very well that the colonel knew very well that Dwight had offered his victim good private compensation, which was much more satisfying to that victim than seeing his assailant prosecuted.

But all that was, as they say in America, 'off the record'.

Bobby went on:

"I got a shock, too, when Roy Green turned up again in the dark garden. I had had to keep him in my mind. His actions were suspicious, though I was always inclined to accept his explanation that he got rid of the Blythe motoring gauntlet because he didn't want to have to explain how he and Miss Ursula happened to be where they were when they found it. His presence that night in the garden was merely due to his curiosity about the digging he and Miss Ursula had seen. It nearly cost him his life, though, when he barged into Blythe in the dark. And I didn't like it a bit when he turned up again after having promised to see to Wright and to get help. The explanation was simple enough. The constable on the beat found my car with Wright unconscious in it, and very naturally drove off in it to report and to get Wright attended to. Roy, not finding the car where I said it was, came back to tell me it was missing."

"I must admit," the colonel interrupted, "that I was often very much inclined to think it was Miss Anne herself who was guilty."

"I don't think you would have, sir, if you had seen her and realized how strong and genuine was her feeling for Anderson," Bobby answered. "If there had been any suggestion of his leaving her, it might have seemed more likely. But there wasn't. The £5,000 gift from Anderson was no motive, since it wasn't at all likely there was any question of Anderson's wanting it back so soon. I wasn't too sure of Mrs Jordan though. She talked a good deal about never trusting a man. That might easily have meant she didn't trust Anderson. I even wondered if, having made the £5,000 secure for Miss Earle by removing Anderson who might have claimed it back, she intended to secure it for herself by removing Miss Earle. I had to give that idea up though when it began to be clear that she was Miss Earle's mother."

"Wasn't clear to me," observed the colonel. "What made you think of that?"

"She knew so much," Bobby answered, "as, for example, exactly where Miss Anne was deserted. Yet when I pressed her to explain how she had identified her as her sister's child, she told a good many lies. It seemed pretty clear she identified her as her niece because she knew she was her daughter and that she knew all the details of the baby's abandonment because she was responsible. That meant the father was probably a Midwych man, and the scrap of conversation Constable Smith very improperly overheard, and Osman Ford's occasional and secret visits to the cottage to see a woman with whom he was certainly not carrying on any intrigue, made it pretty clear he was Anne's father and that Mrs Jordan was trying a little blackmailing. I felt all that was clearly implicit in the evidence."

"Implicit perhaps," agreed the colonel, "but hardly clearly. Still, you did manage to worry it out."

"It only concerned us," Bobby continued, "so far as it explained what was suspicious in Osman Ford's behaviour. By that time I felt all the suspects were more or less eliminated, except Blythe, and yet there seemed no possibility of securing proof against him—proof to satisfy a jury."

"Wouldn't have been the first time," the colonel remarked, "that a murderer perfectly well known to the police, had escaped for lack of satisfactory legal evidence."

"I doubt if we should ever have succeeded, but for that poor girl's resolve to get it, even at the risk of her own life," Bobby said slowly. "Once again, suspicions, reasonable enough in themselves, were directed to the wrong quarter. Just as Osman Ford and Castles both wrongly suspected Anderson, so she wrongly suspected Osman. The anonymous letter she sent Osman and that he showed Blythe for advice, accused him of being the murderer, claimed to be from an eye-witness, and made an offer to remain silent for fifty pounds. Her idea was that if Osman were innocent he would ignore the letter. But if he came to the meeting she suggested in the abandoned cottage garden and actually handed over the money, then she would know he was guilty and that would give her the proof she needed. Unfortunately, Osman showed the letter to Blythe, really expecting him to consult us. Blythe, not unnaturally perhaps, fell into a panic. It must be a trifle upsetting to a murderer to see a letter claiming that the writer had been an eye-witness of the crime. True, addressed to the wrong person, but disturbing all the same. Only too clear, he would naturally think, that the truth was on the verge of coming out. He felt he had to know and he made up his mind to eliminate the eye-witness."

"You don't think there was any truth in Miss Earle's claim?" the colonel asked.

"I am sure there wasn't," Bobby answered, "For one thing, Mrs Jordan's evidence is quite clear that Anne came back to the cottage after seeing Anderson drive off and that she went straight to bed. The poor girl only said that to try to secure a confession and was quite indifferent to the risk she knew she ran. It was more than a risk. It was a certainty. I don't think in her then mood, she cared. Blythe dug in advance the pit in which he meant to bury her body. Unlucky for him that young Green, and the Harris girl saw it. Blythe used a spade taken from Roman Ends farm. He hoped that would direct suspicion towards Osman if the body were discovered. No doubt his chief hope was that it would never be found. Probably he also intended, if the body were found, to give suspicion a tilt towards Osman by repeating the story of the anonymous letter Osman had received. Just as well for Osman that he changed his mind at the last moment and instead of staying away, taking no notice of the letter, as he had promised and as Blythe had advised, that he went there to see what was really happening. He had shown himself so restless and uneasy all evening that it's no wonder Mrs Ford followed him."

"I think that clears up all the points," Colonel Glynne said slowly. "A strange case, and I think strangest of all is Anne Earle herself. A fine character, a strong, unusual character, but just as Blythe let himself be warped by his over-devotion to Hopewell House that led him in the end to fraud and then to murder, so the girl let her mind be warped by her mother's desertion of her. She was strong, but circumstances were stronger, and only those who have conquered circumstances have any right even to hint a judgment. That must be her epitaph."

THE END